THE CHAPEL ST. PERILOUS

MICHAEL RANDS

Hardback ISBN: 978-1-7377525-1-6

E-book ISBN: 978-1-7377525-0-9

Printed in the United States by Bayou Wolf Press, Mobile, Alabama

Bayou Wolf Press

Mobile, Alabama

USA

www.bayouwolfpress.com

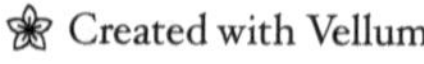 Created with Vellum

I don't remember coming home. I recall the morning clearly, but the rest of the day comprises flashes, and then a long darkness that starts around midday. When I woke this morning to the sound of heavy knocking on the door, I was completely naked.

Antoinette and I had not been lovers. She was my housemate, or more accurately, my landlady. The tension had been there from the outset. Good sense had prevailed for the first few weeks, but a pair of clowns can only walk along a tightrope for so long. And as I lay in bed, listening to the sound of beating fists on the front door, I assumed that in a state of blackout drunkenness we'd crossed the great divide.

I pulled on my pants, put on a t-shirt, and looked out the window onto the small street next to our house to see two, three, four police cars. Even though everything else in Chickasaw is old, the police cars are brand-new. I washed my hands, splashed my face, went down the stairs, and opened the door. Two large male officers stood there.

"Marcel Swart?"

"Uh... yes, sir."

They'd found Antoinette's car, they said, down by the swamp, and clothes, or pieces of clothes, and blood.

"Do we have your permission to search the house?"

They moved into the doorway with such authority I felt incapable of resistance. I stepped aside, mumbled yes, certainly, come in.

With gloved hands they invaded every corner of the kitchen. As I watched them rifle through drawers, I kept wondering if I should stop them, demand they leave. But I was a tenant, after all, and my only thought at the time was— do not get yourself into any trouble; make them believe you're a good person, then they will like you, and they won't harm you.

Upstairs a young officer dug through my underwear drawer. He found a packet of unopened condoms, held it up, turned it about—to make sure, I assume, that none had been used. If you've ever been singled out for a bag search at customs you know what it feels like to suddenly doubt everything about yourself, to wonder, if just for a second, *Am I carrying drugs?*

Only here the fear ran deeper. There was something in my drawers, something beneath my bed, or in the bags I had not yet fully unpacked, that marked me not as a drug user, but as a murderer. There was something about a murderer's socks, or his underwear, or the stain on his shirt pocket, invisible to most, but to the trained eye as clear as surveillance tape footage and a signed confession.

"Would you be willing to come to the station, to talk to us?" the young officer asked me. He looked to be in his early thirties, neatly shaven, hair trimmed. I could see beneath his jacket he had the kind of body that comes only through daily workouts, through a disciplined lifestyle. "Sir?"

"Umm. Why do you want me to come down to the station?"

"Like to ask you a few questions. You'd drive yourself down there."

I agreed

I wished I'd asked for time to shower, eat breakfast, change into something that made me look less destitute. As I brushed my teeth I noticed all our toiletries had been unpacked, left lying on the bathroom counter, and spread across the table next to the window.

A Northern Cardinal landed on the branch just a few feet from me, separated only by a thin pane of glass. I wished to be that bright red bird. Then I remembered for the first time since I'd woken that morning—*I am a wealthy man. I have money*. But the thought brought me no comfort as I walked down the stairs, into the living room, out the front door.

It was cool outside, the road damp. It must have rained the night before. Droplets lined the dark windows of my 1970 Ford Torino. The leather seats were cold this morning, and as I started the engine, that awful smell of burnt flesh filled the car. He was warning me of danger; I hadn't heard from him like this in a while. My chest tightened; my arms and fingers were cold.

I followed the police cars down Grant Street, past the public swimming pool, the library, the white, wooden Episcopal church, the park, the rows of wooden houses, some well-kept, others falling into ruin, past the old trucks parked on the lawns, past the cats, always the cats, everywhere, and the park, and the trees that reach across the street, leaves touching in the middle. There was a sign: *Re-elect Sheriff Jones*. Directly across the road, in front of one of the better preserved houses in the neighborhood, stood a campaign poster for his rival: Jefferson Lee III, whose eyes stared out from beneath his black hat and clawed into my soul. The smell of burning flesh was so strong I almost retched.

I followed the cops right onto Route 43 and up to the humble station, faded redbrick, like an old schoolhouse, better suited to this time-forgotten neighborhood than the shiny cars now parked in front of it.

Inside the station I was asked to sit on a wooden bench.

"Do you want a coke?" Sergeant Alexis, the younger officer, asked me.

"Sure." I tapped my pockets to show I was up for it.

"Don't worry."

He paid close attention to how I pulled back the tab, my hand trembling slightly. I looked into his light blue eyes, smiled.

The interview room was tiny, more like a cubicle. A single surveillance camera in the top right-hand corner peered down at me. When the door opened, a different, older man—with gray hair, a gray goatee, a silver cross around his neck, podgy in the way men over sixty often are—came into the room, I saw the road that lay between me and the needle. Alabama's black soil would be my rest.

"Detective Drew Franklin," the older man said, as he sat down. "You've met Detective Alexis."

"Yes, sir."

"You don't come from 'round here," Franklin said.

He had a deep Alabama accent, and there was something awful about the man's eyes, as if they'd been whisked up from hell, burned by the fires.

"No, sir."

I didn't feel obliged to give him more than that.

He put his fist beneath his chin.

"You live with Antoinette Dubois?"

"I do. She's my housemate. Landlady."

I took a sip of coke and watched his eyes as they watched my hands.

"Just a landlady?"

"How do you mean?" I took another sip. Something shifted in both of them, like dogs who smell fear.

"Did you two ever get intimate?" Alexis asked me.

"Did you have sex with Antoinette Dubois?" Franklin leaned in closer.

I saw my fingers as these two men saw them, fumbling, playing with themselves, fidgeting.

"We wanted to be together... sometimes..." I stammered. I heard myself as they heard me, a guilty man, caught in his lies.

"You wanted to be with her?" Alexis asked.

Then Franklin: "But she didn't want to be with you."

"It drove you crazy."

"No, no, no." I tapped the desk with my knuckles, a sudden rush of anger fueling me. "You don't know anything."

"Then tell us."

"Educate us."

"You don't even know that she was... that she is dead."

"Nobody said she was dead."

"You're treating it like a murder. You're treating me..."

"We're treatin' you like what?"

"Nothing." I looked down.

"Her car," Franklin continued, "was found down by the Chickasaw creek. Blood. Pieces of torn clothing. Her panties were found in the car. All been sent to the crime lab. Soon, we'll have DNA. We'll know everything we need to know. But by then it's gonna be too late. So you got somethin' to tell us, tell us now. Then we can help you."

"I would never." I partially crushed the coke can. "I could not do, whatever you're thinking. You haven't found a body."

"Are you concerned about us finding that body?" the younger man asked.

"Does that worry you, son?"

"No, it doesn't worry me."

"You don't care if she's alive or dead?"

"Of course I care. I hope you find her alive." I looked up from the can, stared into the older eyes, the younger eyes, back. I could not outstare them; I looked down.

"Would you be willing to submit to a DNA sample?" Alexis asked.

"Yes, I would. I want to help you."

"Good," Alexis said.

He exited, leaving Franklin and me alone. The older man wrapped his right hand around his clenched, left fist, and squeezed.

"If Antoinette Dubois is alive, we want to find her. And we *need* to find her soon. If she's dead, we gotta find the son of a bitch that done this."

"Yes, sir. I want to help you."

"What kind of animal does somethin' like this? Murder a young woman, and throw away her body like a piece a trash?"

"Why do you keep talking about her body, like it's already been found?"

He twisted the thick gold ring on his finger, moved it up and down.

"Clock's tickin'." He placed his hand on my wrist. "If she's alive, we need to find her now. Sometimes these sickos hold onto their victims for a while. Or, she may just have had an altercation, but managed to escape. If you know somethin', you need to talk." He pointed his finger at the space between my eyes, leaning so close to me I could feel his breath. "What you not tellin' us?"

"There's nothing... sir." I felt the back of my head shake.

"You know what's going on here at the moment?"

"Sir?"

"Sheriff's election one week today. I know I shouldn't be talkin' about this. But the stakes are too high. The soul of our town's at stake."

"I understand, sir."

"And you know the politics here, what's going on here now, extends way beyond this little town."

"Yes, I know, sir."

"You part of that cult, son?"

"It's not a cult."

He grabbed my wrist and slammed my arm against the table.

"Goddammit. You know Maggie?"

"Never met her."

"You know what these folk think of her, don't you?"

I looked up at the camera. What kind of game was this old man playing? Was he trying to create a faux-intimacy with me, to trick me into giving him what he wanted to hear? Or was he really on the side of re-electing Sheriff Jones?

"They can't hear us." He glanced up at the camera. "They can only see. Now you need to speak and you need to speak quick before my partner gets back in here. I'm the only pro-Jones man in this building. You understand?"

"I hear you, sir. But what do you want me to tell you?"

"You know how they gonna make this look. Media gonna be all over this, like flies 'round shit. They gonna say you done this 'cuz you part of that cult. You know how things work round here, huh? Folks don't take kindly to nothin' that smells like... voodoo or black magic."

"I didn't come here to be a part of that..."

"What else would some outta towner like yourself be doin' here?" He stared at me for a long time, and I did my best to hold his gaze, certain now that this was all an act. He was no more for Jones than was anyone else in this building. He wanted to drive Maggie and all her followers out of town. "Well, did you do it?"

"Did I do what?"

"Kill her?" My hand shook as I reached for the coke can we both knew was empty. "If you killed her you need to tell me, so we can protect Maggie. And cut you a deal."

"I didn't..." My voice trembled.

"You looking at the needle, son. If you fess up, we can save you from that."

"I didn't do it."

Alexis reentered. He wore blue plastic gloves and held a long cotton-tipped swab, which he inserted into my mouth. The tip brushed against the soft wall.

"You drinkin' last night?" Franklin asked as Alexis left the room.

Telling the detective I couldn't remember what had happened since sometime around midday would be as good as signing my own death warrant. I knew I had to start talking, but the longer I waited the colder my mind grew. I had to invent. If I'd woken up at home, in my bed, then I must have been at home in the evening. And we may very well have done what we often did.

"We drank in the lounge. After dinner. That was common."

"You drank in the lounge?"

"Talking; listening to music. That was very normal for us. That was how I, how we, often spent our evenings."

"How much you drink?"

The back of my neck tingled hot; spots of sweat pierced the skin.

"A few glasses."

"And then?"

"We finished up. We went to bed."

"You went to your bed, and she went to her bed?"

"We didn't have that kind of relationship, sir. We were friends."

"It ain't no crime sleepin' with your landlady. 'Specially not if she's young, and you's young. I don't see no ring on your finger."

I held up my hand to show him he was correct.

"Means you were sleeping with her?"

"No, sir. I didn't say that."

"Mr. Swart, last night, you and Antoinette Dubois, by your own admission, were alone in the house you shared, drinkin' into the night. Next mornin' she's missin', and her car's found down at the Chickasaw Creek, bloodstained clothes. You understand how this looks, son?"

"Of course I understand, how it *looks*. But I didn't do anything wrong."

I looked up at the camera in the corner and pictured the other room full of cops, watching me, trying to decide if I sat like a killer, drank coke like a killer, spoke, breathed, moved like a killer.

"I'm the most senior detective in this station. If I tell 'em I want time alone with you, cameras off, you better know they gonna listen."

I looked up at the ceiling. Closing my eyes, I tried to recall the events of yesterday, but the last images I could access were on Maggie's island.

"You want me to turn off the cameras? We can talk alone, if you got something to say."

He dragged his chair across the room, climbed onto it, and fiddled with the wires at the back of the video camera. For all I knew, this was just another trick, another attempt at creating intimacy. But as his hand rested on my shoulder, I felt genuine comfort for the first time since I'd woken up that morning. Sitting opposite me again, he asked: "Cigarette?" He took a pack from his pocket and held it toward me. He had thick fingers.

"I wouldn't mind one, thank you."

"I love these things." He lit one and handed it to me; lit his own. "I don't care what they say. I'll go to an early grave a happy man 'fore I give these up."

I wanted to say something clever, but nothing came to mind.

"Maybe you want to back up a little bit. Tell me about yourself. How you come to be in this part of the world?"

"How far back do you want me to go, sir?"

He took a drag of his cigarette, resting his elbows up on the table.

"I want to help that girl. I want to find her. You want to find her too, don't you?" He pointed at me with his cigarette finger.

"Of course. I haven't lied to you."

"I ain't here to call you no liar. But if you won't tell me what happened last night, then maybe you can tell me what happened to bring you to this little town of Chickasaw. Outsiders like you, they come here for one reason." He raised his index finger. "And that reason is Maggie. And anyone who comes to be with Maggie, well, they had something go wrong in their life."

"Ha." I laughed involuntarily, put my cigarette on the edge of the table, wiped my sweaty hands on my pants. "That's a bit presumptuous, isn't it?"

"Tell me I'm wrong."

I sat back, crossing my arms over my chest.

"How do I know that camera's not filming us? How do I know you really side with Sheriff Jones?"

"We can go someplace else, where there ain't a camera.

We can take a drive, if you like. My colleagues here, they know I got some... how d'ya say? Unconventional methods."

I didn't know what to make of that. Had he just confessed to me that this was all an act, a way of getting me to drop my guard?

"I'm the only Jones man in this station. I want to keep Chickasaw unique. I know some folk say Maggie does weird things, but she does good work. She helped me." From his wallet he took out a lottery ticket, which he placed on the table in front of me. "Won a hundred fifty thousand dollars on this one."

"Things went bad for you after that?"

"Didn't understand why."

"And she helped you?"

He nodded slowly, pursing his lips into an inverted smile.

"How much time you got?" I asked him.

"As I told you, son, time is tight. But you our best hope at this moment of figuring out what's going on. Now, I know I was pushin' you earlier. That's my job. But I trust my gut. And my gut says you ain't harmed that girl." He took my arm and held it tight. "But I'm the only one on your side. And I tell you for certain, I'm the only one who want to help keep Maggie safe. That election's in one week." He got up and walked to the door. "Come on. I'll tell 'em we're takin' a ride, just you and me."

"Okay. Let's go."

"1970 Ford Torino," he said, running his hand over my car. "A true classic."

"Sure is."

"But we gonna take a ride in my car," Franklin said, pointing at an unmarked black truck. "We can smoke in here.

We'll take a drive down to the water, to where they found her car this mornin'."

"Sounds good to me."

We pulled out onto Route 43.

I took a deep drag on my cigarette and looked out the window at a white house rotting in the ground, a dog chained to a tree, barking at us as we went by. Calm settled over me as I exhaled. I was an innocent man, and soon enough I'd be able to prove it.

CHAPTER 2

This story starts on a farm in North Carolina, in the foothills of the Smoky Mountains. Like most of the places I stayed during that season of life, I did manual labor and in exchange was given free board and lodging. The farm was owned and run by Jim Meer, grey-haired, ponytail-wearing, vegetarian—somewhere between a hippie and a survivalist.

My mornings were devoted to teaching online English lessons and writing; in the afternoon I'd do labor around the farm. It was a beautiful place. Surrounded by forest and mountains, far from civilization, I started to see society (distant and noisy) as highly overrated. I lived alone in a single-sleeper A-frame, deep in the woods, far from the main house.

Jim's home, a rickety wooden building built on the edge of a ravine, had a library containing a handful of novels, but mostly books dealing with organic farming and spirituality. That's where I found Carl Jung's essay *Synchronicity*, in which Jung argued that there were, of course, causally related events, but also events not causally related but connected through meaning, and that individuals open to these moments experienced forms of precognition that could not be explained away as mere coincidence.

One of the examples he cited had him sitting at a desk in his office, back to the window, early evening, talking to a patient whom he'd been trying to counsel for many years. She was highly educated and fiercely rational (she had, Jung said, a Cartesian worldview), and he was unable to help her in any way. Then during one session the woman recounted a dream she'd had the previous night in which she'd found a gold and blue scarab. Just then Jung noticed a sound behind him and turned to see an insect trying to fly into the room. He opened the window and there found a seasonal rose beetle that under the light had a blue and gold carapace. He handed the beetle to the patient, saying, "Here is your scarab." Her rational skeptic shell broke and she started to experience break-throughs in therapy.

Synchronistic events, Jung said, were always at play in the world, visible to those rightly attuned to their presence.

I'd often suspected the universe played these kinds of games, but drawing close to such knowledge had frightened me and I'd retreated to my skeptical side—*it's just the pattern-seeking mind imposing patterns on the world.* But during this time on Jim's farm—a time, I believed, of growing enlightenment—I started to feel so close to the universe that I could not ignore the signs it showed me; I could not pretend not to see them.

Small synchronistic moments occurred frequently, daily in fact. But here's the one that changed everything: I had a dream I was walking along a road through the woods. Although it looked slightly different, I knew the farm was Jim's. At the end of the road I saw a redheaded woman dressed in green, sitting on a tractor. I walked up to her and she said, "Money can be easy to find. Come this way." I followed her and she pointed to a chest buried in the ground.

I opened it and saw that indeed it was filled with gold coins. "That *is* easy," I said. I took handfuls of coins and dropped them into my pockets, but when I touched the sides of my pants, I noticed the pockets were empty. Then the redheaded woman reached into the chest, took out coins, and placed them into her own pockets. "This is not your way," she said.

Two days later I went into the living room of Jim's house and there sat a tall redheaded woman. She was a new arrival and had come to work on the farm for a few weeks. Charlie was her name, and although she did not wear a green dress, she had a pair of green-framed sunglasses that she wore when outdoors. Tall, physically strong, and very funny, she was a great person to have around. We hit it off immediately.

A week later Jim came driving down the road on the tractor he used around the farm, and sitting on the back was a young Japanese man; his name was Satoshi Nakamoto. He only stayed for three days, and we didn't get to talk much, but when we did, we got along well. I walked alone with him one evening, and he spoke with deep conviction about a change that was coming.

"For too long," he said, "governments and banking monopolies have ruled the world, and controlled the fate of man. They believe they are our gods. But we will free ourselves from them. There is a new way."

"What is it?"

"It's something we have been working on, and now it's finally growing fast." Jim came driving down the road just then on his golf cart. "I'll leave a book for you, so you can read more about it," Satoshi said. The next day he was gone, but he'd left the book on the doorstep of my A-frame.

It was called: *Cryptocurrencies and the New World Order.*

The book was only a month or two old and had been published by a small, specialist press. I'd heard the name Bitcoin before, but had filed it away in the same section of my brain in which I'd filed the names of tree and fish species I'd heard rattled off by passionate enthusiasts—interesting, but useless. Yet as this book had it, as Satoshi had suggested in our too-short conversation, Bitcoin and other "cryptos"— as the in-crowd apparently called them—promised to upend the established world order. It was the first time in modern history that ordinary individuals could bypass fiat currency, the mechanism through which governments, with their violent monopoly on taxation, in collusion with central banks, controlled the system of welfare and warfare—the lifeblood of the state. The book was a manifesto, and while I was deeply skeptical about its central claim—that the very institution of The State was in its final days—I felt pulled to find out more.

I disappeared down a digital rabbit hole, and by the time I hit the bottom I'd learned that it would be easier for me to buy something called a CFD (cash for difference), a highly esoteric investment that mirrored the rise or fall of stocks and currencies. CFDs were purchased at high leverage, another concept I'd heard of but had not previously understood. I found a CFD trading site that offered a leverage of 1 to 1000, which meant that while a single bitcoin cost $2,500 at the time, I could, for that price, control $250,000's worth. Leverage meant extreme vulnerability. At one thousand to one, the price need only drop by a few dollars for the entire investment to be wiped out. Of course, the opposite was also true, and for every dollar it increased, I would earn a thousand dollars. At that time, I had to my name $2,500.

If I could make my fortune this way, I'd be able to pursue my true passion; I'd be free to write, free from the burden of compromise. Since graduating, I'd promised myself I would *become a writer.* And If you want to write, you can't just confine yourself to books. You have to get out there into the world and *live* a little, but I wasn't too excited about getting tied up in some dead-end job that drained my soul. So I'd opted for menial jobs while hunting for the perfect story, believing that great riches would come when I found it. But that's not what happened. Perhaps Fate preferred the order reversed. First I'd get the money.

Money equaled freedom. Freedom from toil; psychological freedom; but most importantly freedom from compromise and endless sacrifice. I saw myself as a fool tangled in a web of idiocy, compromise, and sacrifice, all the products of my own poverty. Wealth would clear that all away. I could write about anything, aim for the highest ideals in my work and not have to worry about groveling for approval from the masses. Absolute freedom. That's what I wanted, and money was the ticket. I felt free to admit this to myself now.

"Freedom." I said the word out loud, and it felt good. "Money and freedom. No more sacrifice." I said the words again: "Freedom. Money. Sacrifice."

I saw the road ahead of me, and it was filled with light.

Charlie was still living on the farm, and she and I had begun to refer to one another as "bro." I don't know who started this, but late one afternoon when we'd finished feeding logs into a shredder to make sawdust, we sat on Jim's tractor smoking a joint, and she said, "You know, you're like my best bro right now."

"Best bro?"

"Yeah, best bro."

These words left her mouth at the exact moment I became stoned, and I felt in them a depth of affection I had not known in a long time. I told her then about the dream I'd had of a redheaded woman, and how she'd been sitting on a tractor, and how, of course, I'd had this dream before she arrived.

Her jeans were rolled up above her knees and her legs and black boots were covered in flecks of mud. Her hair hung loose, and I could see (and she'd confirmed this for me in recent conversations) that she had not showered in days. Neither had I. We both smelt rank and ripe. Like farm people.

"Well, you're my best bro, too."

"You close to your family?"

"That's a tough question to answer. I suppose so. We immigrated here when I was sixteen, about eight years ago. My parents split up."

"Is your family religious?"

"My father used to be very devout, and even, you might say, traditional. But his ideas have grown and changed. I don't know what he believes anymore."

"Your mother?"

"She's remarried. To a Southern Baptist. My father never got remarried. Why do you ask?"

"Had a chat with my mother earlier. She's super religious and quite poor. She has to take payday loans, from sharks, and then she still gives lots of her money to the church."

"Ouch."

"She belongs to the Prosperity Gospel movement. Heard of it?"

"Sure have. You do right by God and He'll make you rich."

"And you have to plant the seed. The financial seed."

"But He hasn't come through for her yet?"

"Not yet." She playfully kicked my foot, squashed the joint on the edge of the tractor and put the roach into her pants pocket.

At night I'd turn off the lights in my cabin and stand on the tiny porch staring into the dark woods, listening to the sound of the river, the night birds, the insects. That evening I walked off the porch and followed the pathway deep into the woods, with only the pale light of the moon to show the way. I sat on a large stone at the edge of the path and stared through the trees, towards a patch of forest that seemed to glow brighter than everywhere around it. The air was cold; steam left my mouth with each breath.

Now, of course, logically I should have been frightened by Charlie's story of her mother's failed attempts to rig the Divine System, but instead I felt a supreme confidence that this was a sign, the final part of the dream's prophecy. *That is not my way*—not my way to *lose* the money, as Charlie's mother lost hers. I needed to perform an act of trust, make a pact with the universe, or perhaps even with God Himself.

The logical part of my mind, the part that said—*you will lose all your money, you know that*—I ignored. I had to place all my faith in the irrational, or as I renamed it, the *trans-rational*. I threw a stone into the woods and listened as it bounced, rolled, crashed through the forest.

A rustling sound followed, too heavy to have been caused by just the stone. A deer, I thought, or some other animal. Hooves on rocks. I didn't pay it much mind, but perhaps if I'd known how important this moment was, how I would return to it again and again in the months to come, I'd have paid closer attention to what lay there in the darkness.

Back in my A-frame I opened up an online trading account with one of the supposedly reliable CFD trading platforms and transferred $1250. Bitcoin was trading at just under $2500, and with the 1:1000 leverage, I was able to purchase $125,000 worth of CFDs, that would track the rise or fall of the commodity. Yes, I owned a virtual representation of a cryptocurrency, surely the most abstract, esoteric investment a human could hold. But this did not frighten me. On the contrary it gave me confidence, as it mapped neatly onto my current state of consciousness—abstracted from the physical world, freed from old constraints.

Everything I had read about trading suggested that an amateur lost money because he lost his nerve. Making money on the markets was as much about controlling the chorus of fearful voices inside you, as it was about making intelligent analyses. I promised myself I would not check on my purchase again for forty days and forty nights—the number had obvious biblical significance, and I felt safe in it. I promised myself that I would also actively avoid all news about Bitcoin.

For the first three days this was tortuously difficult, but as the hours and days passed, I felt myself letting go of the offering (half my wealth), making peace with the fact that I'd never see it again, that it had been a sacrifice of a kind that would not be repaid immediately, and not necessarily ever with a return of cash.

"Sacrifice." I said the word out loud. "Sacrificial. Sacrificed for... What exactly? Freedom?" I lit a cigarette and smoked on my balcony. "You want freedom. But the sacrifice. It has its own... desires and agenda." I snuffed out the cigarette.

Charlie left, the other temporary visitors moved on, until only Jim and I remained on the farm. He'd decided to take a vacation—he did this once every few years—down to South America, and offered to pay me if I would stay alone on the farm and take care of the dogs. I accepted his offer. He left. I moved into the main house. I slept on the couch in the lounge, with the fire always going, the dogs on the floor, the shotgun on the kitchen table. Aside from feeding the chickens and dogs, and restocking the wood for the fire, there was no work for me to do. I read a book about meditation, watched a few lectures on how to do it, and immediately loved the practice. I did it for two hours each day, an hour in the morning, an hour in the evening. Every two weeks I'd go into town to stock up on supplies. I bought a few cheap journals, and wrote extensively, my thoughts rambling, unstructured, but—at least to me—intriguing. Somewhere in there was the great story I'd been born to tell. I read the *Tibetan Book of the Dead*, walked through the forest, ignored all news completely.

Forty days passed, and on that very morning I received an email from Jim explaining that he'd decided to extend his stay for another two months. I was welcome to leave, and he would find someone else to come take over for me, or I could stay, and he would compensate me for my time. I told him I'd stay. I'd now receive more than I had given up in the sacrifice.

In the back of one of my books, in black permanent marker, I wrote: *Sacrifice is real. Not metaphorically speaking. Must investigate further*.

I could not lose now, and so I decided to recommit myself to not looking. The day before Jim returned was exactly one hundred days since I'd made my sacrifice. When I'd finished my morning meditation and poured myself a cup of coffee, I sat at the old table in Jim's kitchen and looked out on the thick trees that grew along the river. I felt the house creek and shift in the wind. I logged onto my trading account to find that my balance was sixteen million dollars.

I closed my position and cashed out.

CHAPTER 3

I paced and smoked all day, waiting for the money to transfer out of the trading account into my PayPal. When it arrived, the needles of anxiety were all, in an instant, plucked from my flesh. *I am a wealthy man*, I thought. *I've achieved freedom from the burden of life. I can do as I please, write what I like.* I fired Jim's shotgun into the night sky, drank a glass of moonshine; when the buzz from the liquor wore off it was not the electric crackle of anxiety that returned—but rather a burdensome weight, as if on sobering up I'd remembered a terrible crime I'd committed in my drunkenness.

This was not how I'd imagined being wealthy would feel.

Jim arrived late the following afternoon. His skin was tan from the holiday, and streaks of blond showed through his grey hair. His beard had grown. At the kitchen table, we shared a vegetarian meal (cooked by myself), and I extracted a few highlights from his holiday.

"I made some money on the stock market," I told him, by way of partial confession.

"Good man." He raised his glass of ginger beer. "You made a lot?"

"A fair amount." I considered the words, then rephrased: "A considerable sum."

"Very nice."

"So, you don't have to pay me for staying here. I'm fine."

"Oh no." He looked up at me. "I'm paying you for it. A deal's a deal. A pact's a pact." He placed an envelope down in front of me. "I drew this on the way back here. Two thousand five hundred dollars."

I gave him a hug that evening before I went off to sleep, for the last time, in the A-frame out in the woods. The next morning, I left before sunup and arrived in Nashville around lunchtime. Why Nashville, you ask? I'd decided I would head out West, and Nashville was west of where I'd been, and drivable in a day. I checked into a roadside motel, bought myself a six-pack of beer, and worked my way through it as I watched television, checking PayPal every hour to make sure my money was still there.

I left the next morning, early again, just as the sun rose over the interstate. That night I lodged in a Motel 6 on the outskirts of Baton Rouge and ate a catfish po' boy at a place recommended by the woman at the front desk. After dinner I lay in bed drinking beer, checking my balance again before sleep.

I left after breakfast the next morning and continued my journey westwards. As the I-10 cut into the bayou, and swampland opened out on either side of me, I felt a sudden sense of freedom. There was something admirably arrogant about the people who'd sunk these concrete slabs into the water, who'd decided that swamp would not be an obstacle to the mass movement of our species.

I flipped through the regular mix of radio stations—country music; evangelists; country music; evangelists; country music; evangelists—the talk of hell resonating with me in a way it had not done since I was a small child. This was the feeling I'd tried, and failed, to conjure when writing my thesis on Dante's *Inferno*. I'd argued that as modern readers who read hell only in symbolic terms, we fail to grapple properly with the text. My supervising professors hated every sentence I wrote, said I was wasting my time if I didn't offer a contemporary reading. I rebelled against my professors, and went my own way, partially. I'd still wasted my time with logic and argument that satisfied their rigid brains. Regret remained in my body, like branches in mud.

I pictured the bayous at night, the skeletons of the long-dead floating up to the surface and coming back to land, telling tales the living did not want told.

Past the bayous, I stopped at a busy gas station and bought myself a white cowboy hat, a black belt buckle with cross-pistols, a five-hour energy drink, a large coffee, and a bottle of water. Two hours later I crossed the border into Texas, feeling the kind of thrill I imagined bandits of old must have felt as they realized they'd outrun the law.

There was no contract with an invisible force, no meaningful signs or signals. I'd bought into Bitcoin just before it began an historical run that had created a new class of millionaires. Like railroad investors of the Gilded Age, I'd seen an opportunity and I'd taken it; the rewards were rightfully mine, and I would enjoy them. I'd keep going 'til I reached California, find myself a small cottage in a small town, somewhere near the ocean. I'd live out my days in bliss, doing only what I wanted to do with my time, answering to nobody. I was free.

· · ·

It took me an hour to get through the Houston traffic; I drove fast on the other side, not to make up for lost time, but because driving fast is fun. Texas turned from green to brown, the desert stretching out on either side, ahead, behind, dusty and infinite. Like the bayous, these were corpse-swallowing lands. The bodies of armadillos marked the passing miles. *Poor creatures*, I thought. Their evolution stopped in a time before trucks. Buzzards flew overhead, and everywhere there were tires, mangled, ripped apart like mutilated corpses in a warzone. Each passing tire seemed to look up at me, like the skeleton of a man who'd gone before, a promise that what lay ahead was not welcoming.

Perhaps if I'd been more attuned to the mechanical warning signs put in place by engineers, and not these mythical warning signs, I would have known in time that something was wrong. Then again, perhaps they were—each in their own way—warning me of the same thing. I'd never seen smoke pour up through the hood while driving. I wanted to stop but there were trucks behind me, trucks to my left and my right. As I turned off the radio, the roaring sound of these awful machines filled the car.

The hum of the American highway is a violent and unforgiving sound.

The next off-ramp was two miles away, but I made it. I pulled onto the side of the road as smoke roared out the front of the car. I popped the hood open, threw water onto the engine, coffee after it. The smoke-pour slowed, but didn't stop. If the engine was going to explode I didn't want to be near it, and honestly there was nothing more I could do. I was too ashamed to wear my cowboy hat, embarrassed that I'd even thought of buying a cross-pistol belt buckle. I unclipped the buckle and threw it down the dirt embankment toward the thorn bushes; I held the hat in my hand.

The town I'd stopped in was called Comfort. I tried not

to think too much about that, or what it might mean, but I could not escape the sickening feeling that some cosmic scorekeeper had punched me square in the gut. A simple *change of perspective* would not be sufficient to get me out of this contract.

It being Sunday accounted for, I suppose, the fact that the main drag was totally empty. On dirt lots in front of the rusty storefronts sat petrified trucks that looked as if they'd been abandoned in the Depression-era. A hundred yards or so ahead of me, an actual tumbleweed rolled across the street, crashing into a bank of blown-out tires. *Big Dave's Truck and Car* read the sign that dangled over the store.

The shop was closed. I put my face against the glass, looking into a dark room that seemed to function as both an office and a storeroom—spanners and wrenches hung from the walls, dusty ledgers lined the table. As I stepped back, I noticed the number for after-hours emergencies, dialed it, and got through to a man named Chuck, who said he'd be there within the hour.

He arrived on time, in a truck not much younger than the skeletons that haunted the road's shopfronts. He was a short man, stocky. He wore grease-stained dungarees and had black-rimmed fingernails, common amongst men who do real work with their hands.

"What seems to be the problem?"

I gave him a general explanation, and he drove us towards where I'd abandoned my little red Toyota Corolla. I walked close behind him, offering a string of mumbled excuses. He paid no attention, spat on the dirt by my car, and was able to tell me within less than a minute: "Engine's finished."

"So... what can I do?"

"Couple days 'til we can replace it. Couple days, maybe a week."

"How much?"

"Can't tell you offhand. We better tow this one."

We returned with a pickup truck and towed my car back to the shop.

"I don't know if I can wait here a week," I said. "Are there other options?"

"Well…" He put his hands on his hips, looking up at the cloudless sky. "You could buy yourself a new one. I just got one in the other day. You wanna come have a look?"

I followed him behind the store, and there he pointed at a black vintage automobile. I know nothing about cars, but I knew there was something about this one. The lines were sharp and deliberate, the face muscular. A man with money did not drive a Toyota Corolla. This car here was far better suited to the new Marcel.

"1970 Ford Torino. We'll have to sign ourselves some papers, but we could have you driving her outta here tomorrow morning. What ya say?"

"I'll take her."

CHAPTER 4

The next afternoon I arrived in Van Horn, the kind of town that only exists because it's located midway between two other towns. A seven-foot pile of tires stood in front of a sign advertising Fried Chicken and Diesel. Signs for motels and gas stations dotted the street as it narrowed off in each direction toward desert mountains. Buzzards circled overhead, dark against the perfect blue sky. I could not have demanded that Texas be more Texas.

The purity of the experience helped to cleanse my mind, rid it of those silly fears that I was complicit in something. Just like an American fairytale, I had my money and I was heading out West to start a new life in the sun.

How did I get the money? Wrong question. Of course we've all heard of the scoundrels, and the arch-scoundrels of capitalism, the fiends who jack up drug prices to drive up their share price, and the banks that launder drug money, and the Wall Street banks that drive good people into bankruptcy, and the medical industry that charges criminal fees for standard procedures, and the micro-lenders who step in pretending to help, only to drive the poor suckers further into debt. But I was not one of them. The persons on the opposite end of the contract had not been conned into short-selling Bitcoin. I had not conned them into anything, or forced them at real or metaphorical gunpoint to hand over any money.

I felt the burn of the cigarette near my flesh. I'd been so lost in thought I'd forgotten to smoke. I was parked in the Motel 6 lot. I took a long drag, blowing the smoke up against the ceiling. The smell of cigarette smoke was replaced by a faint scent of meat, and then an overwhelming stench like bacon burnt on a flame. I gasped for air, and would've had to jump out the car, but just as fast as the smell came, it vanished.

I booked myself a week in the Van Horn Motel 6. Not an obvious choice for a newly-minted millionaire, I know, but the remoteness of the town, the fact that it seemed to exist only as a stopover for truckers and road-trippers, the sense of purpose and purposelessness that gave it—all this made the town appealing to me; it mapped nicely onto my current psychological position. I ate lunch at Chuy's Mexican restaurant, dinner at the local steakhouse; the next day I'd switch lunch and dinner. I drank a lot of beer. I was gaining weight, but I didn't care. The millionaire's bulge, I'd call it. I'd get rid of it later.

On my third day in town, as I drove down the main drag —off to buy beer—the smell of burnt meat filled the car. I tried to keep driving, but the stench intensified to the point where I felt myself dizzying, my eyes filling with water. I swerved to the side of the road, opened the door, got out the car. My eyes watered and I coughed heavily, spitting on the ground.

Across the road from me, a man dressed all in black moved behind a set of tires, before, it seemed, mounting a horse and rounding the corner. I made to follow him, but a force outside myself clamped me to the sidewalk. Then, up ahead at the intersection—less than a hundred yards from where I stood—a massive semi-truck blasted through a red light, killing no one, only because no one was there to be killed.

I cannot say with mathematical certainty, that I would have been right in the firing line had I not pulled over just then. But if you've ever had to extract a plastic shopping bag from liquid that's been frozen, and is now partially thawed, you will know what I mean when I say I felt my soul leave my body. If you do not know what I'm referring to, then I ask you to think on it a moment, please. Imagine pulling a plastic bag out of something semi-frozen. Imagine further that the something frozen is animal blood. The association is likely an unpleasant one, which is not to say that one day when the soul leaves the body for real, the experience will be unpleasant. But this is a story—I'm speaking now specifically of this moment I describe—of a soul that had already planned for its departure, packed its bags, said its farewells, informing perhaps various associates in the spiritual realm, leaving behind only the fleshy vessel it had once called home in the dark.

I assume that you do not picture the soul (if you picture it at all) to be a plastic shopping bag. Neither do I! But when it is deprived of its moment to soar, and when it has been planning for this moment and is then robbed, it becomes un-transcendent, and plastic-like, a mockery of what it had dreamed it would become, and this then is the problem, because the flesh rejoices that it has not died, but the soul inside it is bitter. Perhaps this is avoidable in certain circumstances, for instance if the soul and the flesh learn in the same moment of the fate and then the reversal of the fate—which is to say, they are in lock-step. But when they are at odds with one another, when the soul longs for its freedom, and the flesh rejoices in its continued existence, problems arise. Or so I believe. So experience has shown me.

I bought whisky, not beer, lay on my motel bed, buzzing drunk, then dull drunk, smoking, staring at the hotel fan. The mystery of my predicament had deepened. I hypothesized that the great cosmic string-puller had mistakenly chosen me for an important mission, spared me, armed me, and had yet to realize that I lacked greatness. Or perhaps—and this was far more terrifying—there had been no mistake, and I had been called to perform some higher function, only I did not know how to respond to the call. This is, I suppose, the problem with turning your back on tradition. The call comes, but you have no framework in which to place it. The feelings have no meaning; they point in no direction. Like a feral human who has never seen another of his own kind, trying to come to terms with sexual cravings. Instead of knowing the Divine Beauty of True Love, he humps trees and jerks off into rivers.

That's when I decided, in my drunken, smoky state, that I would continue westwards to Los Angeles, to see my father. That was obviously the reason I'd decided to head this way, whether or not I had known that when I began.

I left the next morning at sunrise.

CHAPTER 5

"**S**wart."

I gave my name to the nurse (Helen, according to her name badge) working the front desk at the center. Deliberately mispronounced, as always, for the sake of the kindly American.

I had to give it to my father; even here, when by almost all standards, he'd hit rock bottom, he was living in the lap of luxury. This was not his first time in rehab, and I assumed it would not be his last. But if you have to do your time somewhere, then a facility like this one, in the hills of L.A., is hardly the worst place to be.

Helen led me down a wide corridor, the type one finds in upmarket hotels, designed to let in air and light, leading off to various small gardens and large rooms. I passed nurses and doctors, I smiled at patients (inmates?), and yes, I did have that sense of smug self-satisfaction one tends to get when encountering failure. One of the darker seeds planted in the human heart; one that has flourished through the ages.

The feeling died completely the moment I saw him. Seated on a wicker chair, dressed in a brown bathrobe, a cup of tea in one hand, an unlit cigarette in the other, he looked like a member of the terminally ill. The nurse nodded at me. I thanked her, but before I could face him—he'd not yet noticed me—I ducked into the bathroom, took out my phone, and made sure I still had the money. I did.

I walked up behind him and placed my hand on his shoulder.

"Marcel?" He put the unlit cigarette in his mouth. "What do you think of the view?"

"Quite spectacular," I said. Brown hills dotted with palm trees, condos, and mansions. In the distance, the ocean. "You've done well for yourself."

I pulled a wicker chair from a nearby circle of chairs. My father smiled gently. His shaved hair had the same salt and pepper shade as the few days of stubble on his chin and cheeks.

"How'd you find me?"

"Mom told me where you were."

"I suspected as much."

"You still have her listed as an emergency contact."

"At her insistence. How's old Baptist Pants?" This was a nickname we—but mostly my father—had given to her new husband, a well-to-do, overweight, Southern Baptist lawyer.

"He's fine."

"Still wearing a bowtie to the dinner table?"

"He wore a bright yellow one on Thanksgiving."

He burst out laughing, leant forward, slapped his leg. "If only I'd known what I was bringing that poor woman to. I'd never have forced her to leave South Africa."

"I'm sure she's forgiven you."

"Ah." He clicked his tongue, waved his hand in the air.

He looked up at me with his sad blue eyes. The last time I'd seen my father he'd also been in rehab. I knew that time he'd had no intention of giving up drinking. Driving drunk and high on painkillers, he'd crashed his car through some respectable person's front gate and smashed into their stone fountain. As part of a plea bargain, his lawyer had him agree to attend three months of intensive rehabilitation at a court-sanctioned center.

"Why are you here this time?" I asked him.

He made a joke of looking over his shoulders, left, right.

"Come on," I said.

"I came here of my own free will. But the more interesting question by far is, what are *you* doing here? You move out to LA?"

"I just arrived this afternoon."

"And you came straight to see your pa?" He put the cigarette behind his ear, took a sip of tea. "This place is not free, you know."

"I'm sure it costs a lot." I wasn't going to make it that easy for him. If I was here for money, he wanted me to confess my intentions up front. He would probably give me money if I asked, but he didn't want this whole—how would he put it? this whole *performance* to have a *certain subtext*. He was, in his way, honest to a painful fault. But then, it wasn't that he didn't like subtext, he just didn't enjoy another actor controlling the subtext. He liked to be in charge.

But I was in charge today. I'd let the moment simmer. "I'm assuming it's private."

"It's private, yes."

"I've heard some insurance plans do pay for this kind of thing."

"That's right." He bit his knuckle, exhaling as if he'd just taken a drag of a cigarette. "You didn't come to talk about health insurance."

"No, I didn't come for that."

"You know I always welcome a visit." He smiled. This was not true, of course; we both knew it, and knew that the other knew it. He was a friendly man, but a private one. Deranged in some ways, and also brilliant. He'd probably been the greatest historian of his generation in South Africa. Not that anyone recognized him on the street, there or here. He came from a line of brilliant and dysfunctional men. His name, Andries, was his father's name also—thankfully my father was not so narcissistic as to name me Andries III—and his father had been a renowned journalist, a critic of the Afrikaner Nationalism that had led to Apartheid. But also an outsider, rejected by his Calvinistic *Broeders*, seen by many as a traitor. *His* father, my great-grandfather, was a general in the Boer War, a personal friend of Jan Smuts.

All this had meant a great deal to me as a child, but over here nobody knew who any of these people were, and most wouldn't care if they learned. It set my father free, I suppose, and also, I feared, drove him insane.

"But why today?" He reached over and rubbed my knee. "Not that you need a reason."

"What if I told you I came because I wanted to get your advice?"

"Advice?" His eyes lit up as he pointed about himself. "I feel duty-bound to remind you of my situation. I told you that came here of my own free will, and that's true. But it would be amiss of me not to... submit to the fact that there are... how should I put it? Extenuating circumstances."

"I don't need to know all the reasons why you came here." I paused, realizing that this may not, in fact, be true. If I'd entered into some celestial contract, and needed to puzzle my way out of it, there were no facts that could be dismissed unknown. "Or maybe you should tell me."

"Nothing so dramatic as last time. I was offered a job here, at a small college. A *liberal* arts college. Job starts fall semester. I came, as I said, of my own free will. I see this as a fresh start."

"Most impressive."

He raised his teacup, as if he were proposing a toast with a champagne glass, and bowed his head slightly.

"So I am worthy, then? To offer you my advice?"

"You've always been worthy."

"Ja." He put the unlit cigarette in his mouth. "Your mother was a first-generation immigrant to South Africa."

"What's that got to do with anything?"

"When she left, it didn't rip her apart, like this." He made as if he were yanking an organ out of his body. "My family had been there for more than two hundred years. *Your* family." He'd given me this spiel before, about leaving the homeland. "To separate yourself from the culture can be dangerous. You become an orphan in this world. Even if you're adopted, you'll always be the stepchild. Viewed with suspicion."

"Even here?" I pointed out at the city. "Half the people who live here were born somewhere else."

"I'm not different enough to be a curiosity. Nobody cares about my story. Nobody cares."

"You're persecuting yourself."

"Contributing to my persecution, perhaps." He smiled. "But I did not invent the conditions of it." His fist beat the edge of his chair. "Perhaps this is a better analogy. It's like loving a woman who cannot be faithful. Or being the lover, and never the husband."

"You once told me whites, in South Africa, Afrikaners, were an orphan culture."

"Severed from the parent culture, yes."

"Well, you're not in Europe, but you're in the... what do we call it? The West. Aren't you? Maybe you're no longer an orphan."

"Come on. Your speech is riddled with ellipses because you don't believe yourself. I'm an orphan of orphans. I'm the sailor who, kicked out of the navy, joins a band of pirates, only to be discarded by his pirate brothers, left on a sandbar in the middle of the ocean. Ahoy, look, the gulls they come for my flesh." He looked about frantically, swatted the air as if he were under attack, fully committed to his own drama.

I hadn't witnessed many of my father's tirades. He'd not been prone to such theatricality when I was a child. But after immigrating to the States, rants of biblical intensity had become standard. I'd moved away from home after two years in the country, and my mother was left to deal with his increasingly bizarre behavior. She'd telephone me sometimes when my father was out of control. I remember listening once as he jumped up and down, screaming—my mother informed me that he was yelling out the window, and so I have that image in my head—at the *heathens*, and also at the gods, who tossed him about like a piece of trash in the ocean, indifferent to his suffering.

If only you could have seen him when I was younger. He faced the world with great equanimity, was self-reliant to a fault, would never have thought to blame the world for his shortcomings.

"I'm sorry that you feel persecuted."

"*Feel* persecuted. That's a way of silencing me. The way you *feel* is not aligned with how things actually *are*. Adjust your mind and things will get better."

"You're sitting in California. The sun's shining. You have money, and food, and you sleep each night in luxury."

"Vanity of vanities."

"So he quotes the Bible."

"I'm sorry, Marcel, but you came for advice. This is what I have to give today."

He drank the rest of his tea and placed the cup on the ground; he dragged on his unlit cigarette. It seemed appropriate that he was quoting Ecclesiastes. Had I come here chasing after wind?

"I came into some money," I said, taking myself by surprise.

He looked at me intensely with those dark blue eyes, deep as glacial lakes.

"Yes, you haven't come to ask for money. We've established that."

"That's not what I'm saying."

He took another drag of his unlit cigarette, pretended to exhale, then crushed it on the edge of his chair. He threw the mangled, unsmoked stump into his teacup.

"Yes," he said, when he saw me watching him. "I know what I'm doing. I smoke a pack, sometimes two, a day. Unlit. Better on the lungs, better on the heart."

"Same toll on the wallet."

"Quite correct. So you've come into money. You have a new job? You sold something?"

"No and no."

"You've become a bandit, and you're heading out West to escape the law."

"Closer, but not quite."

"Enough with the guessing game."

"Have you heard of cryptocurrencies?"

"Heard of them, yes." He paused, then looked at me with a mad intensity, as if he were seeing me for the first time. "You made money in that racket?"

"I... yes, I did." As I smiled, a gentle, warm current flowed through me. Fatherly approval. For the first time since coming into the money, I viewed the win as an actual achievement.

"We talking big bucks here?"

"Yeah."

"My boy." He raised his hand, and we high-fived. "How much?"

"More than what you're thinking."

"In the tens of thousands?" I shook my head. "Hundreds of thousands?" Again, I shook my head. He paused before saying the next word: "Millions."

"Well over ten million."

He looked across the city, silent for a few moments before taking another cigarette from his box, placing it unlit in his mouth, and dragging on it. "Let's go drinking then. I'm getting out of here." He pushed himself up from the chair, then looked over his left shoulder, his right.

"That's not why I came here."

"I'm joking, boy." He sat down again, took another drag. "But wouldn't that be fun? Huh? Damnit, I feel like lighting this thing. Me and you on the town? One night? Father and son."

"You're in rehab, for God's sake."

"The son has come to lecture his father."

"I came for advice, I told you."

"You want investment advice? I can put you in touch with the right people. You want legal advice, talk to old Baptist Pants."

"That's not the kind of advice I'm looking for."

"How much exactly are we talking?"

"Sixteen million."

"Sixteen million?" The 's' came out in a hiss, and his accent sounded terribly South African. He shook his head in disbelief.

"That's right."

"Your great-grandfather—if you take inflation, and currency conversation and all that nonsense into consideration—he was a dollar millionaire. But not your grandfather; not me."

"He deserved to be rich."

"Deserved?" He spat out the word, as if the very concept deserved scorn.

"He was a General in the Boer War; a lawyer and a farmer. He was from *that* time. A real man."

"And what? We're not real men?"

"You may be. I got rich from trading cryptocurrency CFDs."

"We're in the grips of the information revolution; knowing how to be a *great* farmer is not where it's at. You understand what you need to understand in this time and place. You're a member of the miraculously adaptive human race. You are a Homo sapiens. A wise man."

"Me? A Homo sapiens? You're too kind, Dad."

He smiled and crushed his un-smoked cigarette on his knee, throwing the stump into his teacup.

"Is that why you came? To get fatherly approval? Well, you have it. I'm proud of you, my son."

"Thank you. But it's not because of skill that I got this money."

"Why did you get it then?"

"Luck."

"Luck; skill. Different words for the same thing. You're lucky to have a skill."

"No, not that. I feel like... someone who won the lottery. Celestial good fortune. And..." I felt as if a cork had been pulled from my chest and my words bubbled up freely. "Before it happened I made a... compact... I don't know, and I don't understand."

He listened intensely, nodding as I spoke. "I understand."

"You do?"

"I know why you wanted to see me."

He placed another unlit cigarette in his mouth. Seeing my father deep in thought is like watching a god before he speaks the fate of his subjects into being. And this was the other thing about him—crazy as he was, mad in his judgments sometimes, he had a way of being completely non-judgmental when ideas were brought to him. He listened in a way that no one else I knew listened. Truly. Deeply. With an open heart.

"Before I came here," he said, "I was trying to stay clean on my own. I did the rooms. I kept bumping into a man—in two different rooms—he'd won money in the California Lottery. He told me about a different kind of support group he attended, specifically for people who'd suddenly come into money. Some had won the lottery; others had inherited a small fortune from a relative they barely knew. And as often as not, the money sent their lives into chaos."

"Because they were irresponsible with it? Or because they believed... they'd tampered with the spiritual order?"

"He said some things to me, things I think you'd find interesting. I have his number. You should meet him. You should go to one of their meetings." He nodded, and for the first time since laughing at his vision of *Old Baptist Pants* wearing a yellow bowtie to dinner, he smiled. "I'm glad you came to me about this."

"I am, too."

I held his hand and we looked out across the city of Los Angeles. I felt so happy right then, warm and accepted.

<h1 style="text-align:center">CHAPTER 6</h1>

The meeting took place in a dimly lit side room of an Episcopalian church in Echo Park. Frustration and misery pulsated from the group, who sat in a circle on plastic chairs. The Moneyed Unfortunates, I'd been told, was their nickname.

I sat next to a middle-aged white woman with a freckled face and long brown hair. She wore a server's uniform.

"Just done with the night shift." She wiped her nose with the back of her wrist, then made a show of sniffing under her armpit. "Diner down the road. No time to shower, no time change."

I paused, trying to think of something to say. "I'm Marcel." I offered her my hand.

"Denise."

From her pocket she took a bright pink phone and flipped through pictures, landing on a teenage girl sitting on a bike, smiling. "Don't get to see my daughter anymore. You don't have to share." She put her phone away. "It's just my nature. I'm an over-sharer."

"Yeah."

A broad-shouldered, tall black man in a red jacket, planner under his arm, strode into the center of our group. We all stood, sat again.

"Who's not here?" He asked, as he took a seat in the middle of the circle. "There's seventeen of you. Someone's missing."

"And we have a new person," Denise called out.

I raised my hand.

"We'll get to you. So, two people missing." He scribbled a note in his planner.

"Karen's not here," said a middle-aged Asian man, across the circle from us.

"Kevin?" The host turned on his chair. "How's the cancer?"

"There he goes again." A barrel-chested white man in a chef's outfit spoke in a booming voice. "How's the cancer? This guy should be chairman of the sensitivity committee."

"It's okay," Kevin said. "I'm happy to talk about it. Two years remission."

"You want to ask him about his wife's sex life?" the barrel-chested man asked.

"Ex-wife. Yes, she's still with my brother."

"Jesus Christ," I muttered louder than I'd intended to.

The host turned on his chair and looked at me. He was a striking man: taller than me by a few inches, bald, chiseled facial features.

"How rude of me," he said. "I was abrupt earlier. I should have welcomed you at the start."

My body found itself back in Catholic boys' school in South Africa and raised me to my feet.

"Marcel Swart." I almost added *sir*, but caught myself just in time.

"My name is Dr. Rose. Virgil Rose."

"Hello Dr. Rose." I sat down again.

"You didn't need to stand, Marcel. Welcome to the group. Let's give Marcel a warm welcome."

"Hi, Marcel," the group chimed.

"It's your first time, Marcel. You're welcome to tell us what brought you here. Or if you'd rather listen a while first, that's okay, too."

"Maybe listen a while first."

"You want to hear about what happened to me?" the barrel-chested white guy called out. "Buncha thugs smashed up my car the other night. I've already lost all the fucking money, and shit like this still happens?"

He pointed at Dr. Rose who remained absolutely calm, nodding his head.

"I hear you, Dan. But let's remember what we spoke about last time?"

"No time limits. No expectations. Yeah, yeah. I hear you, man. But my life is a fucking pig circus. I'm living with my mother again. Jerking off to porn in the evenings." A few "urghs" and headshakes. "What? What? My point is I used to have a girlfriend and I didn't have to do shit like that. I had a job."

"We're here to support one another." Dr. Rose turned about on his chair. "Not to judge."

"I lost custody of my daughter," Denise called out.

"I have cancer," said an old, frail-looking woman who clutched a handbag close to her stomach. She had a hint of a Southern accent.

"Oh, I'm so sorry, Mrs. Dern," said Dr. Rose. "Do you want to share more?"

"Not really." She held open her right hand to reveal a rosary. "I've been praying. But I fear God no longer listens. He shut me off when I turned away."

"You don't know that."

"My husband, he always told me gambling was evil. So I

didn't go to the casino. But I liked it. I liked to play a bitta poker, you know?" She smiled at the group. Mrs. Dern appeared to command more attention than the others. "But then I dreamed about those numbers. I kept dreaming about them." A look of horror came across the old woman's face, and now as she glanced about the room none of our faces registered for her, I could tell. She saw something else. I felt my stomach tighten, my jaw clench, as I remembered that night on Jim's farm, the rustling in the forest. The sound of hooves on rock. "Then my poor husband died. And now I'm sick. Why, Virgil?"

"There isn't always a why."

"But I need a why," she said as she gripped the rosary.

"I need a why, too," said Dan.

"Keep praying, Mrs. Dern. You're in the land of chaos."

"I'm old, Virgil. I'm not afraid of dying. What I'm afraid of is not knowing. Not understanding what this world is. I knew more a few years ago than now. I just don't want to leave this world in confusion."

These words burrowed through my veins like cold roots.

I made it to the end of the meeting without having to introduce myself, and stayed afterwards to help Dr. Rose put away the chairs.

"You look like a smoking man." He placed his hand on my back.

Outside, the street had filled with hipsters off to get morning coffee, walking their small, yappie-type dogs.

Although he'd positioned himself one step below me—a conscious choice, I sensed—his eyes were level with mine. He had the kind of build that came from bench-pressing twice your own body weight.

"You need certain vices," he said, holding up his cigarette.

"If you try to drive them all out and become a saint, you push too far. Then it all flips. You turn into a monster."

"Sounds like a good reason not to quit. Thank you."

We smiled, laughed for a moment.

"Those people you met in there." He pointed at the church building. "They're hurting. Hurting bad. All of them. Each person has their way of expressing pain. And it can look a little... strange, at times."

"I didn't come to judge."

"I'm an open book. That's how I cope. I've found if I open, others open. I'll tell you my story. Good?"

"Please."

"I was in and out of the foster care system. On the street at seventeen. I'd flat-lined twice by nineteen. Happened a third time at twenty-one. But that time was different. Soul left body. I was awake. Alert. The most alive I'd ever been. It was beautiful. And when I came back, I no longer felt afraid. All the pain had gone."

I wanted to tell him about my moment in Van Horn. But his experience was transcendent and beautiful, the way it should be, and if I started talking about plastic packets and semi-frozen blood, he'd take me for a savage.

"A few months passed in absolute bliss. I still slept on park benches, but now I felt safe and perfectly loved. I'd never known what that felt like. But it didn't last. I never returned to the old world. Instead, I moved into this in-between space, between the harsh, physical world, and the realm of perfect peace."

"But the rules were different. For instance, I'd have a dream about an old lady dressed in blue, and the next morning I'd wake to see that lady sitting on the park bench opposite me."

"But how does this all relate to money?"

"You ready to go deeper?"

"That's why I'm here."

"Some people hop off at this station. And I get it. I get it. But, like I said, I put the truth out there as I've experienced it. How others judge, that's their business."

I said again: "I'm not here to judge."

"This in-between realm is where the gods live, and ghosts, and other strange beings." He squashed his cigarette on the steps. "Another?" He lit us each one. "The evil ones know us well, and how to manipulate us."

"They know we love money?"

"That's what I've concluded. So, one night, when I was still living on a park bench, I woke to a rustling sound in the bushes."

The hairs on the back of my neck stood up. My chest and shoulders tingled, hot.

"I don't remember exactly what happened. But I followed this... thing into the trees. I was living in the park, just down the road there." He pointed vaguely away from the church. "I heard whispering and laughing. I looked down and saw numbers scribbled in the sand. Next thing I knew it was morning. I was lying on the bench."

"If this story has a tragic ending, I'm not sure I want to hear it."

"The in-between part is pretty exciting. I won a whole lot of money on the lottery."

"I don't mean to be rude, but it sounds like your life was at a pretty low point when this happened."

"There are worse things than living on a park bench." He reached into his jean pocket and took out a can of espresso, cracked it open. He finished it in one gulp. "Most folk don't come here till something's happened. What's happening in your life to bring you here?"

"Curiosity. That's all." We both knew I was lying, and knew the other knew, but my flesh knotted up, and held my experiences captive. If I told him what'd happened, I'd solidify the recent past, make it real in a way I wasn't ready to. "I'm a writer. Always looking for new stories."

"These peoples' lives aren't your food."

"I know that."

Moving his face closer to mine, he stared into my eyes.

"Come on. What you holding back?"

He dropped his cigarette into the espresso can he'd just emptied down his throat, then held it out towards me. Wooden bracelets rattled up and down his arm as he put the can into his back pocket.

I remained silent, afraid that if I framed what had happened to me in his terms, I'd bind myself to an awful path. I didn't want to end up like those people in there.

"I made some money. Online trading."

"We don't get many traders here." He pulled a baker boy hat from his jacket pocket and placed it on his head. "You're not a professional, are you?"

"What does it matter?"

"Those folks tend to be hard-nosed rationalists."

"I'm rational."

"I'm not criticizing you, friend. You're open. They tend not to be. In the short term they think they know what's going on. In the long term, terrible destruction awaits. It comes as a surprise. You at least have your eyes open."

"So something bad is going happen to me, and I can't escape it?"

"You could try get ahead of it. But that's a plan I've always seen fail."

I felt my chest tighten. The world seemed too close, the sun too bright.

"I should leave now."

"Join me for coffee. I get my mid-morning caffeine at a quiet spot five minutes from here."

. . .

Sitting at a sidewalk table, I felt repulsed by all the humans that passed by, like they were insects, as were their little dogs. They seemed too close. Scuttling, creeping, crawling. I scratched at my arm and the underside of my face.

He took a box of snus from one of his many jacket pockets and placed a portion under his lip. "There're a few things you should consider." He took a sip of coffee. "If you've entered this realm, that's where you are."

"The world is just..." I searched for a word, but nothing seemed fitting. I couldn't say mundane. The world had never been mundane. I'd wanted to say something like *same-ish*, but clearly even that wasn't true. The sound of scraping shoes on the sidewalk as passersby drifted along, felt invasive, like a toothbrush on a blackboard. And then, even closer and more uncomfortable, like waking to a stranger massaging your scalp. "The world is here."

"And you are in it. And it is in you." After taking another sip of coffee, he gazed about, a look of serenity on his face. "Sometimes there's turbulence and you have to ride it out. You're not the captain."

"That's not reassuring."

"Isn't it? Stop fighting and resisting what can't be controlled."

"And do what? Sit at home, wait for my life to pass by?"

"No, it doesn't move that way." With his index finger he traced a pattern on the table. "A spider web. For them. The ones that live in this middle realm. Time does not move linearly as it seems to for us. It's all complete. The living are already ghosts."

"I don't like the sound of that," I said. He turned his large hands palms up. "Can't I just undo this? Or, what if I... take my money and enjoy it. Forget about all this stuff."

"You're free to explore all options. Keep your imagination independent." He tapped the side of his head. "That's very important."

He took a twenty dollar note from the same pocket that stored the snus, and placed it on the table in front of me, then got to his feet.

"You're a messenger of doom," I said.

"No. I've been here long enough to know that if you're meeting me, something's happened. As you experience it, these events lie in the future. But you should stop thinking about the future and the past as you used to. Think on their terms."

"What if I need to speak to you again?"

"Here." He gave me a card. "Anytime."

He turned sharply, the soles of his shoes screeching on the sidewalk.

As he left, a thought that'd been scraping at the edges of my awareness, like a cat locked outside in a storm, burst in. This was the table I'd sat at the day I'd argued with my supervisor about my dissertation. We'd talked about Dante. I'd told him it was futile to consider divine beings as purely metaphorical.

"For the text to come to life, you need to face it on its own terms," I'd said.

"I do. Your reading lacks maturity." Professor Martin Huffman was his name. He was a large man. The glasses, the Harris Tweed, the elbow patches. And what business did a man in his forties have vaping? "You give this classic no more respect than a Dungeons and Dragons campaign."

"I give it more respect than you do."

"I'm embarrassed to turn this in to the rest of the committee. Why are you citing evidence for angels appearing to modern people?"

"Because I've changed my mind about this stuff. I think there's something there."

"Then you must leave academia."

I doubled down on my position, and in the final draft added sources I knew didn't hold up to academic standards. The defense was a dog show. Huffman—who should have been in my corner—offered me up as a sacrifice to the committee. He described me variously as a demon hunter and a vampire slayer.

We skipped the traditional post-defense dinner. He did not get a thank you card from me. In the weeks that followed I boiled with righteous indignation. I'd lie awake for hours at night arguing with Huffman, replaying the defense, only this time throwing sassy comebacks in his face, and winning over the rest of the committee to my cause. I dreamed about Huffman and that committee room. He lived inside me like a parasite, and the more I argued with him, the more powerful he became, and the stronger my convictions grew.

This infection reached its peak about three weeks post-defense. I lay awake from one a.m. to sunup, rolling about like a sick dog, howling in the head, but by morning the fever had broken. Three weeks after that I didn't give a shit. I could barely remember what we'd argued about, came to see things from his perspective, even began to assume he was right. Or, at the very least, as likely as I to have been right. Perhaps we were both right. Or both wrong.

I considered writing him, apologizing for my stubborn defiance. I thought about it, and thought about it. At first the desire was strong, but I didn't act on it, and slowly, like the argument-infection, it faded.

All this passed through me in the time it took Dr. Rose to make it to the end of the street. Like a teenager with a crush,

I hoped he might turn around and look back at me. But he didn't.

I paid for the coffee and walked along the street away from my car. That this memory flashed through my mind right then had great significance. The moments were connected through time, space, and meaning. I imagined bringing forth the conversation with Rose as evidence against Huffman. It's like what Rose had said about time. In the realm I'd entered, it did not flow in one direction. My conviction during that past conversation had been fueled by the certainty I'd already gained in the future.

My fists clenched as I imagined dragging Huffman by his collar, throwing him into the middle of the support group.

"See this, you ivory tower wanker. Real people battling demons."

I stepped into a craft beer bar and ordered an expensive IPA. Sitting at a wooden counter in the almost empty shop, I drank it quickly, stepped outside, and called my father.

We drove along the Pacific Coast Highway, windows down. He lay his head against the doorframe, a look of absolute serenity on his face. We bought Coca-Colas and sat on a bench overlooking the ocean, both smoking cigarettes, mine lit, his not.

The noise of the morning still ground away in my mind.

"Dr. Virgil Rose," I said. Gulls flew overhead. Not a cloud in the sky. "He gave me bad news."

"The man who ran the session?"

"Yes."

"I wouldn't wed myself to his views."

"I'm not."

"Yet he has a hold on you." He crushed out his unlit cigarette and took another from the box.

"I had an experience." I described what had happened at the coffee shop that morning. "It's a powerful, synchronistic moment."

"Beautiful. That's a gift, not a sentence handed down from above." He raised his hands toward the sky.

"A gift?" I said. "A box of darkness, maybe."

My father shook his head, stretched his hands across the bench, and lay his ankle on his knee.

"I had a dream about you last night, Marcel."

"You did?"

"You were a small boy. Three, four, I don't know. You came running toward me, and I picked you up. You looked so happy." He smiled at me. "Come on, let's go down to the beach."

We swam in our boxer shorts, and as the evening came we watched the sunset from the hood of the car. When I dropped him back at his rehab center, he said to me: "That moment is a gift, not a sentence handed down. Life is a gift, not a sentence handed down."

The next time I saw him he was dead. Lying in the morgue, his face had swollen and his neck seemed too wide.

CHAPTER 7

I'd been given the keys to my father's apartment, a two-bedroom place a couple minutes' drive from the community center. At ten a.m., on zero-hours sleep, I unlocked the door. Inside, I opened the curtains, the windows; the apartment smelt stale and unloved. On the kitchen counter, a half-drank coffee mug had transformed into a petri-dish, in which grew a thick layer of green and blue mold.

Books and magazines lay spread across his living room, some in neat piles, others in the ruins of piles that had fallen over, some on his coffee table, others on the shelf that would, in a normal lounge, have housed a television. Stacks of records in crumpled plastic covers—one almost as high as myself—marked out the corners of the room. There were unopened boxes and dirty plates with forks and knives stuck to them, and whisky tumblers marked by the yellow residue of the liquid they'd held. On the floor, half-hidden behind a pile of records, I saw the whisky bottle. I poured four fingers into one of his dirty glasses, pushed aside the papers scattered on his couch, and sat down for a good half hour.

I avoided direct eye contact with myself as I opened the mirrored medicine cabinet in his bathroom. According to the police report—or I should rather say, according to what the rehab center told me was in the police report—my father had been found in his room, dead.

I'd read about fentanyl—ten granules and you'll have the high of your life, eleven granules and someone gets a 3 a.m. call. Where had he found it? When?

A seasoned abuser like my father must have known he was playing with fire. But suicide? That seemed impossible. He'd always been an optimistic man. There was even something optimistic about his drug use—he went looking for answers that could not be found on the page, that could not be lifted up from documents, transcripts, interviews.

Two of the four whisky fingers down my gullet, I had the courage to enter his bedroom. It was surprisingly neat, the bed made, no clothes on the floor. On the bedside table sat a framed picture of him with me and my mother.

I pulled the door shut, went back to the couch, and wept violently, like a person I didn't recognize. I knew nothing about this disoriented man who found himself in a strange apartment in Los Angeles. I poured the next two fingers down my throat, pushed all the pages off his couch onto the floor, lay down, and crossed my arms tight around my chest. Closing my eyes, I waited for the pain to subside.

I dreamed I saw my father sitting in front of a low table playing a game. He was dead, and I knew he was dead, but still I could talk to him. I asked if I was the reason he'd died, and he looked up at me, then his face swelled and he fell to the side, bloated like a corpse in the sun.

I woke to see I'd missed a call from my mother. We'd spoken in the early morning just after I'd seen the body, and she'd told me that when we'd taken care of the immediate business—her phrase—I should come stay with her and Charles for as long as I needed. But there were few things that seemed less comforting than living under the roof of Old Baptist Pants, watching him waddle about the house, holding his puffy hand in the evening as he said the prayer over dinner. I told her thank you, but that I didn't think it would be right for me. Thankfully Charles was in the middle of an important case and so he couldn't come out with her.

I picked her up at LAX the next morning. My mother, Donna Smith nee Swart nee Shellsworth, is tall, and all her life she's worn her dark hair at least to shoulder length; she doesn't leave the house without makeup on, without her clothes carefully selected for the occasion. Today she wore all black, including her black glasses. She put her arms around me, holding me for a long time.

"My dear son. I'm sorry."

"Me, too. I'm sorry. I mean, for you. I'm sorry for you, too."

Back at his apartment I showed her the picture I'd found next to his bed. I knew it would break her, and I knew it was cruel, and I knew also that she had to see it. She wiped the tears from beneath her eyes, placed the photograph face down on the couch, and sat next to it.

"Why did he have to live this way? Like a pig. He was such a brilliant man. So smart."

"I know."

"The place smells like rot and mold. When did he last clean it?"

"I don't know."

"It doesn't matter now. I told him a thousand times when he was alive."

"It's not your fault."

"Of course it's not." She looked about the room. "We had fun together, didn't we?"

"We sure did."

She laughed, turning away from me as she wiped beneath her eyes.

"I shouldn't have left when I left," I said.

"What? Our house? Of course you had to leave. What were you going to do? Stay at home forever? Live in our basement? You had to live your life."

"But he was fine back then, wasn't he?"

She huffed. "He was... I don't know what he was. I never did." She patted the couch. "Sit next to me." We put our arms around each other, and stared at the floor.

She booked us each a room in the DoubleTree Hotel downtown. We ate Chinese takeaway together in her room and made our way through a bottle of wine. After the meal, she took a box of cigarettes from her bag and smoked out the window.

"I thought you'd quit?"

"I'm a social smoker again. It suits me better."

Even in the privacy of her bedroom, with no one but her own son to see her, she wore an evening dress, makeup, and although she'd taken off her high-heel shoes, the black stockings she wore were clearly high quality. I walked over to her, taking a cigarette from my own box.

"Does Old Baptist Pants know?"

"Old who?"

I laughed as I lit up. "He never said that in front of you? Makes sense."

"That's what Andries called Charles?" She shook her head, but a mischievous grin crept onto her face. "That's so him."

We both ashed our cigarettes at the same time, gazing down, twelve stories, to the street below.

"How are you doing for money? You're still offering those online lessons?"

"I am, yes."

"And you have your shrimp boat money?"

"My shrimp boat money, huh?"

"That's what it is, isn't it?"

"Yes, Mom."

"Why don't you come out to Charleston? We can help set you up there."

"I don't want help setting up in Charleston."

"You've always resisted help."

"No, I haven't."

I squashed my cigarette against the window ledge and threw it away. Of course I'd never looked at Old Baptist Pants's financial records, but I suspected that he and I belonged now in a similar financial category. I so wanted to tell her this.

But she was not like my father, she would want to know every little detail about how I came into it, how I planned to use it, if I'd paid the right amount of tax—which I surely had not, possibly would not—and so I'd have to sit down with Old Baptist Pants for legal advice. All the while, the dark guest, the curse, would be there. I could not bring it into their home.

"Do you go to Baptist Church?"

"With Charles?" She threw away her cigarette and closed the window. "I go with him, yes."

"He knows you're a Catholic?"

"Of course."

"But he doesn't know you smoke?"

She sat down opposite me. "Why all the questions?"

"You were questioning me earlier."

"I'm your mother, I get to question you." She smiled as she topped up both our glasses.

"I guess you don't drink that much with him either."

"Baptists are allowed to drink."

An awful image erupted in my mind, of Baptist Pants stripping naked, climbing atop my mother, his belly crashing against her. Why would she submit to such torture voluntarily?

I paused a moment, taking hold of her arm. "I love you."

"I love you, too, my dear son. We should get some sleep."

The next morning we went to the morgue together and signed papers. She didn't want to look at his body. Then we drove across town to the rehab center he'd been staying in, and were shown to the office of the director, Stan Newman. One of the slimiest characters I'd had the misfortune of meeting, Stan stank up his enormous office with the kind of aftershave worn only by swingers and gigolos. He wore a muscle top, a fake tan, black glasses that rested on his greasy forehead. Pure California sunshine streamed in through the office's many windows, and he sat in a chair—on the same side of his desk as we did—with his legs wide open, as if to say, *check out my cock.*

"How could you let this happen?" my mother asked him.

"We share your sadness, Mrs. Swart. It never gets any easier." He sank lower in his chair.

"I'm not Mrs. Swart."

"What should I call you then?" He was totally unapologetic.

"Donna Shellsworth is my name."

"Donna Shellsworth, let me tell you, we did everything we could to help him. But patients are free to come and go. This isn't Abu Ghraib."

"And they pay in full up front, I suppose."

"Of course. We have a ninety-five percent success rate."

"How could anyone disprove you? It's unfalsifiable nonsense. That's the kind of figure fly-by-night institutions put on their brochures."

"You're upset, Mrs. Swart. Mrs. Shellsworth."

"Oh, don't be patronizing. My son saw Andries the day before he died, and he said his father was doing well."

I'd said no such thing, but I didn't want to contradict her in front of this man.

"We had a different view, I'm afraid," the bronzed man said, shifting about in his chair. "He'd been saying some rather... peculiar things in the group meetings. He kept going on about the spiritual order, and curses." He tapped his right temple. "Not healthy."

"Why are we here?" I stood up, gripping my mother's arm — too hard, I quickly realized.

"You're listed as next of kin, Donna. We have to give you the belongings he left behind."

"How many weeks did he have left here?"

"Two."

"You should refund that money. I'm sure you'll fill up the bedroom. Make double the money. What kind of incentive is that?"

"We don't do refunds. We have a ninety-five..."

"Percent success rate," she cut him off. "Yes. You've already quoted that bullshit statistic. He died on your watch. What kind of business is this?"

"Come, Mom." I took her arm. "Let's get his stuff and leave."

"We have some pamphlets at the door," Stan said. "We offer discount rates to the family of alumni, as well as military..."

"Fuck off," she said as we left his office.

. . .

It was easy to convince my mother to have the funeral in two days. I was terrified that something would happen to her. I needed her to leave as quickly as possible. This caused a horrid pain, since having her around made things better. I could think clearly, and the days progressed in an orderly fashion—I ate all my meals, slept at a regular time, with the aid of Ambien. Old friends in South Africa sent their deepest condolences but none could make it to the funeral. A counsellor at the rehab helped round up the mismatched group of people my father had called friends in the last months of his life. The withered faces, the tired looks, told me these folks had seen it all before—a man appears to be on the mend, but the next day he's in the cold chamber with a tag on his toe. The priest said a few words, but I was hardly paying attention; then the hearse drove off and two days later we stood outside LAX again.

"You're always welcome, you know that, right? And you can stay for as long as you want."

"I know."

"Take this and don't argue with me." She handed me a check for ten thousand dollars.

"Mom, I don't need..."

"I said, don't argue with me. I love you."

"I love you too."

She turned to wave as she entered the terminal building, then blended into the crowd.

My father's office was windowless and tomblike. An unsmoked cigarette balanced on the edge of an ashtray, and in honor of my father I smoked it, unlit, as I glanced over the stacks of books that rose like small towers in a wasteland.

Two of the three major book piles were filled with works on the Anglo-Boer War, not surprising given that two of his ten published works had focused on the conflict. On top was his old copy of Virgil's *Aeneid*. I skimmed through it. Every page had more handwritten notes on it than lines of the original poem. It was not surprising to find this book here either; he'd been obsessed with it since boyhood. But beneath that— I felt the world open up like a pupil exposed to bright light— was a well-worn copy of Jung's *Synchronicity*. Places in the book had been marked out with orange and blue stickers, and in my fumbling haste I opened to a page, at random, where I found a passage about the Boer War underlined in pencil. It referenced the writing of J.W. Dunne. During his time serving in South Africa in the British army, he'd had a dream about a terrible volcanic eruption in which four thousand people died days before a volcano in Martinique erupted, killing forty thousand. Strange, I did not remember this passage from when I'd read the book on Jim's farm. Stranger still, what had my father been working on? Academic reputations were not built on the back of Jungian ideas about precognition.

I poured another glass of whisky and rolled my left arm in circles, breathing deeply, the pain growing sharper, no longer the pain of the soul but the pain of the physical blood-pump. Was it possible to die of a heart attack at my age? If this was the working of the curse, then ordinary medical explanations didn't matter.

A tap against the door. Another tap, a knock, a tap. The beetle flew across the room and up inside the silver lamp-shade. It danced about, casting a shadow across the pages, then fell down and landed on its back, tiny bug feet twitching in the air. The pain in my chest completely vanished. I picked up the beetle. The carapace was hot. Holding it close to my eye I saw it was indeed shiny blue and black. It wriggled about on my skin, jumped into the air, and flew out the room.

A gift, not a sentence handed down.

That's what my father had said.

I cried again as I smoked the unlit cigarette.

CHAPTER 8

Virgil Rose and I sat in the courtyard of a Persian restaurant, smoking peach-flavored tobacco through a hookah. We shared finger foods. Since my father's death I'd felt like a man missing the side of his body.

"You knew this was coming for me."

"A man who lives in Tornado Alley knows a tornado's coming."

"That sounds indifferent."

"Almost all humans are deeply deluded." He took a drag on the hookah, blowing the smoke toward the night sky. "If you saw there was nothing to be done, you'd stop hurting right away."

"Are you a nihilist?"

"No, no. I saw the world from the outside once, for a brief moment. I realized how... comically futile it all is." He took a sip of his drink. "But that only made me love humans more."

"I want to be where you are. Where there's no pain."

"I live where you live, friend." He pointed around him. The courtyard had filled up. Glass-encased candles flickered between groups of friends, and shadows danced across the tables. "I feel the same thing these people feel, but I remember what it's like not to."

"Feeling is so difficult."

"Yes, it is. If you want to get through, you need a path."

The last time I'd sat on this chair I'd been opposite my father, a few days after graduation. He'd been in town for a meeting. When I told him the story of my defense he'd laughed and hit the table. It hurt, even though I knew he was laughing at them, not me. Nothing in the world had been more important to me than that pain, and it had to be respected. Then the hurt faded, and the memory of my father's laughter faded too, or so I thought. Now when it came back to me, it did not mock.

"What path are you talking about?" But before he spoke, I answered my own question: "When I graduated university, my father reminded me that I should pursue something that mattered."

"That can be a path, yes."

Virgil took a newspaper from the leather satchel that hung over the side of his chair. He placed it in front of me. In gothic lettering: *The Chickasaw Gazette.*

"If I was your age and had no binding ties, this is where I'd head."

"What the hell is this?" I asked, flipping the paper around.

I cast my eye over the cover story.

"There's a sheriff's election in two months that'll determine the fate of this little town."

"And why do I care?"

"The work I do up here. That meeting you attended." He tapped his chest, then the newspaper. "We're all seeds of this. If this place falls, we all fall."

"I don't even understand what you do."

"You know what happened to you. You're a rich man now. You think there's no price tag?"

"My father's death is not connected to this. It's mad to think that way." Dizzy, I stood up, hot balls of anger in my flesh.

"You know what you know. Take this. Read it. Think about it."

◈

I sat in my father's office sipping whisky.

The lead article in the *Chickasaw Gazette* described an upcoming sheriff's election in the eponymous Southern Alabama town. For eight years a sheriff named Chuck Jones had protected an enigmatic woman known only as Maggie—some said her name was Magdalena, others just Maggie. There were no pictures of her on file. Maggie's organization, known as The Farm—officially a "cultural organization," but believed by many in the area to be a cult—sat on an island in the bayou near Chickasaw. Some described her and her followers as Satanists; others believed they were harmless weirdos.

Eight years earlier, a young woman had gone missing from the neighborhood, her body found floating in the muddy waters of the bayou. The angry residents—blaming Maggie and her farm—elected the fire-breathing Jones to drive her out of town. Within a year of coming to office, however, Jones started preaching a different message: Maggie's Farm was a positive influence on Chickasaw; she and her followers were not only benign, they contributed to the town and helped give it its unique flavor. *Keep Chickasaw Unique* became the official slogan for Jones's first reelection campaign. Crime had dropped during his tenure. The murder had been pegged on some out-of-town drifter. The strongest dissidents moved out of Chickasaw, replaced by people who didn't know or care about The Farm. The anger faded. Maggie and her people barely featured in the mind of the town. This state of peace had been maintained for years, and two more elections. But then Jefferson Lee came to town.

He was first spotted at a railway crossing. Even in the small-town-South, a man gets noticed when he arrives from nowhere on a black horse. Pictures of Lee appeared in the newspaper the next day, and soon enough videos of him riding around the town erecting "Chickasaw is Contested" signs started to appear on Facebook groups and YouTube Channels. By the end of the month, an enormous "Dial 800-TRUTH for the TRUTH" billboard had been replaced by a 5x life-size image of Lee atop his black stallion, beneath the words: *There's a New Sheriff in Town.*

❦

Two nights after our meeting, Virgil Rose came to my father's apartment. He wore tight jeans, red suspenders, and a yellow shirt. We shared Chinese takeout.

He told me that if anyone could make me whole again, make me right with the spiritual order, it was Maggie and her people on the farm.

"But you'll need to put in the work," he said. "You'll have to give them a full picture."

"How do I do that?"

"Find out where you are."

I felt a jolt of excitement.

"Maybe I could write about this." I took a sip of whisky. "This sounds like an incredible story. A crazy sheriff's election in the Deep South; a cult."

"Don't call it a cult. And don't go there thinking like this. You're going with the judgement mindset, with the feasting mindset, like the world is your meal. How can you be helped if you think that way?"

"I can be helped." I finished my whisky. "The work I do will save me."

"Oh, you are a dramatic artist, now?" He smiled.

"I'll get lost in my own story. I'll find a way to free myself."

"Good night, Marcel."

He let himself out. I poured myself a fresh glass of whisky.

On my father's desk sat the stained and worn copy of *The Aeneid*, the old Bible he still carried everywhere with him, and a collection of newer books marked with colored stickers. I looked through these books, and I looked through his notes. What struck me most was the sense of urgency and optimism that filled each page. He'd written down dates and names, constantly referenced his father and his grandfather. At some point he started talking directly to his father and also his grandfather, as individuals and then as a collective. The thoughts in his notebook were not far off from ideas I'd heard him express when alive. Living in South Africa, he'd been convinced that the Afrikaners, his people, were an orphan culture, a failed offshoot of a more mature civilization in the European homeland. This explained their atavism, their desire for an ethno-state, and their brutal treatment of Black Africans. This, and of course the fact that they'd been so terribly mistreated by the British, who'd burned their farms and locked up their women and children in razor-wire camps where they'd died by the thousands. My grandfather's own sister had died in one of these camps.

At the very core of the traditional Afrikaner belief, was the covenant they'd made with God. When I was a young child, Afrikaners still celebrated the Day of the Covenant, marking the Battle of Blood River in 1838, when our ancestors, the Voortrekkers, had been outnumbered by the Zulus hundreds to one, but had been victorious. Huddled on the inside of a laager, the Afrikaners had made a pact with God and promised Him that if they were victorious, they'd understand the victory as a sign God intended for them to have that land, and in turn they'd forever hold that day as sacred. We stuck to our word, celebrating the day of the Covenant on December 16th every year.

My father found it appalling. How could God take the side of one group of people over another? Then, in answer to his own question, he'd point out that God had done this throughout the Bible, taking the side of the Israelites, encouraging them to carry out massacres and genocides.

This was a point of contention between my parents. My father would say: either God acts in history or he doesn't. If He acts in history, then He approves of violence. If He doesn't act in history, then He's not who we claim He is. My mother would respond that we humans use His name to justify whatever we want to do. So He doesn't act in history, then, my father would say. No, He does, she'd respond, but He doesn't condone violence. And so the argument would go back and forth. Later, when I'd moved away from home, I realized that this argument had nothing to do with God, or His nature or His motives. When two individuals realize they can no longer coexist, because their natures conflict, they conjure up strange beliefs that cannot be reconciled.

My father had convinced himself that if he moved to Europe he'd feel less isolated. Then he wrote a book about a group of Boer War Veterans who'd toured America after their defeat at the hands of the British. Afrikaners, who would, in a few generations be internationally villainized, were welcomed in the United States at the turn of the last century as virtuous losers. They had, after all, stood up to the British Empire. Or alternatively, they were like Southerners, defeated by the mighty industrial North. These traveling Boers were popular in the North and the South of the United States; they were popular across the vast open spaces of the country. They toured for years, dressed up like Boer Cavalry, set up camps as the Boers had done, told tales of battles bravely fought. This book of my father's became popular with American academics, and he was offered a fellowship at Boston University, where he was subsequently offered a teaching post that initially lasted six months, after which he came home, contract for a tenured position in hand, and convinced my mother and me that our future lay in the United States. He and my mother argued, again directing their anger at one another through abstract ideas about culture and displacement, and so on; but in the end she relented and we moved.

Three years later, after I'd completed my first semester at university, my father started to crack. One night while we were drinking beer together he told me he'd come to realize that he was *thoroughly African*. He now dismissed his earlier rants about the need to be reattached to the European parent culture as the final thorn of inherited racism which he'd finally plucked from his soul. Now he suffered from a far more painful longing, he said, a longing for spiritual completion, a longing he recognized everyone struggled with, no matter where they lived. This eternal yearning was nameless and formless, but culture and history gave it a different name and a different shape, and of course a unique solution or platter of solutions. But now he realized that moving away from his true home only made the longing worse. He loved Africa. He loved the sights and the sounds and smells. He loved the people. And he missed, most of all, the black people.

Having already spent a semester at a liberal West Coast

university, I understood how these utterances would be received by American progressives.

"They'll condemn you as a racist," I told him. "Don't say things like that in public."

"How could they consider that racist? I said I love black people."

"Yes, but they will see that as a form of racism, and they'll feel it is their sworn duty to defend people of color against the utterances of a white man."

He waved his hand and dismissed what I'd said. I should have been more patient and tried to explain this new culture to him more thoroughly, but I suppose I didn't fully understand it myself, nor did I realize quite how disturbed he'd become. A semester later he was let go for inappropriate remarks. He'd been labelled a white supremacist, which he considered ironic, given that he'd spent most of his career brutally criticizing his fellow Afrikaners and their white supremacist system, Apartheid.

So began his descent into martyrhood. My father genuinely despised the Apartheid system. But as an Afrikaner critic of Afrikaners, he'd had a place. He was the trouble-maker of his tribe, but still he was of his tribe, and there were enough others like him to ensure he had friends. He'd had a place in that world, but he never found his footing in this new land. He was too old to get on board with the central project of modern American humanities: critiquing whiteness and its intersection with patriarchy and capitalism. And since—at least in the parts of society he inhabited—the majority of people identified as outsiders criticizing the mainstream, he would have had to join the mainstream to be an outsider. His nature, his deepest instincts, meant that he had to be an outsider. And as an Afrikaner under Apartheid, this nature had aligned with the abstract values embraced by his intellect. But in this new world of American academia, the values of his intellect would have been aligned with the proclaimed values of the academic mainstream, the ones who held the power. And he knew that the values of those in power always served the primary goal of maintaining that power, and so were never what they claimed to be. So to be true to his nature as an outsider, he'd have had to be against those in power whose stated values were values he shared.

This was the terrible bind he'd found himself in. I understood him so well now, in a way I never had when he was alive. It was his complete disconnection that drove him to the opioids. When he was high the pain went away and he could think clearly again. That's why his writing seemed optimistic. And of course it was the drugs—and, if I needed a higher reason, the loneliness—that killed him. Not the curse I'd brought with me. My earlier superstitious thoughts embarrassed me.

But the very night I came to that conclusion I had a terrible dream. My father was tied up and dragged into an old-fashioned bank with marble floors and gold bank teller grills. The mob fastened him to a pillar and fired rounds into his body, leaving his bloody corpse out to hang.

I woke with my heart pounding, body covered in sweat. I checked my bank balance, then made a donation of one hundred thousand dollars to a non-profit rehab center. They wanted to meet with me, but I told them no, I would remain anonymous.

I walked the streets in a state of frenzied anxiety. The buildings leaned in on me. The sidewalks jumped up at me. I heard the scrape of hooves. That night I felt so afraid something would get me, I slept outdoors on the complex roof. I feared sleep. I feared the thoughts I couldn't silence. These thoughts were as real as my legs, and they were monsters.

I tried to meditate, but the darkness I found there was not peaceful. Moss-covered skeletal trees growing from a black lake. Below the surface of the water, restless beings shuffled about. They were always there, as cramps in the legs, and headaches at night. A knot in the stomach, a knock at the door.

So I drank whisky and smoked on the balcony. I walked through the streets and visited all-night diners. When I slept I returned to the same locations in my dreams.

There my father appeared to me.

"Why don't you go for a run?" he said.

I gave myself a day to detox then set out in the early morning. I ran past a homeless woman pushing a shopping cart filled with trash. She'd been in my dream last night, hadn't she? I turned to see her and stepped into a hole. I fell to the ground, rolling to the edge of the sidewalk, away from the road. The grazed lines on my knee turned red. A sharp, stinging pain followed.

At home I nursed the wound and bandaged myself up. I donated a hundred thousand dollars to three different homeless shelters. I cooked myself steamed vegetables for dinner and listened to NPR. I felt like a decent human being. Even the sting in my knee felt good.

But that night the cramps in my legs intensified and I struggled to sleep. When I did sleep, I dreamed of leeches crawling from my flesh and then I woke, but did not fully awaken, into a paralyzed state. I had turned into a leech and I drank the blood of a gigantic creature.

I stumbled through to the bathroom and vomited into the toilet. I flushed away the red water, wiped my mouth clean, brushed my teeth.

I parked my car in the lot where I'd sat with my father the last time I'd seen him alive. As I ran along the cycling path my shins began to ache, then my knees and my spine. Someone followed me; now they were gone. The air felt too cold.

Lying on the couch in my father's apartment, I researched my latest symptoms. I had not been aware that every twenty seconds someone in America broke a bone due to osteoporosis. Was that what I had? The Research Foundation received a generous donation.

But the nightmares continued. A homeless man with piercing blue eyes held out his arms toward me. The sleeves of his hoodie fell back to reveal raw stumps in the place of hands. When I ran that afternoon I found the same man on the streets.

"Let me see your hands, please."

"What?" He had two hands, stained black, wrinkled.

"Wait here, please."

I drew out ten thousand dollars and gave it to him in a brown envelope. He stared at me, down at the money, back into my eyes.

"Don't tell anyone where you got it. Be careful with it."

I put in an order for a hundred thousand in cash and picked it up the next day. I drove around the city handing out envelopes to homeless people. All the while I heard the clickity-clack of hooves. Something followed me. I felt increasingly nauseated. At home I washed myself, stuck my finger down my throat, and vomited.

The fire alarm woke me at 3 a.m.

The toaster had caught fire. I burnt the edge of my arm as I unplugged it from the wall.

A heavy knock at the door.

"It's all right," I called back. "I've got it under control."

I waited.

No response.

The sound of hooves clacking down the corridor outside.

I had to drink whisky to sleep, and still I barely slept, tossing about in nightmares all night, the sound of heavy footsteps lurking just behind me.

I woke to the sound of my phone vibrating on the table next to the couch.

A number I didn't recognize.

"Mr. Swart, my name is Janine Bakriss."

She worked for a law firm putting together a case against New Morning Rehab, where my father had died. Numerous ex-employees were coming forward with stories of gross negligence.

"Your father... And I'm very sorry to tell you this. It could be painful to hear. Your father was left in the room for twenty-four hours before they contacted anyone."

"No, that's impossible."

"I realize this is painful, Mr. Swart."

"But, that..." I remembered his words again: Life is a gift, not a sentence. "We drove in my car. We swam in the sea. We spoke. We sat. We watched the sun on the water."

My hand turned limp and the phone fell to the floor.

She tried to call back, but I ignored her.

I phoned Virgil Rose.

"What's happening?"

"You're stuck in between. Get down to Maggie's farm."

"I don't want to be a crazy man."

"Get down to Maggie's farm."

"Can I go as a writer? I'm looking for my big story. I'm not sick."

"Go however you want to go, just get down to Maggie's farm."

CHAPTER 9

Early evening light faded off the branches of the Southern live oak; one squirrel chased another along an electric wire; a pair of dark birds shrieked about the garden; and the smell of hot roasting flesh filled my car.

"What are you trying to tell me?"

I parked in a narrow street outside the old, white, double-story manor with blackened windows, a closed-in porch, and ivy-covered pillars. At the edge of the well-trimmed lawn stood a sign that read: *Re-elect Chuck Jones*. Beneath it, hand-painted, the words: *Keep Chickasaw Unique*.

Although this street, like all the others in the neighborhood, was quiet, an undercurrent of unease flowed through it. Turning the final corner, I passed an old man wearing a Vietnam Veteran's cap, sweeping his street. He looked at me, cold and unsmiling. Across the road, in a black truck with a Confederate license plate, a younger man in a trucker's cap drank from a brown paper bag. He stared at me.

A screen door slammed. I looked toward the old house. From the porch, the woman I recognized from the advert online, Antoinette Dubois, mid-twenties, dressed in a pair of knee-length dungarees, came down the stairs and across the garden towards me. She had shoulder-length, dark red hair. A thin film of sweat glistened on her pinkish face. In her hand she held a screwdriver, which she now placed in the front pocket of her dungarees.

"Marcel? You find the place all right?" she asked in a thick, Deep South accent. She wiped her hand on the front of her thighs.

"I found it fine, thank you."

"Some folk have trouble with GPS here."

"I'll admit, I was surprised to find an Airbnb in Chickasaw, Alabama."

"We do good business. Some other folk will probably come and go while you here. Got bags you want to take up?"

"I have a bag in the trunk."

"Cigarette?" She took a pack from her dungaree pocket and held it out toward me.

"Yeah, thank you."

"If you have any trouble with money, just let me know."

"I'm fine, really."

"I know why folks come down here."

I decided to let the matter rest. I took a drag of the cigarette and looked up at the beautiful tree in her garden.

"Live oak. Two hundred years old. Hundred years older than this house. See that sign?" She pointed at the porch wall. "Says this home's historic. You'd think they'd wanna preserve a home like that. But without me, this place would be like half the others you see 'round here, just a pile a nails and wood. Bought it over a year ago. Worked on it every day since."

"It looks beautiful."

She rested one hand on her hip as she smoked with the other, looking up and down the street like a head warden, daring any of her neighbors to rattle the bars. She squashed out her cigarette. "Let's get your bags inside."

I followed her through the screen porch into the kitchen.

"This here's a work in progress." The kitchen did not look too good. Open cans of paint lay on the floor, wires hung out of a scratched-up hole in the wall. "But this room." I followed her into the lounge. "This here's my showroom."

"Looks great."

A large couch sat against the back wall in front of the window, and looked over a coffee table to a closed-off, painted fireplace. Matching white fabric chairs sat at either end of the room. An oil painting of a scene I recognized but could not quite identify hung above the fireplace—a walled city burned, as people ran for their lives. A strange image to have in your home.

"Careful. Stairway's real narrow," she said.

I followed her up the tight, creaking stairs, across the rickety landing, and into the bedroom that would be mine. To my great relief, it was, like the lounge downstairs, in good order. A large window looked straight into the trees that lined the alleyway behind the house. A simple wooden desk, a queen bed, a carpet on the floor—I'd be perfectly comfortable here.

"I'll let you settle in." She climbed onto the desk, fiddling with the AC vent in the ceiling. "This thing's been driving me crazy. You just let me know if there's a problem." She hopped onto the floor. "Come find me downstairs when you're ready."

Door shut.

I sat on the bed and breathed in the smell of the room. Thoughts settled in my mind like powder snow falling in a snow globe. A sharp loneliness pierced my side like a spear. If my mother knew where I was, what I was doing here, she'd think I'd gone insane. I hadn't returned her calls. I'd texted, said I'd call soon.

As evening deepened, I lay my father's books and notepads on the desk. Next to them I placed my own notepads. The best explanation I had for my being here was this: I'd come to write a story. I'd come to report on the upcoming election, and on Maggie's Farm.

My arms and legs felt unusually stiff, as did my back. Four days of driving could do that, I suppose.

As I stretched on the floor, my mind drifted outwards and back through time. Twenty-four hours, they said, my father lay dead in his room at the rehab. I'd run over the timeline a thousand times. No one else had seen us on the drive. Had I told my mother when I'd last seen him? Had the lawyers phoned her?

I focused all my attention on stretching my back and legs, until the dark thoughts dissolved.

Antoinette sat in the kitchen, her legs dangling off the edge of the workman's bench-cum-table. A mason jar filled with red bubbly liquid and ice cubes sat next to her knee. She took a sip.

"Finished work for the day, so I'm drinking. You want?"

"What is that?"

"Ain't everybody's medicine." She hopped off the table, opened the fridge, and brought out a carafe of cheap-looking red wine and a bottle of ginger ale. She took some ice cubes from the freezer.

"Never seen that combination before. Is that, like, what, a Southern thing?"

"Nah. Just an Antoinette thing. You want?" She placed a mason jar in front of me.

"Well... sure. Yeah."

The muscles in her freckled forearms tensed as she poured wine into my cup. She threw in a few ice cubes and poured in the ginger ale, which bubbled up, stopping half an inch short of the lip.

"I'm not a heavy drinker," I said.

"Don't need to make no excuses for me, sweetie. Drink all you want."

Her answer confused me, but my own motivations confused me more. I suspect I wanted her to see me as someone different to her, different and better. Different, and better, but also indifferent to my own superiority, willing to mingle with the common people as if they were my own. But she seemed either genuinely blind to any class markers I thought I had, or she assumed I'd come here because my life was falling apart and I needed help.

"I have an interview set up for tomorrow." I took a long sip of my drink and felt the alcohol work its magic, massaging away the tension from the inside.

"That so?"

A better version of me came online.

"How long have you been in this town?"

"Grew up in North Alabama, but I been here now, let me see, three years, three and a half. Something like that. Not in this house the whole time. I done up another one then came here. This place was a pile a trash. Didn't even have plumbing or electricity wires. Put it all in with these two hands."

"Very impressive." I looked around at the walls, half painted, half bare. The electric cords still showed in places, but I could see order emerging. For a moment, I felt awe for this person I barely knew. "I'm trying to put my mind together. You're doing that with this house."

She cackled, slapping her knee. Then when she noticed I wasn't laughing: "Oh, I didn't mean to offend you."

"No, you didn't. You didn't."

She put her hand on my arm and a pleasant tingle passed through me.

80

"I really didn't mean to upset you. I just thought you were making a joke, since this house is such a mess."

"I like metaphors. Building a house is often used as a metaphor, to the point of cliché. But suddenly, now, as I looked around your house, the image felt... fresh, alive."

"You got a strange mind."

"I'll take that as a compliment."

"You should." She smiled and refilled my glass. "When I think about fixing this place up, I think about the people who gonna live in it after I'm done here. I imagine some folk who ain't even born yet living here. I think of a happy family in this kitchen, and that makes me happy."

"Beautiful. That's so... selfless."

"Well it makes me feel happy, so, maybe it's selfish."

She smiled again.

"I noticed a Chuck Jones sign in your garden."

"Keep Chickasaw Unique." She raised her glass. "Is that how come you came down here now? So you could get to Maggie's Farm 'fore it's too late?"

"I've come down to write about this place. I'm not really, a, a, seeker, in the usual sense. In the sense of people who usually come here."

"You come to write about it?" She tilted her head. "And you don't have no problems you need help with? You ain't going to Maggie's Farm?"

"Well, I want to go there, of course, but not to get, uh, help in the usual way."

"Who you writing for?"

"I pitched the article to a bunch of publications." I heard the evasiveness as I spoke these words. "And I'm excited for what lies ahead." What a cliché. I scratched the side of my head.

"Well, whatever reason you're here for, I'll tell you something. Jefferson Lee, he's going to turn Chickasaw into a regular redneck town. But we're unique." She finished her drink, refilled the glass.

"Do you know Maggie?"

"Ain't nobody know Maggie."

"But you've met her?"

"Come as close as she'd let me."

"What's her real name?"

"Some call her Maggie. Some call her Magdalena."

"What do you call her?"

She lit two cigarettes and handed one to me. Our conversation lulled a moment as we each took deep drags.

"I ain't spoken with her face to face. Now with Jefferson Lee around, more and more folk turning against her. They call her Magdalena, which in their mind, makes her bad. You walk up and down these streets, ask folks 'bout her, you'll get so much darn ignorance. There's so much ignorance in this town."

"You get ignorant people everywhere."

"I suppose. It didn't used to be this way. Even a year back it weren't. But if you talk to these folk..." She blew a long line of smoke up to the ceiling. "They'll tell you Magdalena's running a crazy sex cult. Some folk dream up wild things. Way I see it?" She pointed her smoking hand at the door. "You got crazy ideas in your head, says more about you than anybody else."

"I suppose that's true."

"Back in the day they used to try pin things on her, now they doing it again."

"What did they try to pin on her?"

"You heard about that girl that went missing?"

"Read about her."

"Some years back, this girl went missing in the swamps. Swamps begin about a mile from here, and they're big. Miles and miles. So this girl was missing, and when they found her body it was all wasted away. Tragic. Real tragic. But these folk tried blaming Maggie's group. They say she's doing human sacrifices."

"What?" I almost spat out my wine. "Is this widely believed?"

"Wide enough. Jefferson Lee the third is pushing that nonsense."

"But there's no evidence?"

"Who cares 'bout evidence when you got a good story?"

"True."

"Lee talks about God, country, Jesus. But, far as I'm concerned, Sheriff Jones is more like a real Christian than Jefferson Lee. He's a good man. Here's a picture of me and him." She dug through a pile of junk behind us and handed me a photograph of her in a white dress standing next to the man I'd seen on the posters.

"He's the man I have a meeting with tomorrow."

"No way. Well, why didn't you say so?"

"I... I planned to tell you."

"I'll come with you in the morning. That'll win you some big points."

"Well... okay."

We clinked our glasses, looked into each other's eyes, and I wondered if she wondered, and for a moment felt certain she wondered if I wondered.

Later, as I rinsed my mouth out after brushing my teeth, one unit in my mind conjured up images of her naked as another tried to quell the unrest.

In my room, I climbed onto the desk and peered down into the alleyway outside. Glass-encased gas lanterns lined the narrow path, illuminating the moss-covered live oaks and the half-visible front porches of the aging Southern mansions.

I dreamed of walking down that alleyway. The lanterns fluttered out in the breeze as the sound of hooves following me got louder. My father stood in front of me, smoking a lit cigarette.

"Were you dead when I met you?"

"We're all ghosts."

"I'm not a ghost."

"Where's your body?"

I tried to look down. As my head shifted, I woke with a start. The room smelled of smoke. It was night. My eyes closed and morning came.

CHAPTER 10

Antoinette and I drove in separate cars to Sheriff Jones's reelection campaign office that stood in the middle of a grass lot on the outskirts of town, thirty feet from a train track obscured mostly by pines.

On the front lawn, outside the wooden campaign office, Antoinette introduced me to Jones's wife and campaign manager, "Miss Lucy," a black woman, probably in her early sixties.

"Pleased to meet you, young man." Miss Lucy put both her hands around mine. "I have to get back to the restaurant soon, but I wanted to meet you myself. We don't have many reporters from out of town covering our story." Then to Antoinette: "It's so great to see you, Anty."

"When I heard Marcel was coming to see y'all, I couldn't say no."

"Come on in."

"Well... it's a... an honor to be here." I took the notepad I'd bought last night out of my back pocket and scribbled down: *Office made out of freshly cut wood. Smells like pine.*

"Come this way, y'all."

She led us down a corridor so narrow my shoulders rubbed against both walls.

Sheriff Jones, feet on desk, wore weathered brown leather boots and played with a wooden Rubik's cube. An open rolling paper covered with tobacco lay next to a pile of books, including a Bible. Shelves filled with books and files lined the edges of his office. He had no computer and no windows.

"Antoinette, my girl." He put his feet down. "Come over here."

"So good to see you, Sheriff."

They two embraced for a few moments.

"I didn't know you were coming to see us."

"I wanted to introduce this man myself. He's staying over at my place."

"Is that so? Well, you already in my good books then, son. Pleasure to meet you."

"You too...uh... Sir."

"So, you doing good business over there, Anty?"

"I sure am. We can host your victory party that side, if you want."

"Haha. I love this gal." He put his arm around her again. "You keep safe. I'll make sure we come visit you sometime soon."

Antoinette said her good-byes and slipped out the door.

"Ruth," he said to his wife. "You didn't bring me lunch?"

"Come on, Sheriff," she said. "You're dieting this week."

I scribbled down: *He calls her Ruth. She calls him Sheriff.*

"I don't recommend trying a new diet when running a re-election campaign," Jones said as he sat back down at his desk.

The sheriff had a mustache and wore a black hat. Although he had an intimidating presence, he was the kind of man one wanted to please. Or at least, I wanted him to be pleased with me, to *like* me.

He flicked a switch on his desk, turning on an extraction fan in the wall. He lit his freshly rolled cigarette.

"I've downgraded to rollies. This way I only do five a day. If I win this campaign, or should I say *when*, I'm going to quit for good. Feel free to join me, if you do."

"It's been a while since I smoked in someone's office." In fact, I thought as I lit up, I'd never smoked in anyone's office but my father's after he'd died. "My dad, uh, he was smoking unlit cigarettes at the time of his death."

"Unlit?" He leant forward, elbows on the table. "Why on earth would a man do that?"

"Part of his plan to quit." I felt my throat tighten up as I spoke about him. "He'd, uh..." I laughed now. "He'd even crush the cigarettes when he'd finished with them."

"So it didn't even save him money? Ha ha. My father's still alive. Ninety-three years old. Let me tell you something about him. He has perfect health. Unearned. Utterly unearned." He counted on his fingers, starting with the thumb. "Smokes every day. Drinks whisky like water. Eats whatever he wants. You know what he says his secret is? He doesn't worry. Says he never worried a day in his life."

"Is that even possible?"

"I just know what he tells me."

"Do you mind if I write this down?"

"Go ahead."

I made some notes.

"That's why I tell my wife not to worry about my diet. But she says I got my mother's genes. Mommy died at fifty."

"I guess you never know."

"You're the first reporter from out of town to cover this election."

I shifted about on my chair, uncomfortable. I scribbled some meaningless note on the page. He stared at me intensely, then smiled.

"What's your *angle*, Marcel?" He grinned as he leant forward, both elbows on the desk, smoke wafting up from his right hand.

"Well..." I swallowed. "Here's what I understand. You got elected as a... can I say, conservative sheriff? But then at some point, you... changed tactics. But you've been reelected many times over."

"Yes, you can say conservative. If you want to be elected as a black sheriff in the Deep South, you got to make Genghis Khan look like a liberal."

I laughed uncomfortably.

"One hand on the Bible, other on your gun." He placed his hand on each as he spoke. "But I always told the truth. I was a member of the Constitutional Sheriff's movement when they first elected me eight years ago. They wanted me to drive Maggie and her people out of town, and I planned to."

"But you didn't?"

"That's right. I didn't."

From his desk drawer he retrieved a badge and handed it to me: *Re-elect Sheriff Jones.* A picture of his face.

"Would you wear this? Show your support?"

I pinned it to my shirt, then made more notes on my pad. "Would you mind telling me what... caused you to change your mind?"

He paused for a long time.

"Some of my voters were disappointed with me." He looked over my shoulder, like he was looking into the distance. "Just twenty years ago, Chickasaw was not a town you wanted to be in after dark, if you were black." He gave me a sharp look, raised his eyebrows.

"But that's... uh, changed somewhat?"

"I never understood why Maggie had chosen this place.

That little island where she operates. Pirates' Cove. Out there in the bayou."

"But now you understand why?"

"No. All I know is that she needs somewhere to be safe. And it's my job to keep her safe."

"But you were elected to drive her out?"

He squashed his cigarette in an ashtray made to look like a truck tire. I did the same.

"That was the apparent reason. The reason on the surface." He ran his hand horizontally, at eye-level. "But there was also a hidden reason. That only became clear later."

The Sheriff let me shadow him. On the first day we took lunch at his wife's diner, an old wooden building with white tiled floors, framed newspaper articles, and Alabama sports memorabilia hanging on the walls. Classic cowboy movies played on the two television screens. Work crews in blue overalls and yellow reflective bibs sat at tables across from police officers and firemen.

"There doesn't seem to be much... tension," I said as I ate a piece of greasy, delicious fried chicken.

"They like my wife. Very loyal to her. And folks 'round here, they'll smile to your face, all right."

One of the work crews had shifted on their chairs, so they all had their backs to us. I felt like I was in school.

We spent the afternoon parked beneath the trees near the Chickasaw creek, opposite an old white, wooden house, rotting in the ground. A chained-up dog slept on a tire beneath a tree.

"It's been a quiet few days." Jones rolled a cigarette, letting the excess tobacco fall into the hat resting on his lap. "You glad you came all the way down here?"

"Something in me knew I had to come down here. I have to see Maggie's Farm."

"Blind Willie McTell." He reached for the radio and turned up the volume. Ragtime music. A deep, blues voice. "I grew up listening to this."

"I've been hoping you'd tell me why and how you ended up... changing sides... as it were." I took my notebook out of my jeans pocket.

"It doesn't matter why. What you have to figure out is why *you* came down here. You say you came to cover the story, but that's only the surface reason. What's the hidden reason?"

"I know why I came. I know why I was drawn to this place."

"Are you sure?"

"Yeah, I'm sure."

I needed to shift the conversation, so I asked Jones how he'd felt when he first saw the sign Jefferson Lee put up on the edge of the town

"My grandkids woke me up early Saturday morning, the only day of the week I get to sleep in. They were screaming and hollering. We all piled into my van and drove across town. Well, since you're down here, you've probably seen the picture."

"I sure have."

"He took down the sign advertising the Truth, and replaced it with a picture of himself on his black horse. *There's a new sheriff in town*, the poster said. Can you believe that? Going off like he'd already won."

"Shameless."

"To tell you the truth, it felt good to be that angry about something. I hadn't felt that way in a long time. I pulled my gun out the holster and fired six shots into that smug face. My granddaughter, Rose, stared crying. *He's going to come kill us pawpaw*, she said. I picked her up. I said: *Not unless he goes through me first.*

"Sure enough, Jefferson Lee had registered himself to run for sheriff. The election was six months off. I hadn't even thought about it 'til then. And if Lee hadn't shown up, I wouldn't have thought about it at all. By this point, the election was a formality. Don't mean to brag, but I'd become a pretty beloved figure 'round here."

"I know." I made some notes on my pad. "So what happened when you shot his face out?"

"Some folks say it was a mistake." Jones sat up straight in his seat and pointed at his chest as he spoke. He'd become animated now. I could feel the righteous anger. "But you think you can come into my town, and erect a sign proclaiming yourself as sheriff?" He pointed out the window. "Look, I believe in democracy. But this man doesn't even come from here. He doesn't have the courtesy to introduce himself.

"When I first ran for sheriff, I was angry. I was fire-breathing angry. But before I announced my candidacy, I went and introduced myself to the incumbent. We sat on his porch and drank tea. My father would have been chased off that porch, but Sheriff Simons's wife, she brought us tea and cookies. There has been some progress. Good. But other things are worth preserving. Dignity. Respect. These are good, Southern virtues. Godly virtues. But that man, Lee, he has none of 'em."

"Do you think he might win?"

"Heck no."

"But he has support."

"Fear is a coal that never goes out. It just takes someone to come and blow on it. Then it flares back up again."

"You came in that way the first time."

"Yes, yes I did. I understand it well."

"You still haven't explained why you changed... sides."

"And you haven't told me why you came down here and ended up living with my God niece."

"When I read about you putting those bullet holes in the Lee signboard, I felt... something in me come to life. I had to write about this."

"But there was something else going on in your life." He turned and smiled at me.

CHAPTER 11

I woke to an email informing me my proposal had been accepted by the publication, Axan. They weren't offering to pay much for the five-thousand-word feature, but that didn't matter. Money was no issue for me.

I bounded down the stairs like a child on the first day of holiday. Antoinette had classic bed hair. She wore short cotton pants and a crumpled t-shirt. A cigarette rested on the edge of the counter and smoke mixed with the smell of frying bacon.

We sat opposite one another eating bacon, sipping coffee. "My article got accepted. Now I have to see Maggie's Farm."

"I'm going to be in your article?"

"I... I haven't figured out all the details yet."

She smiled, picking up a piece of crispy bacon and crunching it loudly between her front teeth without closing her mouth. From her wrist she took a hair tie then pulled her wavy hair into a ponytail.

"I'm sure I can find a way to work you in."

"You sound nervous." She picked up the last piece of

bacon, snapped it in half, chomped her piece, and dropped the other half on the plate.

"I'm not nervous."

Her chair scraped loudly against the floor as she pushed it away from the table. She threw her bare feet up next to the now-empty bacon plate. It took a great effort of will not to stare down her legs toward the white cotton shorts that became even shorter with the movement.

"I have work today." She lit herself a fresh cigarette. "Usually I'd be done 'round five. You wanna help? Maybe I can get done by three."

"Sure. I've got nothing else to do."

In daylight the alleyway behind the house didn't look quite so ominous as at night. Squirrels scampered about in the trees above us. Bright red Cardinals appeared like flashes of paint, then vanished again. The old tree provided shade for us as we leant a ladder against the edge of the house. My job involved handing tools to Antoinette then standing around awaiting further instruction. Just the kind of unskilled labor my university degree had prepared me for.

My thoughts went to that afternoon I'd spent with my father on the California coast. If he'd spoken to me then, shown himself to me, what explained the utter silence now? My mother had written to me again last night, and I'd responded saying she needed to stop worrying. I could tell her mind had started to spin out of control, worrying about me. But I'd barely slept at all, and when the sunlight came through the curtains it brought with it an obvious truth: I only knew the spinning of my own mind. The news my proposal had been accepted gave me that boost I'd needed, a chemical rush that chased the ghosts away. Coffee, bacon, nicotine, a mile-long view down Antoinette's legs had kept the buzz going, but now it faded, and in its place came the shadows. What on earth would I write about? The story I'd pitched them made no sense. I couldn't even remember what I'd written. It was my own cover story: a lie that gave meaning to my strange adventure.

"Get your mind back in it," Antoinette called down at me. "You off in space somewhere?"

I apologized and handed her the next tool.

Antoinette's flushed face slowly regained its original color as we sat on the back stairs eating peanut butter sandwiches and drinking sweet tea.

"We done good for the day," she said. "I'll take you out there now."

We threw a kayak into the back of her hand-painted black truck. The interior smelt of weed and coffee. Upholstery showed through the worn leather seats, and the dashboard was cracked from sun exposure. The radio knobs had come off, and she'd filled up the spaces with cracked, v-shaped matches. A hunting rifle with a thick scope lay in the middle of the single front seat.

The whole machine rattled as she brought it to life. She pushed the long stick into first and we jumped off at such a pace my body sank into the seat; the gun crashed forward as we rounded the first corner. She didn't care.

"Lady Afternoon. That's her name. What you call your car, Marcel?"

"I haven't given my car a name."

"Well, that's a shame, ain't it."

We both opened our windows as we turned down Highway 43, racing over the bridge, past the old train track and the truck-sized American flag that ripped in the wind. The bayou lay to our left and right. Skeletal trees and dark water. She turned sharply down a dirt road, racing over the train track. Now we drove through densely treed swampland. The road twisted right, left, and narrowed.

We parked.

Antoinette unfastened the telescopic lens from the rifle.

We took the kayak down to the water through an opening in the jungle-dense vegetation. The V-shape of boat keels and truck tire marks scarred the mud and reeds at the water's edge. We entered through a narrow opening in the bushes, our feet slurping through the raw mud.

The kayak glided smoothly, dipping a moment, then buoyed up by the water. Dark trees, bushes, vines reached out so we couldn't see more than a few feet ahead, but five minutes of paddling brought us to open water, where nothing of the world we'd just left was visible. I felt badly disoriented. Where was the highway? The train track? Chickasaw?

"That's where we're headed." She pointed to a distant island. "Just a mile's paddle. Don't be lazy."

"I'm not complaining."

Hawks danced above us in the cloudless blue sky, and perhaps it was the exercise, the fresh air, being out on the water, but the disoriented feeling passed quickly and soon all anxiety evaporated. Our paddles slicing through bayou made a soothing sound.

But as Antoinette brought our boat to a stop, and the wake we'd created rocked us slightly, I felt sick, vulnerable, dizzy.

"Is it safe?"

She continued to turn us around until the side of our boat was parallel with the island, still at least half a mile off.

"Ain't nothing safe in this world."

She handed me the telescope. As I placed it to my eye, the island came into sharp focus, the figures on the beach seeming as close as Antoinette. Two men and one woman sat on a fallen tree trunk, smoking something, a joint I guess. The woman pointed in our direction. They crushed out the joint and disappeared into the thick trees behind them.

"They've seen us," I said.

"'Course they seen us."

"What are they going to do?"

The small boat rocked close to tipping point as Antoinette turned around on her seat to face me.

"Tell us the truth now, Marcel. Why'd you come here?"

Her green eyes held madness. I felt the spirit in her rising, a wild spirit whose sense of peace increased in inverse proportion to the chaos around her. A pirate's soul.

"I told you." The words struggled up through my throat. "I've come to write about this place. I have a story. It's been accepted."

The wind blew harder, splashing water over the edge of the boat.

"That ain't the way the geography works. Only certain kinds end up in this town." She took the paddle from the water and lay it across the boat in front of her. "I been here long enough to know. I got my own story, much as you do."

I looked down at the dark water that grew choppier as the wind picked up. How deep was it? How far was I from the land? What lived down there? This thought so closely coincided with a new disruption of the water's surface that the order of thought and event became confused in my mind. Which had caused which? The rugged top of the alligator came toward us, just feet away when it turned and swam toward the island.

"What the hell just happened?"

"Mock charging. Gators don't eat full-grown humans."

"Oh yes, they can."

"Don't change the topic."

"An alligator just came at us!"

"Well, it's gone now. I seen how you ignore your mamma's phone calls."

"How do you know that?"

"I ain't trying to make you scared. I just wanna help." She paused. The tone in her voice shifted to genuine concern. "What happened to you?"

"My father died. That's what happened."

"I'm sorry." She spat in the water. "I guess you loved him?"

"I did, yeah."

The alligator changed direction again, swimming toward the shore, its large, square head now mostly visible above the water.

"My father died, too."

"I'm so sorry."

"Yeah, well. He weren't the greatest. I'll tell you about him someday. We're talking about you. What happened before that?"

"My whole life happened before that."

"Come on, Marcel."

I looked down at my reflection in the muddy water and spat, as she'd spat moments before. My spit floated on the surface.

"I made some money."

"So you should be living the high life. What you doing in a swamp in Alabama?"

"I heard about Maggie's Farm."

"You heard about that island." She picked up the paddle and pointed. "You traveled across the country to visit that island, in the swamps of Alabama?"

"I wanted to show solidarity. I heard they were threatened."

"Pfff..."

"What?"

She raised her eyebrows at me.

"Okay. I've... since I graduated university, and even before that, I wanted to write about something, but I needed the right story."

"So them poor fools out there going to be your ticket to fame?"

A strong gust of wind rocked the kayak. I looked about for the alligator but it had disappeared, leaving not a ripple of evidence, as if it'd never existed.

"I don't need the money."

With her paddle she shifted the boat so we were again properly aligned with the island. Peering through the telescopic lens she said: "They waving the white flag."

"What does that mean?"

"We can land. But you can't go there with a heart full of lies." She sank her oar deep into the water. "Paddle with me."

"My heart is not full of lies."

"Why you here?"

We faced one another as we paddled. This meant she had to row backwards, something at which she appeared rather adept. Her eyes sank into me like hooks through freshly slaughtered meat. I imagined myself lifting upwards toward the sky like an angel held in suspension by the awesome power of God.

But soon my soul felt crumpled and misshapen and my mind flashed back to the day when the smell of cooking meat filled my car and I'd been saved from the truck that flew through the red traffic light. My father's ghost had sent me that message, hadn't he? *The living are already ghosts.* So what then did I have to fear?

"Come back to me, Marcel."

"I'll paddle for the both of us," I said. "You can relax."

"Don't mind if I do." She put the oar across the center of the boat. "But you got to answer my question."

My body came to life as I paddled, and my mind focused.

"If I were to tell you the truth about why I'm here, I'd have to tell you everything about my whole life, from the moment I was born. But that would only be the tiniest fraction of the story. To get the full picture you'd have to go back to the beginning of time, and I'm not sure time even began, or that it moves in the way we think it does."

"Nice poetry, but you still ain't answering me."

"My dead father saved my life before he died."

"Okay?"

"Which means I didn't bring the curse that killed him. At least that's what it appears to mean. But still I know, that's what happened. I brought the curse. I know it."

"And so you think you can't outrun it? The curse?"

"That's what I fear."

"You think you can't escape it by moving through space, and you think you can't escape it by moving through time."

I pushed the paddle with all my strength.

"I fear that, yes."

"So you need to find some place where time and space move differently. But there ain't no such place."

"So what's the point, then?"

"You need a new technology. Something invented..." She tapped the side of her head. "Invented by folk who think in forbidden ways."

"That's right."

"That's how our little town works. That's why this island must be protected." She picked up her paddle and lowered it into the water, slowing our movement and turning the boat sideways. "We're too close now."

Although we were still three or four hundred feet from the island, I could clearly make out the people standing on the beach. Seven of them.

"You have to swim from here."

"What? Are you mad?"

"If ya'ain't meant to be here then ya'ain't meant to be here."

"There's an alligator in the water."

"So? If you're meant to be on that island, you going to get there just fine."

"And if I'm not, I'll get eaten by an alligator. No, thank you!"

"You afraid of the water? Then everything you just told me now is a lie."

I shook my head.

"You said time ain't what it seems. So if you're eaten, you're already eaten."

"But I can still choose if I jump into the water."

"If you don't jump in, means you was never going to be on that island. You won't get to write about it. You won't get the answers you seek."

I looked across the lake for signs of the alligator. The wind had died down now, and the surface was smoother. There were no signs of the animal, but it could be just beneath the surface, hiding anywhere. And how many more were there?

"This is their rule?" I asked.

"First time you go. No other way onto the island."

"Have people ever..." I stopped myself.

I looked up at the sky. Whatever young philosophy brewed in me had no meaning unless I lived it, unless I let it move me through the world in a new way.

I took my shirt off, sliding out of my damp shoes and socks.

"I don't want to flip the boat."

She looked me over with her sharp green eyes. Was that desire? Certainly I felt more masculine than at any moment since we'd met. Up until this time I'd been handing her tools and driving around as a passenger in her car.

I lowered myself over the edge of the boat, and then dropped into the water, sinking like a bag of sand. My legs kicked, powered by their own frantic intuition, as my mind sank down into the dark water. I pictured monsters racing up at me, pulling me down into the abyss. The pain in my legs felt real. As my hands broke the surface of the water, chopping parts of it white, then back to dark green, I pictured my blood spreading out from me, forming a thin layer, mixing with the water, dissipating slowly until it, like me, existed only in someone else's memory.

As startling as gunfire, the sounds of my feet and hands splashing the water pulled me from this trance. Now all I wanted to do was live. I swam so hard my lungs burned, and my muscles burned, but this only drove me more. Each rupture of the water's surface came at me from my hands and feet and also from the piercing of an alligator's mouth. I lost my life a hundred times before my knees scraped against rocks and logs, and I knew I'd made it into shallow water. I ran toward the land, screaming, my hands in the air. Then I began to laugh. I both yelled and laughed as I jumped to my feet, and presented myself to the seven, now eight, who stood waiting for me. They'd folded the white flag up in front of them. I spun and turned to face Antoinette. I blew her a kiss and bowed.

CHAPTER 12

I showered behind a bamboo wall, then changed into the black cotton robe and leather shoes given to me. Antoinette remained in the kayak a hundred feet offshore. The initial eight had disappeared, and I'd been left in the guard of Tran Tran Sui. A white man with olive skin, Tran—as I was to call him—was so tall I felt unsettled around him. My eyes met his Adam's apple. I didn't enjoy having to tilt my head back when talking to anyone. Even at his extraordinary height, his arms looked disproportionately long for his body. The top of his head was bald; bushy, brown foliage covered the sides.

I followed Tran along a narrow path that led from the beach through the swamp pines and the wet bushes. Mosquitoes swarmed about us. My guide pushed aside branches and we emerged into a clearing, a hidden civilization.

"Welcome to Maggie's Farm."

I looked over a hundred, or more, leather tents. In the center stood a narrow, four-story wood building surrounded by a series of wooden structures that held large, woven, leather contraptions that looked like spider webs. A group of women worked at a great loom. Men and women painted on a large sheet. A steady hum came from the bamboo aqueducts as they carried water to collection points. Everyone, dressed in similar attire to myself and Tran, went about their business, not in the least interested in my arrival.

"Come to my home," said Tran.

We sat opposite one another on cushions as a pot boiled on a wood stove in the corner of his tent. A rolled-up mat lay against the tent wall. Dried plants hung from suspended ropes, and a locked wooden crate stood at the far end of the room.

"What do you seek?" Tran asked.

I felt more confident, more at ease than I'd ever felt in my life. The thrill of surviving the swim and a deepened faith in my new worldview had a narcotic effect on my mind.

The words came out so effortlessly, as if they spoke themselves: "I seek a legend." Then my old mind with all its bumps and broken ends returned. I needed to qualify my statement: "I mean a legend in the sense of a map. For my life, you see? To make sense of the events. They seem scattered, but I believe there's a pattern."

"One moment please."

Tran raised an alien-like finger and got up from his cushion. He returned with two cups. The tea was thick as swamp water and tasted like licorice and mint. The man closed his eyes and took a deep breath, put down his mug, and placed both his hands, prayer-like, in front of his face. When he opened his eyes he pointed at me, his hands still in the prayer position.

"For our purposes, for your purpose, too, your story is important. But not in the way that stories are generally important to people."

"What do you mean?"

"Humans are asked to present a story of their life as an explanation, a justification, for why they are where they are, in the current moment, doing whatever it is they're doing."

"That's true."

"We, here, do not believe this has any value. No one can account for their present reality. All we can do is make up fictions to ease the unbearable tension of not understanding anything."

"I see. I suppose I can agree with that. To some extent."

"Of course you agree with it. You are meant to be here. You cannot get here otherwise. There are certain barriers." He took a big sip of tea. "I should rephrase what I said about stories. They fail us because we attempt to use them as mechanistic devices. A caused B caused C." He downed his tea, pointed at me. "That's not how they work." He slapped himself on the side of his bald head and groaned. "The origin of that slap lies in the ancient roots of our universe. And the ancient roots are an invisible fiction." He stood and picked up a bell from behind his sleeping mat, shaking it frantically as he stared at me so I could see the whites of his bulging eyes. He sat down again opposite me. "What is the connection between the head slapping and the ringing of the bell?"

"I'm not sure."

He raised his voice, projecting as if to the back of an auditorium: "If you look for a *motivation* in the modern sense, all you are doing is telling a lie. A more or less convincing lie perhaps. But, the only reason it convinces is because we are accustomed to a certain type of lie and not another. A lie in your own language is still a lie." Now he lowered his voice and slouched his shoulders. "So to speak."

"It is a lie you can understand."

He raised his voice again: "Don't think of language as you

are accustomed to think of it. Don't think of English. Shut up. I said, shut up." He raised his arms, revealing armpit sweat. He put his fingers together. "See how these two connect in your mind. Go on. Close your eyes. I said, close."

I did as instructed. At first my mind fluttered with sparks of half-formed images. Then the pictures settled.

"I see... uh... I see banging. Both involved banging."

"Good. Deeper."

"Violence. I see violence."

"Violence done to self and violence done to bell."

"That's what I see, yes. And then... from that came..."

"Yes, from that came sound. Both man and bell created sound after they were banged. Now you are beginning to think. But as you try to make sense in this new way, you already start to tell a new story. It's still a story."

"A broken one."

"We here, at Maggie's Farm, we need to analyze the data of stories. We are on guard. We are the guardians of the ancient, dark secret."

"What is that?"

"When you learn to think in myth you learn the language of the gods. When you stop thinking mechanistically, you get a hint of their plans."

I nodded. "I agree. I don't know why, but I do agree."

"Of course you do. Now, hear me: we must keep watch for a certain god. A rapacious god. When he comes he wreaks havoc. If we can stop him early, appease him early, we fulfill our goal."

"What's my part?"

"You have to tell us. But you cannot tell us using mechanistic language."

"I don't know how else to speak."

He reached over and slapped me across the face.

"Why?"

He smiled.

"Think don't think. If we are unable to get him, he will destroy everything. Our organization is ancient and we monitor the signs of his coming. We've spoken enough for one day. Now you must get off the island."

Each time I came close to drifting off, I'd feel the murky water I'd swum through. I gasped for breath, sitting up straight.

Dim light from the streetlamps spread over books and notepads on the desk near the window. I pushed these aside, slid the window open, and lit a cigarette. A shadow moved along the narrow walkway, fading into darkness as it left the lamp-lit area.

Sitting on Antoinette's kitchen floor, I drank a glass of wine and smoked a cigarette. I lay awake, half-naked on my bed as the windows turned orange in the morning glow.

With a cigarette hanging from her mouth, Antoinette folded laundry and towels. "Bet you slept well last night, didn't you?"

"I've got to go for a run."

"We got some other guest coming to stay a few days. He's going to be in the room next to you."

"Fine."

I stuck to tree-covered lanes, running past old houses,

with rockers on porches, some empty, others home to a pair of eyes or two. Chained-up dogs barked. I ran faster and faster.

"Waylon!" A large white lady in a tank top and cut-off shorts yelled at her dog. "Get your ass back here!" She walked across the sand-covered lawn.

Black and white flags with the words: *This Town is Contested* hung from the front of porches. *Jefferson Lee* stickers adorned the backs of trucks.

Heartbeat in my ears. But no, it felt too definite, too deliberate and clear, the click and the clack. I ran past a *Chuck Jones* poster, then one for *Lee*. Did someone call my name? Or did I just yearn to be in a place where people knew me? I turned fast and almost tripped. I looked forward again.

My muscles cramped and my heart raced too fast. I sat on the sidewalk and tried to stretch as blood drained from my head. In the distance a dog howled.

Back home, Antoinette helped a middle-aged white man in a tan-colored trench coat carry a bag up the stairs.

"This here's Marcel," she said to the man as I came up the path.

"Pleasure to meet you," he said, offering me his large hand. "Name's Simpson. Dave Simpson."

"Have a great day," I said as I shuffled past them.

I made a donation to the ASPCA .

I sat on the bed with the window open, smoking. When I heard Antoinette coming up the stairs I got up, putting my hand on the doorknob. But as her footsteps got closer they morphed into something else, the sound of hooves. I recalled this sound from my earliest memories, as if it were the beating of my own heart, recorded in the ancient part of my brain that flickered to life when I lived as a seahorse inside my mother.

And the sound had hunted me from before then even, from when I didn't have a face, from when my death had not yet become a possibility.

The skies turned blood red, then black. Families sat outside laughing and shouting. Cigarettes glowed, dogs barked, cicadas screamed in the trees. Stickiness left the air.

We sat together in the narrow room next to her kitchen, Antoinette on the dryer, myself on the washer. An old country song played on a portable nineties hi-fi system, covered with white paint hand marks. After pouring us each a second glass of her special mixture, she moved closer to me.

"Where's the other guest?"

"He's in his room. He's just some kind of traveling sales-man. Last of his kind, he says."

"We're all the last of our kind, aren't we?"

"The poet's back in town. How's your story coming on? You seen the place for yourself now, so you can write it in full color." Her face flushed as she smiled. "You gonna mention the gator?"

"I haven't figured out how it'll all fit together."

"You're a cagey one, Marcel."

"I'm not cagey."

"Bless your soul. I bet you if I asked your mamma, she'd say you're cagey."

"She doesn't know that."

"She knows you better than anybody."

"Possibly."

"And you still ain't called her."

"No, I haven't. Well, what's up with your mother? You always ask about mine."

"My mamma ran away when I was a baby."

"I'm sorry."

"You're always apologizing for things you ain't done."

"I'm expressing condolences."

"I didn't ask for that." She flicked her cigarette ash on the floor. "Like my daddy told it, my mamma was crazy. But like they say, there's always two sides to a story, and I ain't heard hers, and I know for a fact he's crazy."

"No one should abandon their baby."

"There're many things no one should do."

"Maybe it wasn't her fault."

"Maybe it was."

"I'm trying to agree with you."

"There ain't no point in that."

"Whatever I say, you just disagree with me."

"No, I don't."

A moment's silence. Laughter, then the sound of her feet hitting the floor. She finished her drink, dropped the glass into the sink, and marched out the room. "Call your mamma."

I struggled to sleep again that night. When I finally did I heard those hard footsteps. I woke cold, as the sun came in. I tried to run but my knees hurt, my spine hurt. I felt like I'd aged decades in a few weeks.

Dave Simpson sat at the breakfast table, eating pancakes covered in syrup and drinking orange juice.

"This gal sure knows how to cook a good breakfast. You going to join us... what was it? Marcel?"

"I'm not big on pancakes for breakfast. But thank you."

Dave had a very round face and short brown hair. He smiled at me, as if I'd just complimented him.

"Well, I just love these pancakes, Antoinette. This house is wonderful. This neighborhood is wonderful."

I poured myself a cup of coffee and sat down.

"I'm sure glad you like it, sir. We're proud of what we have here."

"If I didn't have to keep moving on, I'd stay a few days extra. I'm a travelling salesman, Marcel. The last of my kind."

"Life on the road," I said.

"That's right. Life on the road."

When Dave had checked out, Antoinette and I sat alone at the table.

I ate a bowl of cornflakes. "Why did you make me swim with those gators?"

"Why you bringing that up now?"

A light drizzle turned to a downpour. The room darkened.

"I guess you won't be working in your garden today."

"I can work in my garden if I want to." She took a deep sip of coffee and stood by the window, smoking. "I have rain boots. I have a rain coat. I have rain socks and rain hair."

"I didn't mean to offend you."

She let out a laugh like a bullet, pointing at me with her smoking hand.

"You wondering why you done swum with that gator? You blaming me for your decision?"

"Tran told me to stop thinking mechanistically."

"And you're going listen to him?"

"Maybe I have no choice. Maybe none of us do. And that's what frightens us."

"Maybe you do have a choice, and that's what frightens you."

I drank the milk and the last few cornflakes out of my bowl, wiped my mouth.

"Tran helped me see my purpose here is twofold. I'll never know why I'm here in this house with you."

She crushed out her cigarette, carelessly blowing a line of smoke in my direction.

"Tell me something." I stood up just as the rain intensified. Now it sounded like gunfire on the roof. I paced up and down in the small space of her kitchen. "The next time I go to the island, I can go alone, right? And I can row right up there?"

"Now you gonna thank me for making you swim with the gators?"

"Sure, I'll thank you."

"You can go there anytime you want now. Long as they raise the white flag."

"I have to take them my father's notebooks."

CHAPTER 14

The kayak fractured the blue sky reflected in the bayou water. I stuck the paddle deep below the surface and rowed away from the land, careful to keep myself steady. I'd stored my father's notebooks in an old duffle bag Antoinette had given me. The thought of them falling into the water frightened me more than my own death.

As my father had travelled down increasingly esoteric paths, he'd become less prolific. He'd broken a book contract, moved from one project to the next without bringing any to completion. But this didn't mean his findings were less valuable, and here lay the remains of his latter thinking. A part of him that survived in this world. Thoughts converted into scribbles on pages.

An eagle circled overhead now, just as it had in my dream last night. Its shimmering reflection circled my kayak like an aquatic creature. The sun moved higher into the sky. How had last night's dream played out? Something had circled above me and below me then, but now, in waking life, the creature below me was a reflection of the one above.

I peered through the gun site to an empty beach. A

moment later a pair of women appeared by the water. They both had long hair. One disappeared, and when she reemerged a few minutes later she held a white flag in her hands. As she waved it in the air, I felt my energy rise.

I hit the beach, my neck, hands, and forehead sweating. My heart raced as I dragged the kayak from the water and hauled out the duffel bag.

"Come this way." Tran emerged through an opening in the bushes. "Follow me."

This time I sensed my arrival had caused a stir. Bodies shifted and eyes followed me.

I sat down in the tent opposite Tran, who placed his long arms across his spidery knees in a meditation pose. The duffel bag sat between us.

From a table next to him, he took a cup of tea and handed it to me.

A man and a woman entered the tent, bowing slightly as they came in. The man sat on Tran's left, the woman on his right. They smelt of fire smoke and lavender perfume. Both had long hair, dark skin, blue eyes. Their ages were difficult to tell. They could have been thirty-five or fifty-five.

As I finished my tea I began to feel pleasantly light-headed, and then it was no longer clear which of the two was the man and which the woman. How had I come here this morning?

"Had I planned to be here?"

"Interesting question," said Tran.

Only then I realized I'd spoken out loud.

"My name is Helen," said the woman.

"I'm Helena," said the man.

They took turns speaking and my eyes shifted from one to the other.

"You brought this across the water."

"These are your father's books."

"And you suspect they are important."

"How do you know these are my father's books?"

They looked at one another and then at Tran. He nodded.

Helen spoke: "Maggie has warned us that we were missing an important piece."

Helena took over: "Our job is to seek unity in the narrative, but also to identify disturbances."

"There is a terrible disturbance at the moment."

"As I tried to explain to you last time," Tran picked up now, "the modern world thinks only mechanistically. The more mechanistically we think, the greater our power as human beings grows, and the more dangerous we become."

"And the more illiterate we become in the other language the universe speaks."

"In the language the gods speak."

"We used to live in the open. Prophecy was accepted. Visions and stories of visitations were believed."

"But now our people are harassed."

"Some are locked away, others mocked."

"I'm not the..." I reached for my empty tea cup. I saw my shaking hand, the way they saw it: evidence of my madness. "I'm not that way." I stood up, swinging the duffel bag over my shoulder. "I came here to write."

"Yes, and we have a room for you."

"No, not like that. To write about *your* situation. To write about the election that threatens you."

"But why do you care?" asked Tran.

"Because. Because I... care about the work you do."

"You've only spent a short time with us."

"I was told about you. I was told by someone who... understood what I was living through."

They let the silence linger.

"Would you let us show you something?" Tran asked.

Their facial expressions registered as both pleading and equanimous, as if they knew they had to beg me, but also that I couldn't say "no".

I followed them down a path that wove through the tents, past this civilization in miniature. Men and women sharpened knives, fashioned spiderweb-like contraptions out of branches and leather, prepared food, sewed clothes. Some turned to watch us as we passed. Sharp eyes; enigmatic looks. We stopped finally outside a tent, similar to all the others.

"This is yours," Tran said.

I pulled the flap aside. In one corner lay a reed mat, in another a knee-high writing desk in front of a red pillow.

"Sleep here tonight," said Helen. "Use the duffel bag as a pillow. This tent was built to dream in."

"I'm expected home tonight."

"Antoinette understands our work." Tran interlaced his long fingers and popped the joints.

Helen and Helena stared at me intensely. I did my best to hold their gaze, but I could not. I threw the duffle bag on the floor.

"Fine. I'll stay for the night."

"Excellent."

"Wonderful."

They put their hands on me and rubbed my back. Was I guest or prisoner? I patted their hands and arms as I stepped away from them into my tent.

"Yes, spend time in here. We'll bring you cool tea. You need to prepare yourself for the evening. The dreams you have tonight are important."

They brought me nuts, dried fruit, and cool green tea, not nearly as swampy as Tran's. I sat on my haunches at the low desk, flipping through my father's books. In his copy of *Synchronicity*, where Jung describes the beetle flying up against the dark window, my father had made some pencil notes. I didn't recall seeing these the last time I'd looked through the book. Or perhaps I'd taken them for waffle at the time: *S.V. II, 165*. But now I remembered that strange game my father used to play when I was a child. He'd have me sit on his knee as he flipped back and forth through his old copy of *The Aeneid*, pressing his finger down on a passage chosen at random. Then he'd read the Latin words out loud and translate them for me. Perhaps he had dreams of my being a serious scholar, the type that might pun with him in ancient languages.

Sadly, Father, that dream of yours did not come to pass. But I do remember the game you played, and I do remember the meaning behind it. It's called Sortes Virgilianae. Early and Medieval Christians had considered Virgil a pre-Christian saint. This is one of the reasons Dante had Virgil guide him through Hell in *The Divine Comedy*. I'd become intimately familiar with Virgil during those tumultuous months that I wrote my dissertation, and so even though I'd still struggle to translate more than a single word from Latin, I knew the line reference by heart: "Now the man Of Ithaca haled Calchas out among us In Tumult, calling on the Seer to tell The true will of the gods."

I folded the two books into one another, the respective pages touching. Like lovers, I thought. Or maybe just friends?

When the night came, the three returned to my tent and opened a flap in the upper part of the right wall so the night sky was visible from my bed.

"Drink this tea. It will calm you."

Helen handed me a cup. Night insects screeched. The

island had no electricity, and the flickering shadows cast by fires danced on the walls of my tent.

"Perfect for sleeping," said Tran.

"Perfect for dreaming," Helena added.

They pulled the front tent flap shut. I lay my head against the book pile I'd fashioned into a pillow and stared through the open flap at the stars. Breathing deeply, I drifted off.

Antoinette and I sat on her porch, our bodies rubbing together. I felt madly aroused, and she began to rub her hands over me. She wore a long dress which I slipped up her body. She wore no bra. Slowly, I pulled down her underwear. Now she lay completely naked before me.

"Come inside me," she said.

I moved to get on top of her, craving her. But from the house came a hammering sound, an awful screech, and I remembered that I'd come here for some other reason.

"Please wait for me," I said, and tried to kiss her face.

She rolled away, pulling her clothes on.

Inside the house the painful, groaning sound intensified.

I found my father in the attic, nailed to a wooden beam.

"Why are you up there?"

"They hung me like this."

I scrambled to lift his body, free him from his own weight. I pulled out the nails. Blood spread across the floor as I lowered him down.

"You put yourself up there, didn't you?"

"Don't tell them what you saw here."

"You expect me to lie to them?"

"Someone has to do this."

Antoinette appeared in the doorway.

"You're the only other one who's seen this," I said to her.

"You expect me to keep your secrets? To tell lies for you?"

"I'm the one they'll ask about this."

My father got to his feet. Blood continued to pour out of him, forming pools on the floor.

"I barely know you," he said, pointing at Antoinette. "I'm doing this for my son. But it will help you. You don't know what may be asked of you."

Antoinette stared at us both in silence.

"Let's take him downstairs," I said. "We can clean him up there."

"He stopped bleeding. Look." She pointed. True enough, he'd stopped bleeding, and the pools of blood on the floor had vanished. "I fixed this place myself. I put up those beams. He's going to pull them down with his foolery."

"He's trying to help us. That's his gesture. Just like building the house is yours."

"Ain't nobody asked him to do that."

"Nobody asked you to do this either. We each do what we can."

She shook her head. "We need to get him out of here."

But when I turned to look at him again, he was gone. I stood up, taking Antoinette's hand.

"Let's go back downstairs. Pick up where we left off?"

"I'm not in the mood anymore. You come find me some other time. I may be ready for you then."

She kissed me.

"Did you dream?"

An explosion of light filled the tent as Tran struck a match, revealing Helen and Helena, one on his left, one on his right.

I sat up. "You're in my room."

"Tell us what you've dreamed," said Helena as he pressed his pen against a writing pad on his knee.

"I thought you'd left me alone."

"We understand this might feel uncomfortable," said Helen.

"But we knew you were dreaming," said Tran.

"And sometimes dreams are forgotten soon after waking up"

"Maybe I don't want to tell you. Where's the cool tea?"

They stumbled over themselves to help me.

"Sharing dreams with someone is very intimate," I said.

"We understand that." As Helen lent forward her hair fell from behind her ears. In this light it flashed grey, unlike Helena's that still looked dark. "And we wouldn't ask this of you unless it was important."

"We know what you did," said Helena.

"Don't threaten him," Helen snapped back.

"It's not a threat. We've all done something like that."

"It's no crime, what you've done," said Tran. "My life had fallen to pieces before I came here."

His companions touched his arms.

"That's why I walk with a limp," he said. "Injecting was the only way to soothe the pain."

"You had bad luck?" I asked.

"The gods hated me." He wiped his forehead with the sleeve of his robe. "I was the most despised man."

"Something brought on the bad luck?"

"Numbers. Money."

"You won the lottery?"

"Oh, I won it, all right." He ran his hand over his head. "For fifteen years I used the same numbers, made up of birthdays and anniversaries. Then my father died and I switched his birthday for his death day. Three six to four nine. I won. But I'd offended." He gestured vaguely at the sky. "Everything was taken from me. But she..." He pointed to his left. "She helped me make amends. I found peace again."

"Why did you stay?"

"Out there, you can only wreck your life once. No second chances."

"You had a family?"

"Two beautiful girls. My wife loved me."

"You stayed here to help other people?"

"I did and I did. For a long time we held it all together. But now we're attacked on all sides."

"*He* is returning, just at the same time as some lunatic wants to defeat the only sheriff who's willing to defend us."

"Throughout our long history, our organization has never known anything like this." Helena took the lantern from Tran and hung it from the center of the tent. It swayed, sending elongated shadows up the tent walls. "We don't have internet out here, so we rely on papers from the mainland." He stepped out the tent for a moment and returned with a pile of newspapers bundled together with string. "These arrived this morning."

"It confirmed what we already knew."

Helena flipped through the newspapers, reading out headlines.

"Lottery winner and family killed when tornado destroys home. Recent lottery winner killed by own gun. Millionaire gambler dies from food poisoning."

"He's not being subtle," said Tran.

As they spoke I felt my heart beat harder and faster. I stood up.

"I need to leave. Why can't I meet Maggie?"

"Tell us, what did you see?"

"In my dream?"

"Yes. Of course."

They huddled around me, Helena itching to write.

"I saw my father."

"Yes? And? What was he doing?"

"He was in pain. He'd... he seemed to have been nailed to wooden beams in the attic of a house."

"Had he put himself into that position?" Helena asked as he scribbled frantically on his page.

"I think so. I can't remember."

"Did you leave him there?"

"No! Of course not. I took him down."

"Oh no, no!"

Helena grabbed me and pushed me aside.

"Leave him alone," said Helen.

"You know what this means, Helen. You shouldn't have done that, Marcel."

"That was my father. And it was my dream."

He took the books I'd taken out and threw them into the duffel bag.

"We need to get this to Maggie. She needs to read all this, and hear about what's happened."

Helena stormed out of the tent with my bag.

"I'm sorry about this, Marcel," said Tran. "But we have to go with him."

The other two left, and I was alone in the tent.

A rhythmic chant came from outside. A hum-drum-lol repeat. A steady percussion; a low-groaning of collected male voices and a single female voice that flew above it all. An angel's voice.

I pulled the tent flap aside. Untamed by electricity the night felt alive. Shadows danced up trees, poles, the sides of tents. Signs of human life—tent sites, fires—were all about me, but where were the humans? The chanting had gone silent. I stood still, next to a tree. An owl landed in the branches above me and let out a mournful cry. The sound of a twig snapping spun my head. A deer watched from the shadows.

And then as if all the world were staged for my experience—as if the steps I'd taken and the exact time I'd paused had been scripted—the thud of drums hailed the return of the choir. I ran past the tents and looked toward the towering wooden building in the center. I knew right away that I was not meant to see this ceremony. I felt uncomfortable, sick, as if worms had hatched inside me.

Naked bodies danced around flames that climbed up toward the spider-web-like contraptions I'd seen earlier, now hoisted halfway up the tower. Pages fluttered about the flames, lifted and propelled by the flames' heat and then sucked in. Were those my father's pages? Surely they would not do this to me.

Like a bruised eye, the half-moon peered down on the ceremony. A group in dark hoods emerged at the top of the tower. From the middle of the group, a tall woman with long, dark hair stepped forward and pushed everyone away from her. She held something—a book—up toward the sky, and pages fluttered from her hands, and is if in a zephyr, they drifted upwards, merging with the darkness.

"You're not meant to be here!"

I turned to see a small girl, maybe four years old, with dark hair and pale skin, standing in the forest behind me.

"Who are you?"

"She's my daughter."

A woman stepped into the light next to her. A man emerged, and then another. Both men had rugged skin, wore dirty clothes.

"You ain't meant to see this," one of the men said.

The other drew a long blade from a leather holder.

"I'm meant to be here. With Tran. With Helen and Helena."

"Don't see none of 'em here." The man had bad teeth, swollen gums. "You wan play with this knife?"

"No."

"Then you better run, boy."

The two men lunged at me. I ran back towards my tent, then turned and bolted for the path that led to the water. The moon barely lit my way, and when I got to the beach, I grabbed the kayak and ran with it into the water. I scraped my shin on a rock as my feet sank into stick-filled mud. One of the men had come waist-deep into the water. I swatted at him with the paddle, just missing his face. But he ducked beneath the water, then shouted back at the others.

"He gone. He gone."

CHAPTER 15

When I woke the next morning, peace flowed through me despite the fact that my body was scraped and bruised. A wet cloth lay across my forehead. Tran sat next to my bed, a writing pad in his hand.

"Antoinette let me in." He placed the pad on the desk. "May I?" He took the cloth off me and touched just below my hairline. "Still warm."

My head pounded.

"I was chased off the island."

"Yes, yes." He started scribbling on his pad. "Tell me all the details. How did you get back here?"

"No, no. This happened to me. Not a dream. Why are you writing it down?"

"Of course."

The man was so tall he had to crouch not to bang his head on the ceiling fan. He was very awkward, uncomfortable in his own skin. He paced, fidgeting with his hands.

"Your mother has been trying to call you. Video call. Your phone kept lighting up." He sat down again and smiled at me. "I almost answered it. You should call her back."

. . .

I looked at my face in the bathroom mirror: scratched and bruised. What the hell had happened to me?

I video called my mother.

"Marcel. I've been trying to get hold of you for over a week."

I smiled so widely she must have known I was hiding something.

"Well? What's going on? Is your face scratched?"

She rested her elbows on the kitchen counter. A suited Baptist Pants waddled past her in the background, holding a plate of food in his hand.

"Morning, Marcel," he called out.

"Morning."

"I'll go up to the bedroom," she said.

I looked at myself in the small side-screen of the computer, fixed my hair, tried to flatten out the puffy skin beneath my eyes.

"Here's our room," she said, turning the camera around to reveal a bedroom out of a home improvement show. Light streamed in through large windows that opened—she now showed me—onto a balcony above cobbled streets. In the distance I could see the ocean.

"Gorgeous," I said.

"Charles was just saying again how you are welcome here, any time."

"Things are going quite well for me here."

"That's good to hear." She coughed a deep, chesty cough.

"Are you okay?"

"Smoker's cough."

"You told me you were a social smoker."

"I've been very social lately. We're talking about you. What's going on?"

"I'm down in Alabama."

"In Ala*bama?*"

"Yes. A story of mine was accepted."

"Marcel. Well done." She settled into a chair on her balcony. "So that's why you're in Alabama?"

"That's why, yes. That's the reason. I'm reporting on a local sheriff's election."

"Okay?" She sounded skeptical.

"It has broader ramifications. That's why the editors took it on."

"That's great. And you're doing okay for money, then?"

"More than okay. I'm doing fabulously well."

"Ha ha, Marcel." She took a sip of her coffee. "That's good."

"You think I'm joking, but the really funny thing is, I'm not." I got up from my bed and walked over to the window. A sharp, stinging pain intensified in my knee—a scrape from last night. "Basically, you could say I've got my life in order."

"I'm proud of you." She put her coffee cup down and coughed deeply into her hand. "You must let me know if you need anything."

"Why are you coughing like that?"

"I've had it for a while now."

"Since?"

"I can't remember exactly. It's allergies."

She certainly hadn't been coughing that way when she came to visit me.

"You need to keep an eye on that."

She stood up and called down to the street: "Have a good day." Then to me: "Charles is off to work."

She turned, leant against the balcony railing, and held the camera away from her face so I could see the street behind her. Somehow, using a single hand she was able to light a cigarette.

"Do you feel sad?" I asked her.

"There are too many things to feel sad about. If I started feeling sad about one thing, then I'd be neglecting another. So instead I just live. And I feel happy."

"I mean about dad."

"I know what you mean."

"So, I'll take that as a no. You're not sad about him?"

"It doesn't mean I don't care. I mourn. There's a life that could have been."

"For him?"

"For him. For me. For us. But look at you now. Your writing career is taking off. You know what you're doing and why."

"Yes. I know what I'm doing. I know why I'm doing it. I know why I am where I am."

I heard the clopping of hooves. I spun around, hopping off the table. My mother began to cough again, drawing my attention back to the phone.

"You have to look into that."

"Stop worrying, Marcel."

"Okay."

The conversation meandered gently, pleasantly, for the next thirty minutes. We laughed a lot. It was wonderful. But then I started to feel uneasy, my heart thumping.

"Let's speak again soon," I said.

"I've been trying to phone you. I'm here to talk."

"I'll be better at keeping in touch. I love you."

"I love you, too."

I crept down the stairs.

They sat across from one another in the kitchen, Antoinette drinking coffee, Tran hot water with a slice of lemon. Tran had rolled back the sleeves of his robe, exposing hairy forearms; his neck and shoulders were matted with dark hair.

"We worried about you, Marcel." Antoinette placed a cup of coffee in front of me. I held her gaze. It was the first time I'd looked into her eyes since we'd almost made love in my dream. Before that moment, in waking life, I'd only been vaguely aware of my desire for her, but now it burned. Did that moment we'd shared count as a moment? "You ain't got nothing to say for yourself?"

"You don't have to worry about me."

"Mother Magdalena," Tran said. "She's reviewing your documents."

"You didn't burn them?"

"Of course not. Why would we burn them?"

"I saw pages burning last night."

"Oh, Marcel." Antoinette gave me a pitying look as she reached for my arm. Her face flushed pink and her fingernails were muddy. Tools stuck out of her dungaree pockets.

"Tell her that's what happened out there, Tran."

"I'm not here to contradict you, Marcel."

"Well you just did contradict me, by not backing me up. Tell her what happened."

"We need your contribution to the story. In its purest form. If I contradict you that dilutes and distorts what you've said."

"That makes no sense."

"Quite true."

I groaned. "How long does this go on for?"

Antoinette took my hand, slipping her fingers between mine. A pleasant feeling surged through my body. I stared into her eyes, looking for the flicker that would tell me if she'd been there last night. But her eyes would not be read.

"Who chased me off the island?" I asked Tran. "Those people were dangerous. They were part of your... cult?"

"What do you think?"

"It doesn't matter what I think."

"Quite right."

"You need to stop agreeing with me." I slammed my empty coffee mug down and stood up. "I'm going outside to smoke."

Shoulder to shoulder, they watched me from the porch as I sat amongst the fallen leaves, smoking. I looked at my hands and remembered them clawing into the mud as I'd scrapped myself up the bank. I must have walked home along Highway 43, carrying the kayak on my back. Even as I recalled the images vividly, I doubted their truthfulness. But I looked up at Tran, and he nodded gently. I understood what he meant. He did not doubt me and I should not doubt myself.

The clouds had been low, electric, ghost-white. I'd stopped beneath the signboard for Jefferson Lee. Sitting atop his black stallion, he gazed across the highway and the bayou, toward the small town of Chickasaw, the town on which he'd set his sights. The holes in his eyes, shot through by Chuck Jones—did they start to glow? Did I hear horse hooves coming along the road? A thick mist came up from the water. A train let out a shrill whistle as it passed over the bridge; the sound of horse hooves intensified and then vanished.

"I need to see Sheriff Chuck," I said.

"Whatever you need to do, Marcel."

A half hour later I sat opposite Chuck Jones in his office. With his mud-stained boots up on his desk, leaning back in his chair, he smoked a hand-rolled cigarette.

"I was almost attacked on the island."

"There are rogue elements. They don't represent Maggie's Farm."

"Who are they, then?"

"Don't fully know myself. Think they're disgruntled ex-members. Or people that never got full acceptance." He put his feet down on the floor and leant forward. "Probably thought they had something useful to offer, but turned out they didn't."

"And now?"

"They roam the bayous. Got nothing left in this world, nothing to offer that one."

He took a large coin out of his pocket and spun it on the table. "Are you trying to say I shouldn't protect them?" He wiped his mustache with the back of his hand, taking a drag of his cigarette.

"What's more interesting is that you would think that's what I'm saying."

He leant forward, stared silently into my eyes for a few seconds, then burst out laughing.

"Good one, Marcel. You should take notes." He pointed at my writing pad, then raised both his hands as if directing a choir. "Give the people a feel for the kind of man I am." He picked the coin up before it stopped spinning. "That's one way out, you know."

"What is?"

"I'm about to tell you something, but I want you to know that there's a counterargument."

"Okay."

I had no idea what the man was talking about.

"You have to pick a side. In any battle. Heads or tails. Jones or Lee."

"Or I can pick up the coin before it stops spinning, and walk away."

"Yes, you can," he said, and spun the coin on the desk. "But then you always lose."

Instinctively, I snapped up the coin. I held it tight in my

hand and felt like I was squashing a small bird. I dropped it back on the table in front of him, like a casino chip.

"Or I could do that. There are many ways to play this game."

He sized me up silently before looking away. Something took possession of him—an emotion and a reflexive suppression of that emotion. I'd seen something of this nature move through my father and other older men. I spun the coin on the table. This was meant as an apology. I felt a chasm open up inside me. Sadness poured in like floodwater through a broken floor.

"Why don't you go meet Jefferson Lee?" he asked me. Now Sheriff Chuck picked up the spinning coin and put it back into his top pocket. All these spins, and we'd never seen it land. "He has a rally tonight on the other side of the river. Antoinette will go with you, I'm sure of it."

"Maybe I will. Maybe I'll even talk to him."

"Good."

He looked offended.

"I'm not planning to support him," I said. "I came here to write an article. I just want to get the full picture, to understand the whole story."

"All you can ever hope to understand is your own mind." His right eye twitched. On the skin below his eye he had some darker spots, like freckles. "If some part of you wants to see those folk driven out of town, then some part of you will be attracted to Lee."

"That's not fair."

"Oh, it's fair." He retrieved his still-smoking cigarette from the ashtray and took a long drag, then squashed it out.

"I don't have a long-standing loyalty to this town."

"So that means all morality goes out the window? *I come from out of town, so I can do as I please.*"

"I'm not saying that."

"You were drawn here because of Maggie, and her farm." He stood up, putting his hat on. I got to my feet. "Go see my rival tonight, Marcel. See what kind of man he is. Thank you for coming by." He gave me his hand.

I left feeling all torn up inside. I missed my father. I turned to look for him, as if maybe he'd be standing there, waiting. But even the wind was silent.

CHAPTER 16

Hard rain fell as I walked through the mushy garden to find Antoinette on a rocking chair, smoking, and drinking coffee. Her knees were muddy, and her wet hair frizzy. I handed her the bag of Foosackly's chicken I'd picked up on the way home.

"You know how to make a Bama gal happy."

The screen door slammed shut behind me. The porch smelt damp.

"I bought us sweet tea, too."

"You're learning fast, Marcel."

Rain splashed through the screen door. Antoinette wiped her hands on her grass-stained dungaree pants. I looked at her fingers and let my eyes drift over her body, making no attempt to hide it. She reached into the packet, taking out a napkin. We ate in silence and watched the rain.

"I have to admit... I have an ulterior motive... to some extent... There's something I need to ask you?"

"Come on. What is it?"

"Okay. Will you go with me to the Jefferson Lee rally tonight?"

Antoinette wiped her fingers on a napkin, rolled the napkin into a ball, and dropped it into her box of Foosackly's. "What the heck's wrong with you?"

"I'm writing about this election. I need to get a full picture."

"That man's evil."

"So, what should I write? There's an election between two sheriffs, one is bad, one is good?"

"You've met Sheriff Chuck a few times. Write about what kind of man he is."

"And write off his opponent?" Her desire to drain the world of nuance surprised me. "Don't you see what's wrong with that?"

"Come on. All he wanna do is drive those folk out of town."

"I was driven off their island last night."

"Not by Maggie's people, you wasn't."

"As I tried to explain to Sheriff Chuck earlier, I don't have a longtime attachment to this town."

She dipped a chicken finger into the sauce and gave me the kind of look a mother might give a child she's angry with, but is about to indulge out of necessity. "Mr. Objective? Mr. Sees it as it *really* is cause we folk's too dumb? We're your story then, huh? Nothing more."

"I want to tell your story accurately."

"You still ain't getting it. Ain't nobody in this town here on accident."

"I get it. I get it." I felt then like someone was watching me. I stood up, looking through the pouring rain, across the street.

Would everything return to normal once I'd given all my money away? Did I have to find the right charity? Was that it? Or the right person?

Antoinette smiled at me, and I knew what I had to ask her.

"How did you end up here? What's your story?"

"That's not what I'm trying to get you to ask me."

"I want to know."

She licked her fingers.

"Come on, sit down." She lit two cigarettes, handing one to me. "I grew up in Florence."

"Alabama?"

"No Florence, Europe, Marcel. What you think?"

"Okay."

"Daddy was a policeman, killed in the line a duty." She dragged deeply on her cigarette, holding the smoke in her lungs, as she saluted. "God bless that man, and God bless America." The smoke rolled out of her mouth as she spoke.

"That's sad." I took the dirty notebook out of my back pocket. "Do you mind if I make notes?"

"Don't go writing, oh, boo-hoo, so sad, poor gal."

"I'll just write down what you tell me."

"I know it ain't good to speak ill of the dead, or whatever, but that man, he was a real bastard. I was shocked when he died, 'course I was, but I weren't real sad."

"But he was a hero in your town?"

"Sure was. I'll give the man what credit he's due. He done raised me all on his own. Mamma ran off when I was just four weeks old. So, I guess, I should be thankful to him. But he didn't love me, or like me. I think I reminded him of my mamma."

"How old were you when this happened?"

"I was sixteen years old. I got a bunch of life insurance money. Tell you the truth, I almost thought my mamma might show up, try claim some a that money."

We both looked across the street at that moment, as if she might suddenly appear there, standing in the rain. But the road was empty. Water trailed down the mosquito netting around the front porch.

"I assume she never showed up?"

"Not that I know of. I only have one picture of her. I ain't looked at it in years."

She put her feet up on the old glass-top wicker coffee table. The rain stopped. The smell of our cigarettes mingled with a new smell, post-rain fresh air. Antoinette stood up, pacing as she smoked and continued her story.

"I had a boyfriend at the time. He was twenty-four years old. When my daddy died, he decided to move in with me. Next eighteen months is like some kind of bad dream. I can only remember flashes. Just images here and there. Always high, drunk. I wake up with a swollen face. Bleeding.

"I didn't tell nobody. My dog died. I became sick. Real sick. Coughing all the time. Spitting up blood. Then he, that piece a shit Shane, he became sick, too. He blamed it on me, said I brought a demon into the house. I *did* brought a demon into the house, I said, and that demon's *you*. I still had a few friends back then, but my best friend, Cindy, she gone died from some strange sickness, and my boyfriend, he tell me it's my fault too. Finally, one night we were fighting. He pulled out his gun and says he's going to kill me. He started shooting. I don't remember how I survived. But the next day, I took my daddy's old gun out the safe. I found that piece a shit Shane sleeping on the couch. He was so stupid he had messages with some other chick open on his phone. Goddamit, some people are stupid. I put the gun to his head, told him to get out my house.

"He started begging and pleading. I made him stand up and shot him in the shin. Then I dragged him to the car. He was skinny as a plastic straw. Weighed about a hundred pounds. I dropped his sorry ass outside the local hospital with his wallet, empty except for his driver's license, so they'd know who he is."

"You never heard from him again?"

"I still have that gun. He knows he show up at my house I'll shoot him 'fore he can shoot me. Same goes for any bad man." She gave me a threatening smile. "If a man turns bad and shows up at my door. Bam. You hear?"

"Loud and clear."

"But things kept on going bad for me. Some point I start thinking, maybe Shane the shit was right and I done bring a demon into the house." She inhaled deeply and blew out a smoke ring. "That money. That's where it started. Now I know what some folks are gonna say: there's a reasonable explanation. But I could feel it in my bones. I started having these strange dreams. I started hearing hooves following me around."

"You did?"

She nodded. "I knew I done offended... something." She looked toward her house, then out onto the street. "I thought of giving all my money away. I gave *some* of it away, but that didn't help. I started using again. Heavy stuff. I was shooting up when I realized I'd gone way off the deep end. So I went to the meetings. That's where I met a man who told me about this place."

"And Maggie set you right?"

"It taken some time, and like I said, I never seen her face to face. But that woman done set me right. If she asks you for anything else. You need to give it to her."

"What might she ask for?"

"The story you're in began before you was even thinking. I don't understand it all, but they explained it to me. My daddy, he was involved somehow. He was tangled up. The gunshot that killed him." She blew out a line of smoke, like a jet stream, then leant forward and squashed her cigarette. "That was part of it. Related. Know what I mean?"

"I think I do, yes."

She put her arms behind her head and leant back slowly.

"I'll take you tonight," she said. "But I'm telling you again: I fucking hate that man."

The rain came and went all afternoon. We set out for Jefferson Lee III's election rally early evening. Antoinette wore a bandana under a cowboy hat, a baggy camo jacket, camo pants, and leather work boots. I made do with a pair of jeans, hiking boots, and a sweater. Smoking cigarettes and sipping whisky from a hip flask, we drove across town in her car listening to Bob Dylan.

"Dolly Parton Bridge," she said, as we drove beneath two massive steel arches and over the river. "That's what everybody calls it." Darkness stretched off in front of us and to our left. To the right lay a coal processing plant, the gothic machinery dimly visible through the fog.

We drove past the coal plant, turning left down an unlit muddy road. Half a mile ahead the taillights of cars glowed.

The muddy parking lot, lit by a searchlight on the warehouse roof, was filled with SUVs and heavyset men in overalls and boots, jackets, and baseball caps. They stood in huddles like the bad kids at school, smoking, not put off by the rain. An American flag had been hoisted up a pole in front of the warehouse entrance. The car to our left had a Confederate license plate.

"We're going to stand out. Do you think we're safe?"

She unzipped her jacket to show me a pistol.

"M1911," she said.

"All these guys are probably packing, too."

"Packing. Haha. Come on. You wanted to come. You wanna write the Great American article, or whatever. Now we're here. You scared?"

"No. Let's do it."

Keeping our heads down we walked through the mud toward the warehouse. At the entrance a woman with the crinkled skin of a smoky boozehound gave us each a pamphlet.

"Y'all take a seat anywhere."

The warehouse, the size of two tennis courts, was already half-full. Many of the men were dressed like Antoinette, and the women—outnumbered maybe three to one—looked, on average, like the lady at the entrance. They wore bright-colored rain jackets, pink, white, orange; one wore a white coat with shiny objects all over it.

We sat in the emptiest row, leaving four seats between us and an old man in a blue rain jacket.

"Y'all get wet out there?" He turned to us and smiled.

"Sure is raining hard," Antoinette said.

A woman a few rows ahead, turned around and smiled. "Guess it must be the global warming." She cracked up laughing. We all joined her.

"You need to keep yourself warm," the old man said, pointing at me.

I nodded and smiled, but said nothing. There was no way a man with my accent would really be here. Antoinette took my hand. "I'll make sure he stays warm."

"That's a good woman," the old man said, and pointed at her. "That's a good woman right there. You got yourself a good woman."

Another old man a few seats ahead of us turned around and pointed at me.

"You better take care of her. Ain't many like her left these days."

"Yes, sir," I said in my best Southern accent. I leant over and kissed Antoinette on the cheek. Her skin reddened and I felt a rush pass through my whole body. She gazed at me, and our eyes did that thing where they hop from side to side, left eye to right and back again. My chest fluttered. The room disappeared. *Were you there on the porch that night? In my dream?*

She looked away.

The room exhaled.

By eight pm—the time Jefferson was set to appear—all the chairs were taken. People stood in the aisle and pressed up against the walls. We stood for the national anthem and made a pledge to a flag that had been wheeled in and placed near the makeshift stage. The lights went down and a single spot lit up a podium. A fat man in khaki waddled on, took the microphone, and sang the praises of Jefferson Lee III: a patriot, a man of God; a man not afraid to stand up for what was right.

The audience hollered back approval. Feet stamped. There were yells and yahoos. The excitement was contagious. I had to remember this feeling so I could bring it back to life in my article. The more I focused on the feeling, the more intense it grew. I tried to describe it to myself, but soon enough, like a lonesome boy on a stormy road, the feelings defeated me. I was one with the crowd. Later perhaps, I could pretend I'd been an objective bystander, but in truth I was no different than my neighbors.

The fat man in khaki waved as he waddled off stage, the spotlight following him. From the darkness behind us came a holler. Now a spotlight revealed a pair of cowboy boots, black jeans, a black jacket and a black hat. The room exploded, and many jumped to their feet screaming as he came onto the stage.

He took the microphone and called out: "Evening y'all! Thank you for coming out in the rain." He was an older man —in his early seventies perhaps—but he had amazing energy and seemed to be in much better physical shape than most of his supporters. "How many y'all love America?"

The whole crowd screamed and stamped their feet.

"How many y'all love Alabama?"

The same response.

"And how many y'all love the beautiful, little town a Chickasaw?"

More screaming and stamping.

Each question got the same response: "How many y'all lived here all your life?" "How many y'all have parents and grandparents who grew up here?" "How many y'all know no other home?"

And then: "So how come we have to drive over the river and meet out here in this warehouse for our meeting?"

From behind us a woman screamed: "'Cause the Satanists took over." Hollers of agreement.

Jefferson pointed at the crowd and wagged his finger as he spoke.

"That's right. The Satanists have taken over. Good, God-fearing people like ourselves have to meet in the dark, because the Satanists have driven us from our own town. And why's this happening?"

"Chuck Jones is a Satanist," came a holler.

Antoinette muttered under her breath: "Y'alls a bunch of Satanists."

I squeezed her arm.

"That's right," Jefferson called, and raised his hand in the air. "Now I'm glad you called him Jones and not *Sheriff* Jones." More cheering and stamping of feet. "'Cause I remember a time when the word sheriff meant something. Do you know that the sheriff is answerable only—and hear me clear when I say this, folks—is answerable only to the American Constitution, to you the people, and to God Himself." The crowd went wild, and Jefferson let the cheering continue as he wiped his forehead and took a sip of water. Then with a swipe of the hand, he brought the crowd to silence. "What kind of a man, can put on a United States of America sheriff's badge, call himself a *sheriff*, and let *Satanists* run his town? We may be tempted to ask: What is this world coming to? But we should not be surprised. The Enemy is always among us. But we will drive him out. For this is God's country. This is America." The crowd began to cheer louder and louder. "This is Alabama! This is Chickasaw!" The screaming reached a crescendo.

"Actually, that's across the river," Antoinette muttered.

"Do you know what they call her? They call her Mother Magdalena."

"Some call her Maggie," Antoinette muttered.

"She's a *Satanist!*" somebody shouted from the back of the hall.

"That's right. And the Satanists who worship at the altar of Magdalena, do all kinds of disgusting things that ain't suitable for public discussion. But I assure you, they evil, and they bold. And in ten days' time, the man who protects them, the man who dares to call himself Sheriff, is up for reelection. And if he wins, those Satanic animals are going to be bolder than ever. And they're going to go on a killin' spree. Killin' good people, drinking their blood. But in ten days' time, we..." He pointed out across the crowd. "We, the people of Chickasaw, are going to send a message to those Satanists and those who would protect them. We're going to tell them, that their time has come. We're going to tell them, that their time is over." The crowd stood up, screaming and cheering as Jefferson worked the people to a wild climax. "We're going to tell them their evil ways will not be tolerated here in God's country. Give me an Amen." The crowd gave him an Amen. "We going to say: not today Satan. Get behind me Satan. Can I get an Amen?" He got his Amen. "We're going to tell them that this is America. That this is Chickasaw... And we're going to tell them... Here me clear folks: There's a New Sheriff in Town."

The crowd roared like the ocean, like the inside of a bomb.

❦

Puddles outside Whataburger reflected its neon orange sign. We sat at a corner table and watched the rain stream down the window. I scooped up ketchup with my fries.

"Let me play Devil's advocate again," I said.

"They're not so bad as you thought they was gonna be. You said it already." Antoinette took a bite of her burger.

"You don't agree."

"I know these folk." She pointed into the darkness. "Those people sure seem friendly at the start. And maybe one-on-one they ain't so bad. But when they're in a group? By the end, you saw 'em. Come on. They were howling like a bunch of crazies. They wanted blood."

"They think they're fighting evil."

"They're under a spell."

"They think we're under a spell."

"But they under one for real."

"And they think you are."

"But they *is*."

"All right." I put a handful of fries into my mouth.

In the dark entryway of her house we took off our shoes and wet coats. This was the exact spot we'd been when we'd almost made love in my dream. I thought of reaching out for her, touching her face.

She flicked on the kitchen light. Her eyes were so green they took a bite from my soul.

"You want to shower first?" She stepped away from me, and stood beneath the kitchen lamp, strands of hair stuck to her wet face. "What you smiling at?"

"We'll meet down after? More wine?"

"You're a boozehound." She pointed at me, coming around the side of the table, hand out. I wanted to kiss her so badly. And she wanted to be kissed, didn't she?

"If you think all them folk's so wise," she took my hand, "then you should listen to what that old man said."

"What did he say?"

"That I'm a good woman." She pressed herself against me, and any doubt I'd had about her desires vanished. "There ain't many like me left."

"But you said they were all crazy."

"Crazy folk can tell the truth." She let go of my hand, staring at me silently. I could feel not only her disappointment, but also her confusion. She knew I was acting against my own desire. "Now I feel stupid. I thought you liked me."

"I do. I've been waiting for this moment."

"So, why you holding back?" She touched her cold hand on my cheek and ran her fingers toward the tip of my chin. "You in love with someone else?"

"No. It's not that." The truth is, until this moment, I'd been unaware of the resistance in me. "It sounds stupid if I try to say it out loud."

"Come on."

"I'm worried I'll curse you. My father died." In my mind I could hear my mother coughing. I saw her on the balcony in Charleston. "I've sickened my mother. I know it. I shouldn't even be here."

She held both my hands and looked into my eyes.

"If I didn't want you here, I'd kick you out. Trust me."

"I know that."

She ran her hand up my back, but instead of melting me, she turned my body rigid and cold. Where had all my desire for her gone?

"Let's just hang out this evening, talk."

"You worried about my heart? I ain't a child."

"Believe me when I say, I want to kiss you." I touched her face. "But I'm convinced something bad will happen to you."

She said nothing for a few long seconds.

"If you was anybody else, I'd think you were the dumbest liar on earth."

"But?"

"I think you're a fool. But I think you believe what you're saying." She stepped away from me, lit a cigarette. "And that matters."

"It doesn't make what I'm saying, actually, literally true. Does it?"

"Why're you arguing back at me? I'm letting you free."

"I want to be wrong."

"You are. Your mind is a mess. But your heart is okay. Now take a shower."

Her empathy caused my desire to rear up again.

"Can we still hang out?"

"Yes. Now get out of here."

We showered, separately, and reconvened in her bedroom, on the same floor as mine—a loft above a workshop filled with half-painted doorframes, rocking chairs, wooden spoons and pipes, saws, hammers, screwdrivers hanging from the walls. The workshop was lit by a lamp with no shade that sat atop an upside-down paint can. Hammer- and saw-shaped shadows covered the walls and ceiling of her loft. The room smelt of paint fumes and sawdust. I followed her up the wooden ladder. A queen mattress lay on the floor. An old lamp on an apple box provided light.

As we sat on her bed, she filled our glasses with her special mix of red wine and ginger ale, then flicked a home-made switch, held together with tape, turning on an extraction fan above her bed. Cigarettes lit, we leaned against the pillows at the back of her bed, like lovers, post-coitus. In fact, the conversation in her kitchen had functioned, in some sense, like sex. We'd paid homage to our primal instincts, admitted that we were fully human and desired fleshly contact. We'd been vulnerable and awkward. And because we'd agreed on our reasons for not having sex, the awkwardness that comes from one person rejecting another was avoided. This was—I now realized—a kind of genius move on our part, and I felt free to talk as I would with a lover.

She opened a wooden box next to her bed and took out a small bag of weed.

"You smoke?"

"I will tonight."

With great skill she rolled a joint.

"Tell me, Mr. Swart, you ever been in love?"

"Dive right in, huh?"

"Answer my question, Marcel."

"I've never been in love, no. Not really. In high school no one would date me. In college, I floated from one relation-ship to the next. I'd think I was in love, but then it'd all end, and soon enough I'd realize it was just another infatuation."

"Maybe you're overthinking it."

She lit the joint, took a few puffs, and handed it to me.

I took three deep, long drags and held the smoke in my lungs, as I asked: "What do you mean?"

"You thought you was in love, right?"

"But that doesn't mean I was in love, ever. You know what it feels like. It's confusion. It's madness. Then it's all over. You love being on your own and you enjoy the peace. Then you get lonely. Or horny. Or both. And then it starts up again, and you become obsessed. Then it ends. Repeat. Repeat."

"Now I see why you wanna be a writer. You're kind of dramatic, ain't you?"

"Just describing my experience."

"Who says that you weren't in love? If you ask me if I was in love..." Just then I became extremely stoned, feeling as if I'd sunk deep below water. "Marcel?"

"Yes."

"Ask me."

"Oh, you actually want me to ask you? You ever been in love?'

"I say: yes. Heck yes, I have."

"With the guy you told me about the other day? I don't need any more joint."

She took a few more drags then put it out.

"That's the guy. I felt all the same madness you're talking 'bout, with one guy, for a long time. I was in love. But it ended, and when I look back, I don't even know that gal who was with him. But who am I to say she was wrong, and I'm right?"

"Well, you can say: I was in love. I know I was. Now I know I'm not. I say: I thought I was in love. Now I know I'm not."

"No, no. You just doing what most folk do. You give preference to the you of right now, and forget about the you of before. But that's just bias, ain't it?"

"Who could trust the me of years ago more than the me of now?"

As I asked that question I slid down on the bed, laying my

head on the pillow. The ceiling came closer until all the world turned white and speckled.

"That's why you got to keep a diary. Trees have rings, and humans have words."

"But you have to cut a tree down to see its rings."

"Nobody will know who I was 'til I'm dead. Then my story is over."

"And you hope someone reads it?"

"Trees die and they rot. New trees grow where the old ones grew before 'em. That's how a forest lives."

"Very few trees ever have their rings counted. Only we humans count tree rings. Most of us don't even care about that."

"Far as we know. There could be a great ring counter, who knows every ring in every tree."

"Like every hair on our heads is counted."

"Like that, yeah. And maybe the rings ain't what matters. You know? Like that's just our way of thinking."

"We appreciate trees for other reasons, too."

"Dammit, Marcel, I'm talking in metaphor here. Come on." She laughed, as she flipped around and slid down on the bed, so our faces were just a few inches apart. "That relation-ship I told you bout, it caused me a lot of pain."

I touched her arm. "I hear you. I'm sorry."

"Was it something I did?"

"I..." Realizing this was a question she'd posed for herself, I cut myself short.

"I've told you how I came to be here. I learned about Maggie through the support groups. But I grown up believing in God. Loving Jesus. So is this wrong, what I done?"

"I don't think so."

"If there's a great-great plan, a plan that covers all and everything, this is just one little piece a that. And *He* knows about it."

"Sure." I couldn't tell if she was talking to me as a conversation partner, or just shooting off a monologue in my presence, and as I became more stoned, I could no longer tell if there was a difference.

"What I'm saying is, things need to fall apart sometimes. And I'm glad for it. It's like they used to say back in the old days. Some things a blessing in disguise."

"We just don't see it at the time."

"That's right." Now she was talking to me again. "We got to have faith the whole plan is there, even if we can't see it."

"But sometimes, for some people, the plan doesn't come together."

"Maybe looks that way from outside. But we don't know what goes on inside other folks' mind and soul."

"That's true."

I was so stoned it took me some time to make sense of the shadow that moved across her ceiling. At first my mind interpreted it as a piece of a saw or a hammer that had come loose and moved through space, unbound somehow from the laws of physics. When I realized it was a bug I shifted up looking for the creature and slipped off the edge of the bed into a pile of her books.

"You're going to make me lose my place."

I held a book out toward her—C.J. Jung's *Memories, Dreams, Reflections*. "Why do you have this book?"

"Ain't no crime." She lit a cigarette and exhaled toward me. I opened the book to the place she'd marked using a one dollar bill. The chapter: *Life After Death*.

"Why didn't you mention this?"

She took the book from me. "He says we should do our best to figure out for ourself what's gonna happen when we die. That way we set ourselves up for the journey proper. Like, we get ready for it, and then we can live better."

"And what if you're wrong?"

"Ain't nothing lost. Just get a big surprise."

"What if God is vengeful?"

"Don't make no sense." She raised her hands in the air as she spoke, like a revivalist preacher. "He, who created the whole universe gets some kind of kick out of allowing torture, for all eternity, of those folk what believed the wrong thing?" She lowered her hands. "You don't even know what you believe one moment to the next." She poked me in the forehead. "Old you, ain't the same as this moment you, and ain't the same as next moment you. You said so yourself, when you was talking about love. That applies to you and all the rest..." She pointed her finger about.

"What about really bad people?"

"Some folk just bad. As I told you, I don't got no love for my daddy. But I don't get all excited thinking about him burning in a lake. I just want him to be better." She raised her hands again, and looked up at the ceiling. "Like maybe God's love burns so bright it burns off all his badness. Why would I get comfort knowing he's gonna to be punished for ten thousand trillion billion years cause he was a jerk for forty five?"

"Some people get comfort from that, apparently."

"'Cause they're sick. I hope they get better, too, and wake from their sickness. I pray for them every night." She raised her voice to a shout and said, "I pray for y'all." She pointed her hand this way and that. "All y'all. I even pray for you, Marcel." She shifted right off the bed and kissed me on the mouth, lips closed.

Three times now I'd come across that book. Three, the sacred number, the perfect number.

"You can sleep here tonight if you want," she said. "'Cause we're comfy now. Just friendly sleeping. In your clothes."

"Bless you," I said, and kissed her cheek.

I followed Highway 43 out of town, driving for ten miles until I reached the dirt road the campaign manager had told me to look out for. I passed an antebellum planta-tion manor tucked off the road behind a black fence and magnolia trees, then nothing but wild bramble, a horse eating shrubs.

At the edge of the dusty clearing stood a blonde woman, probably in her late twenties, dressed in a grey suit. She had a black Filofax in her hand, and she wore black stockings and green heels. I'd never in my life seen a human less matched to her environment.

"Welcome, Marcel. I'm Hailee." She leant over and smiled through my window. Her face had been carefully made up as if she were about to go on TV. She had a strong Southern twang. "You just park over there, 'kay?"

"Yip."

Somehow she managed to transport herself across the parking lot, and stood waiting for me as I got out of the car.

"Mr. Lee the third is very excited to see you." She smiled and offered me her hand. "But he has to finish up a very important conversation with a donor. He'd like you to wait for him on the porch."

She gestured toward the wooden cabin that looked like it came from the eighteen hundreds, complete with a pair of black rocking chairs. A docile black horse tied to a pole a few feet from the porch looked mournfully in our direction.

"I'll bring you some tea while you wait." She placed her hand on my back and gently pushed me toward the cabin.

The horse and I locked eyes. Insects buzzed. Cicadas cried out from the trees. The smell of manure and burning grass mingled with diesel fumes that came from somewhere.

I sat on the rocker and took out my notepad, making a few notes about the location. Hailee brought me my cold, sweet tea.

"Mr. Lee would like you to ask these questions." She handed me a single sheet of paper fastened to a clipboard.

"I'd been hoping to ask my own questions."

"Mr. Lee the third would like you to ask the following ten questions." She ran a lidded pen down the sheet.

"And then I can ask my questions?"

"Mr. Lee the third and I both believe that these are *excellent* questions."

I ran my eye over them, taking in only words and letters, but no meaning. I took a sip of tea.

"This is excellent tea."

She gave me an awfully strained smile, for half a second opening her mouth to reveal peroxide-white teeth. She turned to leave, her heels clacking on the wooden floors. The swinging door banged shut behind her, and a heavy cloud of perfume lingered like a ghost.

I cast my eye over the questions, slower this time:

    1. Can you name three of Chuck Jones's greatest
       mistakes?

2. Why do so many people consider Chuck Jones a
   failure?

3. How did you develop your reputation as a *can
   do* man?

Looking up from the sheet, I took a deep breath and tried to calm my rising nerves, but a dark dread had locked its claws in me. The docile black horse, the crows near my car, even the smell of burning grass or leaves, seemed... off. Something evil hung about this place. The wooden planks from which this cabin was made seemed to have been soaked in darkness.

I listened attentively to the sound of boots on the floorboards. The door swung open and shut.

"Mar-say-al."

His leather boots were speckled with mud, as were his black jeans. He had the hands of an old man, white hairs sprouting from his knuckles. He wore a black waistcoat over his black shirt.

"Mar-say-al," he said again, and I found myself rising to my feet as if under hypnosis. He wrapped his hand around mine and made clear he still had the strength of a much younger man. His eyes were the color of the sea on a grey morning. "Do you mind if I join you out here?"

"Um."

"I brought us each one of these." He took two cigars from his waistcoat pocket. Sitting down on the rocker opposite mine, he bit off the backs and spat them over the edge of the balcony. "That's my horse, Lucy Lae. She's a good gal, coming toward the end of her days." He struck a match and lit both cigars in his mouth, then handed mine to me.

"Well, thank you."

"When the day comes, I'll do her the goodness of settling

a .32 'tween those sweet, sleepy eyes." He brushed some invisible dust off his jacket. "I don't believe in needless suffrin'."

The horse let out a pathetic neigh.

"Don't you worry, gal." He pointed at her with his cigar-smoking hand. He had gold rings on three of his fingers. "It ain't time for that yet. Only when you're in agony." He grinned, baring the pearly whites. "She'll be begging me to do it when the time comes."

My nerves had settled but they'd not been replaced by confidence. I was a freshly injected tooth.

"What you have there?" He reached over for the questions Hailee had given me. "We don't need these."

He set the page on fire and dropped it to the floor where it burned slowly; puffing on his cigar, he stared across the clearing to the brambles.

"You probably wonder why I have to be ten miles out of town."

"Uh, yes, sir." I scribbled notes on my pad.

"Lucy Lae was a younger lady when I came to this town." He crossed his right leg over his left. "She's aged many years since we've been here. I'm speaking in terms of biology, Mar-say-al."

"Yes, sir. Uh..." I dug deep into myself in search of confidence. "Where did, uh, Lucy Lae live before this? Which is to say, where did you come from?"

He rocked on his chair and puffed deliberately on his cigar like he was playing an instrument. Then he blew smoke along the shaft with great love, as if the cigar needed the smoke like a plant needs water.

"I have a library inside, and I think you're going to like it."

Instead of feeling frustrated with him for avoiding my question, I felt guilty that I might have upset him by asking a question he didn't want to answer. And so, as he stood up, I followed him to the entrance like a puppy.

"Should we...?" I paused, uncertain whether we should smoke inside, but he just strode right in.

Hailee sat at a large, rectangular table in the center of what must once have been a family dining room. The fireplace had been closed up. The window panes were thick, blurring the world beyond this room. Heads of various animals mounted on the walls, including one of a white fox that died with a snarl on its face.

"Y'all need some more tea?"

"We're good, Ms. Hailee."

I followed him into his office.

"Shut the door, won't ya? Take a seat."

Through the window behind him I watched a light rain start to fall. The wind swayed the pine trees.

"There are many collectibles in these shelves." He pointed about the room with his smoking hand.

"What a collection." I scanned my eyes over the endless rows of books. "I..." I wanted to say: *I didn't expect you to be much of a reader*. But that sounded rude, and, now that I considered it more fully, entirely unfounded. Why would I have assumed this about the man? But of course, I knew why, I just wouldn't feel comfortable fully articulating it, even to myself: *The hat, the shoes, the accent, and, well, the stuff you were saying*. But you could read lots of books and still turn out crazy.

As these half-formed thoughts jumbled about in my mind, I noticed at the top of one of his shelves a copy of Virgil's *Aeneid*.

"You read *The Aeneid?*" I pointed at the book.

"Arma virumque cano."

"I sing of arms and the man."

He grinned as he took off his black hat and placed it on the table next to him. As he puffed on his cigar, he looked at me with gentle eyes, and I sensed behind the rugged lines of age, a younger man, a child, innocent and playful.

"Do you mind?"

"Go ahead."

I took it down and flipped through the pages. Like my father's copy it was filled with handwritten notes—passages circled, words underlined. I turned to the verse I'd seen referenced in my father's notes. "Now the man Of Ithaca haled Calchas out among us In Tumult, calling on the Seer to tell The true will of the gods."

In pencil next to this he'd written: *It is we who shall tell his will. It is I.*

"My father..." A dark feeling passed through me. "My father was obsessed with this book."

"Well, I'll be damned." He wrapped his knuckles on the table. "Quite literally if I'm not careful."

The door behind me opened and there stood Hailee, an iPad in her hand.

"Yes, sir?"

"I was just knocking on the table."

"Sorry to bother you, sir."

She smiled, but her cheeks barely moved and her forehead remained unwrinkled.

"Turns out Mar-say-el's father is... was?"

"Was," I said.

"I'm sorry, son. *Was*, a fan of *The Aeneid*. This." He picked it up and showed it to her.

"That's wonderful. Sounds like you two will get along just fine. Can I get you anything?"

"I'm fine. How about you, Mar-say-el?"

"Oh, I'm good."

"We're both good, thank you, Hailee."

"You're most welcome."

It was a terribly strained interaction and I wondered what was going on between the two of them.

As the door shut, he leant across his desk, beckoning me with his index finger.

He whispered into my ear: "We ain't fucking."

"Oh." I laughed, and felt myself blush. I shifted about on my chair.

"I know what you thinking."

"Haha. No." Of course, that's what I'd been wondering. "Hadn't crossed my mind."

"We don't need to bullshit with one another. You have a pen and paper. You want to write about me and my campaign. The world out there is hostile to me." He pointed about him, and I felt the same energy I'd felt that night I saw him on stage. "They say I have some kind of a hidden agenda, and when I say this, what I really mean is that. And when I say that, what I mean is this. But that ain't so. That ain't so."

"Is it true that you want to drive Maggie and her people out of town?"

"Listen to your question, son. You make it sound like you've caught me in an act of wrongdoing. There's something evil brewing in this land, and I've been called to stamp it out. Who am I to say no to a higher calling?"

I scribbled some notes on my pad.

"Have you ever played Sortes Virgilinae?"

"What manner of Sortes is that?"

"It's a game. You flip back and forth through the book and point randomly at a line of text. That line tells you your fate. Or so, those who played it seriously in the Middle Ages, believed."

"Never done such a thing, and don't plan to. I cannot entrust my fate to the random flipping of pages."

"My father used to play it. Really, it's just for fun. For the most part."

"Many things that start out as games can take over our lives. I only have time for one game, and this game isn't a game. I have an election to win. And I suspect that you want to help me."

"I, um…" Although I barely knew the man, I felt awful about hurting his feelings. Why? He had an eerie magnetism. "That's not what I've committed to. I should tell you, I've been to interview your rival, too."

"Chuck Jones?" He grinned widely, contempt in his voice.

"Yes, sir."

"Chuck the schmuck. Jones the Bones. Chuck Jones the schmuck bones."

"He seemed all right to me."

"Oh he's all right, all right. But he ain't no sheriff. Let me show you something." He leant down and brought up a silver star-shaped sheriff's badge. "This here badge belonged to Sheriff Wyatt Earp. You know that name?"

"I've heard it."

"Fought in the gun battle at the O.K. Corral."

"Really?"

He stared into my eyes, a look that said: *How dare you question me?*

"So, why did I show that to you?"

"I don't know, sir."

"To remind you that the word *sheriff* used to mean something. Today, we've got a bunch of Satanists living out in the swamps, and the man who calls himself sheriff ain't got the cahoonas to do nothing about it. I had to come in from outta town. Heck, somebody had to do it. There's something evil brewing and I can't just stand by. There ain't no honor in doing nothing, in being silent. Silence was no option for me."

My time on the island flashed through my mind as I tried to decide if I should tell him that I'd been there.

"How do you know these people are really bad? How do you know they're wrong?"

"Oh, oh. Have they started to get to you already? This is what they do, you see. They pervert. They say good is bad and up is down. They praise what should be blamed and blame what deserves praising."

I felt myself resonating with him, like a guitar string coming into tune. His confidence in what way the world ought to be, felt comforting. What clarity. My own confusion became repulsive to me, and I wanted to blend into this certainty.

"Tell me more," I said. And then, half believing it, half knowing it to be a necessary deception, added: "I want to help you."

CHAPTER 18

As I sat opposite Antoinette that evening, in the dim light of her kitchen, a little tipsy, smoking a hand-rolled cigarette, I felt like a man who had something to hide. Like a dirty, cheating scoundrel.

Her hair was wet from showering and her well-worn pink tank top hung down the edge of her left shoulder. She gazed deep into my eyes, tilted her head sideways, and smiled at me.

"You gonna try tell me he ain't so bad, right?"

"I didn't say that."

"But it's what you thought."

"He has a certain... magnetism."

I filled up my glass and hers. A beetle buzzed around the kitchen lamp.

"Maggie's folk came 'round to the house today and left this here letter for you."

I skimmed over the handwritten note.

"They need the rest of the documents from my father's apartment? Is this normal?"

"They wanted something like that from me once upon a time. I know a gentleman."

"A gentleman?"

"He does cross-country moving of stuff like that."

"He'll have to go into my father's apartment?"

"I trust him."

"I'll have to pay him?"

"'Course you will. I can give you an extension on rent, if you need."

"No, I don't need that." I put my cigarette out. "Why would you assume that about me?"

"Sensitive, Marcel."

"I'm sorry. I guess..." I looked her over. I could see the outline of her nipple beneath the thin material of her top. I pictured my lips sucking on her pale neck skin as I undressed her, running my hand right up her thigh, feeling her go wet, and soon enough my lust roared like an ocean. I guzzled what was left of my drink.

Upstairs I heard something. I turned to look. She did not.

"Did you hear that?"

"Old house, makes all kinds of sounds."

I felt her taunting me now with her eyes. She knew how much I wanted her, and knew just how much effort it took for me to resist.

"I had a dream about you the other night."

She stirred her drink with her finger, licked the tip. A ting-tang sound came from above us as the beetle crashed into the metal lampshade.

"Dreamed about me? When you were sleeping right next to me?"

"Not that night."

I recalled how warm her body had felt, how much comfort I'd found in her smell.

"On the island."

"Don't tell me what you dreamed on the island."

"Why not?"

"The dreams you have there, they ain't regular dreams."

"You were there? You know what I'm talking about?"

"I didn't say that." She leaned back on her chair and crossed her legs, flashing me a few beautiful inches of upper thigh.

"I tried to explain to you, why... I can't be with you."

"Shut up, Marcel. Don't talk to me like I'm a baby. I wasn't asking you for nothing."

"I didn't say you were. I feel like something will go wrong." I rested my elbows on the table and leant on my hands. "Something will go wrong, but only if we're together in... waking life. Not there. Not if I find you."

Longing pulsed through me so wildly I almost gave in. I wanted to push the table aside, pick her up off the chair, pull her top over her head, and put my mouth on her nipple. I could taste her skin. My tongue would slip over her stomach, between her legs.

"You wanna have sex with me in your dreams? Romantic, boy."

"But not in just any dream. In the tent dream. Where it's real. Next time. If I find you. Will you?"

"I didn't even say I was there. We shouldn't be talking this way. It's time for bed."

She stood up.

"Can I sleep next to you again?"

"You ain't like any man I ever met. You're like... the opposite of a man. You want the sleeping, not the loving."

"I want it all... Come on. I've just explained..." I raised my hands indignantly.

She smiled at me, putting her hand across the table. Our fingers interlocked.

"Don't get all worked up. Then you won't be sleeping at all. Come on. Bedtime now."

"What's that sound? You don't hear it?" The rattling,

hammering I'd heard in my dream. My body tingled numb, my heart raced. "What is it?"

"Old house. Wind. Night."

Through the murky windows I saw the moon come up from behind the tree.

All night a storm raged in my chest. Never quite asleep, never fully awake, I tugged at the blankets and sheets, fighting for my share. All the pitfalls of a hookup and none of the benefits. Was she right, I wondered as I drank coffee the next morning at McDonald's, was I the opposite of a man? The opposite of a human? Was it because I lacked a soul? Since that morning I'd almost been killed on the street in Van Horn, I'd been living without a soul, or rather living with a soul that had been frightened and wounded. The thing is, until that moment I'd never really been certain I had a soul, not in the same concrete way I knew I had feet and hands.

The sound of obnoxious big-city American accents snapped my mind out of its dream. A group of reporters stood at the counter ordering coffees and breakfast.

"Listen, Lisa, yes, I hear you," one of the women barked into her phone. "Jones is talking to everyone, that's nothing. Any idiot off the street can get an interview with him. Lee's met with no one." A few moments of silence. "We don't know why. We don't know why, *Lisa*. Of course... of course."

"Hey, Julia. Julia!" Another reporter yelled across the room.

❧

Ninety minutes later I sat opposite Lee. He wore the same black outfit as last time. The room smelt of aftershave, sweat, and smoke. His hat hung from a nail on the wall behind his desk. A soft light came through the window behind him, illuminating the grey fingers of smoke that reached up from his cigar.

"Telling a story, Mar-say-el, is like exhaling smoke. It leaves your mouth unified and then it breaks up into a million pieces, each one goes its own way."

I made notes on my pad.

"That's very well put, sir."

"As you said, they clambering to talk to me. They want to know what I got planned. If they want to know, they can come to my rallies. But they can't come to my rallies 'cause they won't be let in." He slammed the edge of his fist on the desk. "See 'em buzzing about like flies. Hahaha." He threw his feet onto the desk and leant back in his chair.

"But, sir... don't you think they're going to write what they want to anyway?"

"I'm only letting one journalist tell my story. And that's you, Mar-say-el. We're going to tell my story right. A story of a good man who takes back a town overrun by Satanists."

I was a small bird in his crushing hand, trembling. Outside, the cicadas' screeching reached a crescendo as some uncomfortable energy inside me wrestled about, trying to escape.

"Hailee," he called. I snapped back. She appeared at the door.

"Yessir, Mr. Lee?"

"You saddled up Betty Lou?"

"Sure have, sir."

"Come on, Mar-say-al, let's go riding."

My horse, Betty Lou, had a coat of mixed black and white. She walked uneasily, like a drunk trying not to stumble. With her head down, she watched Lucy Lae's legs, and kept a few feet behind her no matter how hard I tried to speed her up.

We crossed over a train track and turned down a long dirt road with thick, swampy trees on either side. No sign of human life or settlement. Within minutes it was just he and I. I suppose I'd noticed the gun on his side before, but hadn't thought much of it. Now, it felt pregnant with meaning. What if he decided to shoot me?

Click-clack. I listened to our horses' hooves as they tapped on stones.

"Sir? Where are we going?"

"I just want to take you to a little spot where I like to come, to uh, clear my mind, as they say. Come on Mar-say-al. Let's pick up our pace. Hee-ha."

He kicked Lucy Lae in the sides, and she began to trot. Betty Lou instinctively kept pace. Lee turned his horse off the road, down a muddy path that led through the thick trees. We stopped just short of the water, and he dismounted into the black mud. Shards of light came through the thick foliage, exposing the hidden world of the mulchy forest, alive with insects, frogs, and birds.

"Come on, get down."

I dismounted, landing with a squelch in the mud. A strange birdcall came from the depth of the forest. The horses drank from the water.

"This is where I come to clear my mind."

He took off his hat and tucked it beneath his belt on his back. From his holster, he drew the gun. I felt myself turn cold, but the fear passed as he pointed it into the forest away from me.

"I find the parable of the gun and the bullet to be the most convincing. Do you know that parable, Mar-say-al?"

"No, sir."

"I believe it best captures the work I do. God is a gun,

and Jesus a bullet." He fired a shot into the swamps. Both horses jolted. "Straight is the gate and the narrow the path." He knelt down, resting his knee on a rock, and fired another shot. My ears rang. Betty Lou let out a screech and tripped on her reins as she pulled back from the water. Back on his feet, Lee returned the gun to its holster. "So many wrong paths, Mar-sal-al, and only one right path. Only one."

"Yes, sir."

"And don't try fool yourself into thinking God ain't takin a side. God always takes a side. He has an opinion. He has a preference."

"No doubt, sir."

Why the hell did I keep calling this man, "sir"?

My heart pounded heavily. I felt the raging storm in my chest I'd felt this morning when I woke up next to Antoinette—how far off that seemed, less real than a dream.

"You look pale, Mar-say-al." He stepped toward me, his hand out. "You feeling light in the head?"

"I'm feeling all right, sir." In fact, I did not feel well. "Maybe I should go back."

"You have somewhere to be?"

"No, sir."

"I want *you* to present my story to world. That's why you're here." He pointed at me, confidence and certainty shooting out of him like electricity.

"*That's* why I'm here?"

"That's why you're here."

I caught my first whiff of gunpowder. Then it passed, and the thick scent of swamp returned. A wet silence.

"Why did you bring me here? To this spot?"

"That's where I came through," he said, pointing to an opening in the forest, across the water.

"Where were you before this?"

"This is the starting point. We got to clean up this town,

take it back for the good folk. Get the Satanists out of here. Then we got more work to do. You're gonna help me, Marcel. You're gonna help me."

"Why do you have confidence in me? You barely know me. I have no track record with... work like this."

"I've had many years to hone my instincts. I noticed the passage you opened to in *The Aeneid*."

"You did?"

"And you read the notes I'd made. You understand what a sacrifice is. I'm not talking about a metaphor. Metaphors have betrayed us."

His face tensed up as he drew the gun from his holster and emptied the cartridge, firing at a thick tree in the forest.

"Yes, sir."

I put my arm around Betty Lou.

"That's a good girl. No need to be afraid."

CHAPTER 19

That night I met Chuck Jones in his old house on the edge of town. We sat in his kitchen beneath a light with two dead bulbs and one flickering. We drank sweet tea and smoked hand-rolled cigarettes. His wife brought us meat stew and rice with a large helping of yam.

"Thank you, my Ruthie, my love. Tonight, Marcel, is the night of the week I eat anything I like."

"That's every night for me."

Ruth laughed. "You enjoy that food." She left the kitchen.

"You're young, Marcel, you don't have to be so careful about what you eat."

I watched my reflection in the dark kitchen window as I ate a mouthful of stew. I felt so nervous I didn't have much of an appetite, but the meal tasted amazing and I didn't want to offend my host.

"There were protests across town today," Jones said. "I feel disconnected from my city. I hear about these things happening. I see Jefferson Lee's signs across the town. I just don't understand it. I don't understand what's happening."

"I went into the forest with him today."

"Why are you telling me this? Why were you alone with him?"

I looked over his shoulder, into the darkness of the garden. Why did he not keep his curtains closed? He had no fence, no wall, no guard dogs. His gun, placed in its holster, hung over a chair beyond his reach.

"I felt the need to see him. Again."

With a paper napkin, Chuck wiped stew off his moustache.

"Felt the need? You hearing yourself? You sound like a junkie."

"He has an appeal."

"He wants to change this town. He wants you to play a role that ain't your own."

"What if he sees me here tonight? Why don't you close your curtains?"

"It's a symbol, a gesture. I sit here, light on." He looked up at the flickering bulb. "I keep my pistol in the holster. I leave my door unlocked, curtains open. I eat dinner here alone every night. Done it for years. I ain't got no fence. Somebody wants to kill me, it shouldn't be too difficult. Heck, I even eat dinner at the same time."

I turned and looked out the window behind me. I felt I was being watched.

"I'm not comfortable with that idea."

"It brings a sense of freedom. They're not going to take that from me. Lee ain't going to take that from me."

Minutes passed as we ate in silence. The brown clock on the kitchen wall ticked loudly. Car engines in the distance; sirens. From another room the sound of television and Ruth laughing.

"I suppose I never told you the full story about how I ended up here," I said.

"You hardly told me anything."

"It was a night like this. I only say *like this* because I felt on edge like I do now. I suppose it was, otherwise, a night, just a night. But, it sits in the center. It's the moment everything comes back to. That night, and... another day. A day in a small town in Texas. The day I lost my soul."

"Son, you're saying all kinds of things now. You need to slow down. Be careful you don't say something you're going to regret."

"Why would I regret it? Are you going to use what I say against me?"

"I have no intention of doing that. Eat some of the sweet yams. They're good."

A sound outside made me jump. A gun shot? No, just a car backfiring, or maybe a firework? I breathed deeply, slowly. I took a mouthful of yam.

"What do you mean you lost your soul? That's a... a wild claim. The Bible assures us there will be dark times. Sure, it warns even of hellfire. But I've never heard talk of a man... losing his soul, like... like you might lose your watch. On accident."

"But that's how it happened. We're not all in the same story."

"And you apparently haven't decided which one you're in." He wiped his moustache. "I apologize. I'm being too harsh."

"You're not being harsh. I'm saying things that... hardly make sense. But here's what I think now—if my soul had been with me, I wouldn't have entered into that pact."

"What pact?"

"I'm a wealthy man. A very wealthy man."

"Well... well. I hope you find this residence to your liking, your highness. Want a beer?"

"I'd love one."

He cracked open two cans and handed one to me.

"Cheers."

"So, tell me about this wealth of yours."

"Some might say I won it fair and square. I didn't cheat, I didn't lie. But something happened, something was there, and from the moment I got the money I knew my fate was sealed."

"And when did you lose your soul?"

"I don't think I've lost my soul forever. I can't have. It's still there. Just a little further away than before. It was a road. A road in Texas."

"When?"

"It happened... now I remember. It happened after I won the money. So my whole theory is wrong. Unless it's like they say, and time doesn't... move in a line. I have to leave." I pushed my chair back from the table; the legs scraped loudly on the floor. "I have to go."

"Come on now, son. You're my guest. We're eating dinner. Pull yourself together. What on God's earth are you talking about?"

"I've been told that in the realm of spirits, time doesn't move in the same way we experience it."

"That may be so."

"And I've had some experiences. One experience in particular which more or less confirms that." I took a large sip of beer. "You'll think I'm crazy if I tell you this."

"I already think you're crazy." He raised his beer can. "But I've never met a man I didn't think was crazy."

"I spent an afternoon with my father. I'd seen him the day before, and he was alive for certain then. The next day I met up with him, and we went to the ocean, we spoke, we connected. The next morning I woke to a call telling me he'd died. But not long after that, I got a call from some lawyers, working on this... class lawsuit. Long story short? He'd been dead at the time I met him."

Jones shifted about on his chair, wiping his forehead with the palm of his hand. He coughed.

"Now listen here." He looked over his shoulder before leaning across, closer to me. "Don't go saying stuff like that in front of my wife. She'll think you're talking about spiritualism and voodoo. This is a Christian household. We don't dabble in that kind of stuff."

"I'm sorry."

"Don't say you're goddam sorry. I'm telling you about my wife, and her feelings and opinions on these matters." He spoke in a frantic, hushed voice. "As for me, as I've tried to explain, I'm a sheriff. I don't know how or why I ended up with this task, all I know is that I *must* protect this town, and most importantly that means protecting those folk out there on the water. Those folk on Maggie's island."

"Lee's desperate to get them out of town. To beat you in the election. And... for some reason, he thinks I'm the man to tell his story. He wants me to sell him to the public."

"Why you? And what did you say to him?"

"I don't know why me. When I'm with him, I find myself saying, yes sir, yes sir."

"So you didn't say no? So you're double-crossing the man?"

"I suppose so." A thrill rushed through me, but left me cold. I looked at my reflection and the darkness beyond it. Lee could be watching me right now. He'd never forgive me if he knew what I was doing.

"So how do I know you ain't double-crossing me?"

"I didn't tell him about all our meetings. But I tell you about his and mine."

"Of course that's what you'd say." He took a mouthful of food, chewing his meat slowly as he stared at me. "Want another beer?"

"Sure."

He cracked open two beers and placed one in front of me. I took a deep sip.

"Where did the man come from?"

"I went with him into the forest. And he... pointed and said, *that's where I came from.*"

"He just... appeared? From the forest? Like a mushroom after the rain?"

"Why are you getting angry with me?"

"I just want some sense." He hit the table. "My family has roots here. Generations. Generations. Where did he come from? The disrespect. What makes him think..." His words trailed off. He took a sip of beer, then placed the can down heavily on the table. "Do you have a plan to see him again?"

"He said he'd reach out. In a day or two. Those were his words. But I've got an appointment on the island. And if he knows I'm going there. If he knows I'm visiting Maggie's farm..."

"What'll he do?"

"For one thing, he'll stop trusting me."

"Son, you're staying with Antoinette still, yes?"

"I am."

"I knew her grandfather. I care about her. You better get back home. You better get back there and make sure she's safe."

"You think she's in danger?"

He breathed deeply, looking up at the ceiling.

"Yes, I think she is. I have a... dark intuition. We don't know who this man is, what he is, where he comes from. And we're abandoned here. The world might care for the spectacle, but that's it. This ain't nothing but our little corner of the earth. We must protect it, keep it safe."

We sat in silence.

"I'm afraid now."

"Don't be afraid. You're helping me. I trust you. That's

why you're here. I want you to take something." He left the room and returned with a silver sheriff's badge. On it, the words: *Reelect Sheriff Jones.* "You don't have to wear it, but keep it with you." He pinned one on his own shirt.

"I will keep it with me."

❧

The clock in my car was stuck at 4.50, 16.50 in military time. Take away the zero and it's the line from *The Aeneid* my father had referenced in his copy of *Synchronicity*, the one alongside which Lee had written—*I shall decide.*

I said the line out loud: "Now the man Of Ithaca haled Calchas out among us In Tumult, calling on the Seer to tell The true will of the gods."

The car filled with that awful smell of burning flesh, and through the darkness a figure came toward me. My hand fumbled as I turned the keys in the ignition and drove my foot down on the pedal. The wheels spun on the tar and skidded to the side. As I struggled to regain control, I saw in the rearview mirror a figure in black, standing in the light of the streetlamp where my car had been parked.

Fires burned alongside the roads; protestors blocked the street I wanted to drive down. Gunshots rang out here, there, one, two, ten.

I parked outside Antoinette's house and breathed slowly, focusing on the rise and fall of my ribcage, the steady and slowing rhythm of my heart. The smell of burning flesh had faded as I drove across town, but now it began to intensify again.

"Is it you, Dad? You were dead that last time I saw you. I get that now. But I smelt this smell... when I was in Texas, a week? What? Ten days before you died? I'm giving you your chance to speak back to me now. But you remain silent. Is it because you can't speak to me, or because you won't?"

The specter of my supervisor, Martin Huffman, appeared. I pictured him there on the passenger seat, vaping his apple-scented tobacco, shaking his head condescendingly.

"This is why we don't go chasing demons in the real world, Marcel."

"What a wanker you are, Huffman. Martin Huffman *coma Pee-aych-dee!* If you've already decided what kind of world we're living in then you'll only accept the kind of evidence that affirms this world."

As with all characters summoned up by my mind when it felt the need to replay old arguments, Martin had nothing to say.

"Good night to you, then."

My tire had gone flat. I'd change it in the morning, in the light of day.

Standing in Antoinette's garden I looked up at the tree that loomed over her house like a dear friend, or a curse. Inside I poured myself a glass of wine. Surely it was too early for her to be asleep. But no, it was nearly midnight. Where had the time gone? There were hours I could not account for. And now I noticed I'd missed several calls on my phone, five from Baptist Pants.

A text message from him read: *Marcel, you need to call me. Your mother's condition is worsening.*

He must be mistaken, I told myself. *What's he even talking about? He's always rambling on about nonsense.* I poured myself a large glass of wine and downed it in a single sip.

I sat at the desk in my room, taking out my computer. I'd set a reminder for myself to turn in my article to Axan—it was due in 24 hours. Stashed away in my bag I found a box of 5 hour energy drinks and knocked back two in a row. Then I poured another glass of whisky, lit a cigarette, and started reading back through all my notes.

It was a blessing, I suppose, that I had so little time to complete the article. If I'd had longer I would most certainly have overthought everything, struggling in vain to find some powerful and unifying theme. Instead, I churned out a profile on each sheriff. Sentences such as these were included:

"At the same time every evening Sheriff Jones dines alone in his kitchen, curtains wide open, gun slung over the chair opposite him. He says he's sending a message to the people of Chickasaw: *I'm here; I have nothing to hide, and I'm not afraid.*"

"No one is quite sure when Jefferson Lee III first came to town, and whenever I press him on the issue, he tactfully changes topic. What is established lore in this small town is that within days of his arrival, he'd bought up the largest billboard in town and taken out an advert: *There's a New Sheriff in Town.*"

"The enigmatic leader, known to some as Maggie and others as Magdalena, shows herself infrequently, and only to a chosen few."

"They describe themselves as guardians of an ancient secret, and from what I've learned, they are peaceful and entirely harmless."

I sent it off at dawn and, buzzing as I was with anxiety, I'd yet to fall asleep when I received a reply an hour later.

Weird. Crazy stuff. Intriguing. I love it.

The editor asked for a few changes and wondered if I'd be interested in writing more. Perhaps a series about the election?

I responded: *I'd love to.*

Warm with satisfaction, I fell asleep.

· · ·

When I woke again, mid-morning light filled the room. A voice came from downstairs: Antoinette's. I found her in the kitchen, her dungarees paint-stained, cheeks flushed, strands of hair sticking to her sweaty forehead. She wiped them off with the back of her hand, in which she held a paintbrush. While I'd slept, she'd repainted the kitchen ceiling.

"Mover's here." She pointed at the window to a large white van outside her house. "I been shouting for you. You was off in dreamland, huh?"

"I sure was." I splashed my face in the kitchen sink.

"Dude was up here banging on the door. Now he's fixing to unload the truck. You better go talk to him."

The screen door slammed behind me. A man with long dark hair was unloading boxes from his truck.

"My name's Bryson," the man said. "You Marcel?"

"That's right. Thanks for bringing these all the way across the country."

"Hey, that's what we do."

"Ya'ain't bringing those in here." Antoinette appeared on her front porch, then came down the stairs onto the lawn. "Put 'em in the shed."

"Where will these go? These are my father's pages."

"Ain't no space in my house for all that."

"We can put them in the shed, ma'am," Bryson said. "Caution's best."

We got the last box into her shed as the rain started. It poured down, singing on the roof, rushing through the leaf-clogged gutters. Inside, the three of us sat around the kitchen table drinking sweet tea and smoking cigarettes.

"I got a few days before my next assignment," Bryson said. "I looked online and it said you run some kind of B&B. That right?"

"Sure is."

"You mind if I stay here a couple nights?"

"Fifty bucks a night and I'll throw in a meal. You take the room upstairs, next to Marcel. Sound good?"

"Sure does. Thank you, ma'am."

CHAPTER 20

With my father's pages wrapped in refuse bags, I rowed across the bayou towards the island. The water reflected the scattered white clouds. The morning grey had left without a trace.

My phone rang.

"Marcel, I've been trying to get a hold of you." Baptist Pants's condescending, upper-class, milk and molasses Southern drawl had my fists clenching and set my jaw on edge.

"I've been very busy."

"I told you it was about your mother."

"I assumed you were wrong. I know she's fine."

A long silence.

"Marcel... I don't want to argue with you. Your mother is not doing well. She was checked into the hospital last night. They're doing tests."

"She's fine." My heart raced. The pressure dropped inside my skull. There were ripples in the water around me. "Right?"

"We're hoping so. Of course, we're hoping so. But she

hasn't been well. Coughing. Fainting. The doctors aren't sure what it is."

"No."

"Where are you now?"

"Fishing."

"Can you come here?"

"I really can't right now. I have to deliver..."

"You have to deliver the fish?"

"If I told you what was happening, you wouldn't understand. I just need you to know that... I'm fine. I'm wealthy. Like you."

Silence.

"You're making me nervous, Marcel. I think you really need to get up to Charleston. We can take care of you up here."

"We?"

"I'm confident, as you are, that your mother will be out of here soon. We can all be together then."

"We? I need to finish what I'm doing here. I *need* to. As soon as I'm done here. As *soon*." My throat tightened. I realized I was crying. "I'll get there. Okay?"

As I heard him say my name I hung up. He phoned again, but I didn't answer. With new determination I rowed toward the raised flag on the island.

The kayak hissed as I dragged it up the beach toward the dead tree on which the listless flag-waving committee of three sat. Tran Tran Sui stepped out from the bushes and came toward me. As he leant forward to help with the refuse bags, his gown slipped open, exposing his hairy chest. Unperturbed, he slung a bag over each shoulder and strode back toward the forest. I followed, a bag in each hand.

Sunlight and leafy shadows danced at my feet. Faces

turned our way as we walked through the busy camp; eyes caught mine, some confrontational, some welcoming, a pair or two flirtatious.

"We've made up your tent for you."

An oil lamp sat next to a stack of pages on a low desk. Luscious pillows and a thick red sheet lay over a futon.

"You'll dream tonight." A moment's awkward silence. Tran tightened up his gown. "I must get these pages to Maggie."

"Will I get to meet her?"

"That... I, uh, can't say."

A face appeared at the tent door, then another: Helen and Helena. The grey hair fell forward across their faces.

"Welcome back, Marcel."

"Yes, welcome."

"Thank you. Thank you. Be very careful with those," I said, as the three picked up the refuse bags.

"Of course," said Helena.

"You should relax now," Helen added. "We'll be back early evening with your dinner and calming tea. Now, hang out in your tent or walk around."

"Wherever the mood takes you," Tran added.

Lying on the futon, I clutched the duvet and tried to suffocate the guilty feelings in me. Had I abandoned my own mother?

As I stepped out of my tent, a young woman with brown hair down to her back came toward me.

"Thank you for what you're doing." She put her hands out toward me. Our skin met; our hands clasped together. I tingled with desire. "We appreciate it. So brave. So few would do it."

"Of course," I said, though I did not know what she was talking about. Her eyes kept swimming through me. Was she one of those people who always seem to be flirting, or was she trying to seduce me? I looked back at my tent. She smiled, letting go of my hands.

"I have to get back to work, but I hope to see you later."

"Yes, me too."

As she turned and walked away, I felt eyes peeling skin off me, but no one else seemed interested in speaking. I strolled past the tents, the fire pits filled with ash surrounded by tree stumps, the spiderweb-like contraptions made of wood and leather, and large sheets of paper covered with pictographs that hung from leather straps hoisted between trees.

As I rounded a corner I passed a woman crouching in the bushes, urinating. She smiled at me and waved. A child ran from across the sand road, chased by a grown man. His father, I hoped.

I curled up on my futon and with the duvet wrapped close to me, I read the messages Baptist Pants had sent in the days leading up to our conversation today. Now as I read them I could sense his optimism. He knew just as well as I that my mother would be fine, that we were really just engaged in an elaborate dance, an attempt to get me to go up to Charleston.

But my mother would never actively deceive me. She was sick, yes, just not as sick as the messages implied. And of course—the most ridiculous thought I'd had that must be dismissed out of hand—I was not responsible for her sickness.

But why was I looking for responsibility? Why was I trying to escape from *that?* Why was *that* my first concern?

Hours passed as I lay there frying in repetitive thoughts. It was a relief when Tran, Helen, and Helena appeared at my tent door. The air had cooled; dusk had come.

Helena placed a tray of food on my table.

"Plantains, dried tomato, arugula, and goat's cheese."

"You must have the best," Tran said.

"Your stomach should not be too full," Helena added. "A heavy stomach interrupts sleep. This tea is essential." He poured me a cup, and the room filled with the scent of dried herbs and grass. I took a deep sip. "It eases cramps in the body and cramps in the mind. You'll sleep like air."

"Have you ever wondered how well air sleeps?" Helen asked.

"I can't say I have."

Voices from outside drifted into the silent tent. Tran placed his long arm on my shoulder.

"You don't need to be afraid."

"I'm not afraid."

Music came from outside: a woman's voice singing.

"When you wake up we'll need to hear everything that happened to you," Helena said.

"But you mustn't rush to explain it," Tran added. "Too many words destroy dreams."

"You need to bring it back to us whole and unbroken."

"Like sculpture made out of air."

"But it's the feeling most of all," Helena said as he hit himself square in the chest.

"This is true." I sat down, laying my head on the pillows, overcome by a wave of tiredness. My muscles relaxed, and my posture softened. "If I imagine the very worst thing that can happen, it's not the thing itself I fear, but the feeling that comes with it." I took another sip of tea as the room faded like morning fog, and with it all the faces.

Eyes shut, I heard singing in the distance, and I maintained an awareness—both soft and sharp, like barbed wire in the mist—of everyone in the room with me. "We come to earth to feel. Is that it?"

I stepped out of the tent. The fires had all been extinguished and the pits smoldered. Figures moved here and there, but if they were humans or shadows or ghosts, I could not tell. I knew I must move toward the tower in the middle of the campsite.

A black door in the center of the tower's base opened easily as I pressed against it before stepping into a room strung with black curtains, half-covered mirrors, and large clothes rails, the kind one finds backstage at a theatre. "If I come here in the daylight," I said, as I walked up a narrow, winding flight of stairs, "it will be much different. I won't recognize it. And it won't recognize me."

Reaching the top of the stairs I entered a barren room made of stone. For windows there were large, square holes through which moonlight fell, painting white rectangles on the floor.

"Tran Tran Sui," I said.

The man sat at a piano playing some melancholic tune I didn't recognize. He raised his long arm and waved at me, but by the time I got to the piano he'd gone.

I paced up and down the cavernous room. The emptiness of it felt staged, too empty. Through the window I saw a perfect oval moon the color of a faded pumpkin come up over the trees. Now the emptiness felt natural again; the moonlight had enlivened it.

Movement caught my eye.

"Antoinette."

She hopped onto the windowsill and her legs rested against the stone wall.

"You came across the water to see me?"

"Even you ain't dumb enough to believe that."

She hit the stone ledge—*Come over here.*

I squeezed into the space next to her, half of me pressed against the cold stone, the other against her warm body. With brute confidence I took her hand in mine and placed her fingers to my lips. As she shifted toward me her dress moved up above her thighs, and I wanted her so desperately that all other things—the stone room, the cold air, the cold ledge, the cold white light of the moon—slipped into nowhere. I ran my hand through her hair and our tongues met. My hand traveled up her leg, and as her skin warmed and I felt the cotton of her underwear and the shape beneath it, she slipped off the ledge and moved across the room.

"We can't," she said.

"Why not?"

I stumbled after her as she sat on a wicker chair, sitting at her feet. I put my hand on her knee, and she rested her hand on mine.

"What are you going tell 'em when you get out of here?"

"Why do you care?"

"You gonna say you spent your time getting lucky?"

"They'd understand... I won't tell them."

I rubbed my hand up her leg, but she was no longer interested.

At the far end of the room, she sat in the windowsill; the smoke from her cigarette twisted in the moonlight as it drifted upwards toward the ceiling and out the window.

"You're here to see Maggie."

As I walked toward her I could feel my cock throbbing in my pants, hard as a mallet.

She pointed her cigarette hand down at my pants. "You gonna see Maggie looking like that?"

"Is she an old lady or a young lady?"

"What kind of question is that, Marcel?" She raised her voice. "You ain't doing that with her either way."

"You don't know what I'm doing."

She hopped off the windowsill and came toward me, her smoking hand pointed right between my eyes like a gun, just fired. Her finger grew as large as the room, and I coughed as I breathed in her smoke.

"I know you ain't doing that."

"Well, it worked. I'm as floppy as a puppy's ear."

Her laughter echoed through the room, down the hallway, into the shadows. "Stand up." She put her arms around me. "Go see her. She wants to see you."

The room was a long hallway. The windows were evenly spaced and leaves rode the wind through them, scuttling on the floor like insects. Then, no more windows, and the only light came from candle-filled chandeliers that hung from the ceiling. I walked for hours, days, until it seemed all my life had passed within the walls of this gloomy castle tunnel.

In the distance I saw a light, and when a feeling of hope flickered in my breast, it frightened me, the feeling. It had been so long since I'd felt hopeful. What kind of light was it? Moonlight or candlelight? As I ran toward it, my feet made a new sound, no longer thudding, but splashing. The water came up to my ankles, then my knees. I turned back, hoping I could retreat; there was nothing behind me but darkness so thick it blotted out thought.

I waded on until the water took me up to my waist, and I knew I had to swim.

How long had I been swimming when my hands hit sand? I gasped for air as I pulled myself up onto the beach. I'd entered a cave, the walls lit by a single lantern.

What I saw: Shelves lined with books, pairs of scales, daggers, snakes floating in jars; in the center of it all a silver-haired figure in flowing purple robes. As I crawled up the steep beach, she turned to face me.

"Why are you so interested in my age?"

"Ma'am?" I got to my feet, dusting the beach sand off my knees. "How long did it take me to get here?"

With her index finger raised, she held her hand out toward me.

"Answer my question."

"Out there. In the world out there. People say all kinds of different things about you."

A flash of red as a bird flew from its perch and landed on her shoulder. It sang a gentle melody, then called out my name: "Marcel."

"Kiss my hand."

Acting from pure instinct, I knelt down. Gold rings covered her pale, cold fingers. I pressed my lips against the back of her hand.

She sat on a throne behind her desk, the red bird still perched on her shoulder. I took a seat on a chair no fancier than one found in an old school classroom. The bird hopped down on the desk, onto a pile of papers.

Her skin had a youthful glow, though I could not guess her age. Her face was oval, like the moon; her green eyes locked on me like snipers.

"There's nothing special about you," she said as she shooed the bird off her shoulder.

"Did I say there was?"

"You're at the center of a plot."

The bird returned with a pair of slim cigarettes.

"Marcel," the bird called my name.

"That's right. His name is Marcel. Marcel, call me Maggie."

She lit the two slims, handing one to me.

"Do you look like this in real life?"

"This is real life." She tucked her white hair behind her slightly pointed ears. "Let me end some of the riddles for you. Those who find me when awake call me Magdalena. Those who meet me in the dream world call me Maggie. In the waking world I'm an old woman. In the land of sleep, I'm a young woman."

"But I'm the same in both."

"Are you? I've never seen you awake."

"Ha-ca-ca-Ha!" The bird's call echoed through the cave. Feeling embarrassed, I breathed deeply and noticed how damp the air was. "Funny. Funny. That's funny."

"Thank you, Spencer."

She put her hand out and the bird climbed onto her fingers, hopping all the way up her arm to her shoulder.

"Am I young here? Or old?"

"Take the lamp. Look at yourself in the water."

I followed the bird toward a lamp that hung from a hook fastened to the cave wall. With the lamp in my right hand, I leaned slowly over the dark water, heart kicking in my chest. What would I see?

"Don't!" Maggie called.

I turned to see her right behind me, hand out. The bird took the lantern and flew across the cave, sending shadows crashing against the walls like water at high tide.

"Why not?"

"You don't need to know."

"What do you see?" I turned to her, getting back onto my feet. I looked at my hands, but it was too dark to see clearly what condition they were in.

"In a short while I'm going to ask you to save me."

"How can I save you?"

We sat across from one another, the desk lit by the lantern hung by the bird directly over our heads from the cave roof.

"So much in the world is noise. Even art is noise. And so much of the world is dead."

"I know what you mean."

"The dead are more alive than the living, and in dreams we are truly awake."

"That's true. I know it is."

Maggie leant forward and ran her hand across her cheeks and chin. From her came a force like one feels near the ocean, at once dangerous and peaceful. But she was also sad, and sad not just for herself, but for all the world. My instinct was to comfort her, but the thought that I might comfort the one carrying the sadness of all the world seemed so ridiculous I began to laugh, and she did too. Our laughter echoed like water boiling as the bird darted from desk to lamp and back again, shrieking, calling out my name as shadows of wings flew about the cave and red feathers fell like blood-stained snow.

Maggie sighed deeply, ending the laughter.

"You were looking for life, even as a student. But you were told that angels did not exist."

"My professor? You know him? You've seen him? He has elbow patches, and he vapes. He vapes! Can you believe it?"

"Perhaps he should have smoked opium."

"Ha-ha. Quite possibly."

The bird squawked loudly, and I got the sense it was getting jealous, that it had a possessive streak.

"I've read your father's notes. I've read his books."

"What did you find?"

"A man like your father was destined to go mad in this world."

"It didn't matter that he came to America? He would have gone mad anyway?"

"I'm not willing to speculate."

"But had he found something? Was he onto something true?"

"There is a distance, as you know. The world can be sterile and the world can be magic. Sterility is safe, magic dangerous." She clicked her fingers, and the bird flew about the cave, returning with cigarettes for her and me. "You know what I mean?"

"The living and the dead are equal. We are the ocean and the trees and we don't have to be afraid of drowning."

"Yes. But the price to bring the magic back is steep. It requires a symbolic act that involves blood and flesh. But we will get to that." She took a long drag of her cigarette. "Spencer, bring us wine."

The bird flew across the cave, opened a golden vault, and flew back with a string in its mouth attached to a glass vase filled with red wine. She poured us each a glass.

"Your father was looking for such a moment, a moment where the symbolic order intersects with the flesh."

"Did he find it?"

"If he'd found it and acted on it, we would not be in this position we're in now."

"And what about me? Please tell me. Do you know?" The wine tasted sweet. "Let me know if you know. I fear I'm heading down the same path as he is."

"The night on the farm."

"Yes. That night lies at the center. I've said this many times."

From thin air she produced a gold coin. She flipped it, caught it, placed it on the table.

"You wanted money."

"Of course."

"You thought it would set you free. Did it?"

"Here I am. I'm not free."

"This here." She spun the coin on the table. "This is where the symbolic order intersects with the order of the flesh." She picked up the coin, flicking it into the air. "Most money, of course, you cannot hold. That does not matter. You will toil your life away, blood and sweat, for this. Because of money a chopped down tree is worth more than a living tree. And also, if you do not have any of it, you will die. It summons death and it banishes death."

"We focus on it so hard we cannot see the angels."

"Where did you get that line from?"

"I just said it. I don't know where any of my lines come from. They just appear half-formed in my head, or halfway out my mouth."

"You should pay closer attention to the moment they form. The moment you first notice them. That, too, is a moment where the symbolic order intersects with the flesh."

I finished my wine. The bird immediately refilled the cup.

"You said you'd ask me to save you?"

"Symbolically, yes. But not yet. We haven't finished with money. You tried to give some of it away."

"I did."

"You felt the darkness at your back."

"Yes."

"Sometimes you thought you'd outrun it."

"I wouldn't have come here if I thought I'd outrun it." I took a sip of wine. "What can I do? Can I undo the pact? I don't need the money."

"Of course not." She pointed at me with her long fingers. "Some call it *following passion*, and some call it *being smart*; others call it *revolution*; some love playing its game, others hate it; some give up all the hours of their life for it; it inspires some to master skills, and others to kill. You wake at the time it prescribes; leave home when it demands, return only when it says you may. Modern religion is subservient to it. No church stands on prayer alone. New religions are born every day. They are born at the height of his reign, and they are vicious and sound like the beating of tin. Governments try to abuse it, but in the end they must obey. Of course there are many who realize this." She held her glass up and the bird filled it with wine, then flew across the table and topped up my glass. "But what does it matter? It enables us to do other things, they say. Yes, true, but without it there is no doing. Without it you die alone on the streets. The good and the bad; the faithful and the faithless. Preach from this side of your mouth, or that. There is no freedom. You must arrange your life as it demands. But very few are mad enough to embrace it in its primeval form."

"That's what I did?"

"There's nothing special about you. It could have been anyone. You happened upon the spirit."

"What about all the others who've... you know, won money and then had things go badly?"

"An encounter with him causes harm."

"But why when we win money?"

"He hates lotteries."

"Why?"

"It mocks his power."

"So he punishes these people. He ruins their lives."

"He whispers in their ears; gives them the blueprints." She held her glass up to the bird who refilled it. "But they ruin their own lives."

"And they come here, why?"

"To make tents and sing together at night. To dance, to dream, to acknowledge the deeper truth of metaphor."

"For what?"

"Is that not enough?"

"They believe they're involved in important work."

"They believed the same before they came here."

"But they're trying to stop him."

She laughed. "Nobody *stops* him. You tame him. For a while. You remove the sterility from the world. You bring the magic back."

"But they have roles to play?"

"All of them are points of intersection. Just like you. They've hurt people."

"So it is my fault? What happened to my father... and... also my... mother? Is she okay?"

Maggie raised her hand. "Quiet."

"My role is just like their role? Or different?" Anxious waves rippled through me.

"I'm going to ask you to save me now."

"How?"

The bird hopped off her shoulder and flew around the room, casting its shadow up the walls of the cave. I could hear the water lashing up against the sand behind me.

"You need to make the choice, so I don't have to."

"What choice?" I reached out for her hand but all I felt was air. "What choice?"

CHAPTER 21

I sat up in the tent. Tran, Helen, and Helena stood around me like surgeons, their hot breath on my face.

"What did you see?"

I wiped tears away from my stinging eyes. My joints lacked vitality, like I'd been turned from a marionette into a teddy bear.

"Give me some water, please."

The cool liquid massaged my dying throat.

Tran sat next to me and placed his hand on my forearm. "You need to tell us what you saw."

Helena paced fiercely through the confined space like a man on death row, etching on his notepad. Firelight came through the tent opening.

"Did you meet a young woman or an old woman?"

I finished the water.

"I met a young woman. She had white hair, but her face was young."

Helena crouched before me. "What else?"

"She had a red bird. It knew my name. It brought us wine. We smoked Slims."

Placing his face on his arm, Helena wept. Helen leant over to comfort him.

"How did you feel?" Helena asked, looking up at me through teary eyes.

"I felt... like I was understood."

"Yes." Helena wiped his eyes.

Helen also began to cry, and the bed shook with the moving of Tran's body as he, too, wept. Soon the sound of wailing drowned out the chanting voices from beyond the tent. I lost myself and cried freely. We touched each other's shoulders.

When we'd finished crying, and the tent flaps were opened more fully, I felt as if my soul had been covered with a hot cloth and all the pores were open.

"It's been ten years since I saw her like that," Helena said, as he scribbled on his notepad. "I wouldn't tell those people out there. Many have never seen her that way and some have waited years. Others only saw her once."

"I must see her again. She didn't finish..."

Tran put his hand on my shoulder as I made for the door. Helena shook his head and laughed.

"What?"

"We can't let you go back there," Tran said. "Not until you tell us what she said."

Helena moved to block my exit.

"We're not threatening you, Marcel," Helen added.

"Well. Ha." Helena looked up at me with his grey eyes. His frame was more solid than I'd realized; he smelt of spice and sweat. "We're not... *merely asking* either."

"Don't be put off, Marcel." Tran placed his hand on my shoulder and turned me toward him. "You have something we don't have. Please, don't keep it from us."

"If I can get back to her... if you'll let me."

"On this side? Awake? Pfff." Helena scoffed.

I grabbed hold of his gown and pushed him out of the tent.

Then: a flash of red and a metallic ring like a spoon flung on concrete; a black screen of sky; sand, firelight and shadows; cold ground against my face.

I scrambled up. Tran had pulled Helena's arms behind his back, and dragged him away from me. The scattered bonfires did nothing to dry the cool, wet air. Cold sand wriggled between my toes as I meandered through the fire pits, past circles of men and women chanting, banging on drums. My tent was lost to the darkness; my forehead throbbed; some petty desire wanted me to return to the tent, fight Helena, but I could see the tower where Maggie lived, where Magdalena lived, and I knew that's where I had to go.

The pine trees grew thick around the tower and clusters of fallen branches blocked my path. No one from the bonfires had followed me, only their chanting, and the smell of just-too-ripe branches burning. The door was heavier than in the dream. As I pressed it inwards the firelight exposed a barren stone room.

"Don't go further."

Tran grabbed my gown and pulled me, but I shook free and continued into the empty room.

"I'm sorry for what Helena did," he said. "We have strict procedures. He'll be punished."

I stood at the bottom of the staircase. All the stairs were as black as they'd been in my dream. Light came from the room above.

"Please, Marcel," Tran called after me. He sounded impotent, not angry.

"I'm going to see her."

At the top of the staircase I pushed the door open to find

the same long room I'd found in the dream. The castle windows without glass panes were the very shape they'd been in my dream, only no moonlight came through them. Soft firelight from below clawed at the windows, like Tran trying to call me back. But a much brighter source of light came from a pair of chandeliers, each of which held at least a hundred candles.

By the time I noticed the perch, the red bird was just a few feet from my face. It landed on my shoulder and called into my ear: "Marcel."

Now she came into focus, at the edge of the shadows, sitting in a wooden wheelchair. Maggie's silver hair hung down her shoulders, and washed over the front of her body like a foaming waterfall.

She wheeled herself toward me. Her long fingers were as buckled as tree roots popping out of the earth. As she approached I could smell her age. The room lost its dampness. Green eyes looked up at me.

"You came back. Dear boy. You came to see Magdalena. You decided you would save me, so I won't have to decide. Thank you." She reached her wrinkled hand out to mine.

Footsteps. Tran and Helena took my arms and turned me away from her.

"We must wash you," said Helen. "Come this way."

The next thing I remember, I woke to the sound of fists beating on the door downstairs, and I was in my room, naked. And then I got dressed, let the police in, came down to the station, and now, here we are.

CHAPTER 22

"Well, I feel like I know you a whole lot better, son," Sergeant Franklin said. Both our feet rested on his dashboard. We'd paused for lunch —chicken from Foosackly's—and now we smoked, drank our Cokes. Parked just off the road, in the shade of the wild trees that surround the swamp, we were hidden from sight. But this didn't bother me; I felt calm with Franklin. "Sorry to hear about the tough times you been through."

"I've never told anyone all this before."

"Needed to get it off your chest." He leant forward, putting out his cigarette. The silver chain that held his crucifix was tangled up in his silver chest hair. I caught a flash of black in those dark blue eyes as he put his feet on the floor. "But you leave us hanging. First time you told me this..." He flipped through the notes he'd taken. "You said you drank with Antoinette, in her house, just you and her. Now you gonna tell me about this other fella. This, what was his name? Bryson? He was staying at the house too?"

"Yes, sir. I didn't want to lie to you, but I couldn't... admit to all that was lost to memory."

"I'm glad you came clean, son. But this Bryson fella, he could be important. We can't just sit on this."

"No, he was just a random guy. He didn't do anything to her."

"How you know that? You can't remember." He gripped my shirt. "Son, try recallin' what happened. Everything goes blank just as you appear in front of Magdalena? Maybe we need to go there. Out to the island?"

"No. Hold on a moment." I closed my eyes. Like a fire a hundred miles off in a black night, a new memory appeared on my horizon. "Maggie... Magdalena... She was thanking me... for helping her... She believed I'd save her. And I... I couldn't disappoint her. I couldn't let her down. She'd seen me, you understand? I'd been seen, fully." I looked into Franklin's eyes. There was pain behind the cold blue surface. "I had to help her. Whatever she wanted."

"Of course, son. I understand." Franklin leant toward me as he scribbled on his notepad. The late afternoon sun cut through the trees. From the road came the sound of a semi-truck. I sat up straight, putting my feet to the floor. The memories began to flow again, fast, clear, and suddenly a whole stretch of events became visible. "Keep going."

Tran and Helena led me down the stairs, out into the cold night. Cool sand between my toes; shadows, firelight, the sound of drums and singing. I turned to look back at the wooden building. As my body wriggled, their hands tightened on my arms; I wasn't free.

We walked along the beach then moved back inland along a new path. The air grew colder and with the light of the fires gone, stars pierced through the black above. After crossing a small bridge, we walked along a narrow path where the branches scraped against my arms and face. Now we came into a clearing; flaming torches surrounded a single-story wooden building, in the fashion of a Japanese temple, hemmed in by a moat. The sound of running water drew my attention to a fountain that poured into a stone bath.

"Strip," Helena said, his shoulders and chest pushed out toward me.

"Naked?"

"You promised Mother Magdalena," Tran added in his gentler voice.

"I didn't promise…"

"You said you'd help her." Helena took a step toward me "You said you'd decide, so she wouldn't have to. We were all there. You going to deny this now?"

I undid my robe, paused for a moment with it in my hand, then gave it to Helena. As he took it from me, I regained a sense of power.

"Thank you." I looked into his eyes. "You're a good servant."

He spat on the dirt.

"Have a sip of this. If you want to help Magdalena, you need to do this." Tran took a small glass vial out of his robe and handed it to me. "It'll warm you up."

I finished the spicy, syrupy liquid in one sip and kneeled before the wooden bath. With a head-sized wooden ladle, Tran scooped up cold water and poured it over me. My skin tingled under the chill of the water, but a pleasant warmth glowed in my stomach, now my chest. I got back to my feet, dusting the sand and pebbles off my knees. The stinging sensation in the cuts was pleasant, and I felt at peace.

"Now you must drink this." As if by magic, Tran produced a wooden cup.

I snatched it from him, looked Helena in the eyes, and downed it. The liquid tasted bitter, and the effects kicked in as fast as alcohol, so by the time I reached the small bridge that led over the moat, something had shifted. I felt warm, safe, filled with trust.

We arrived on the other side of the bridge. Helena stepped out of the temple and handed me a black robe. I slipped it over my naked body, tying the strings. It felt good against my skin.

"Drink this," he commanded and gave me another wooden cup.

Wanting more of this raging hot peace, I drank without question. But this one affected me differently: with the bitter taste of the cup still fresh in my mouth, my consciousness began to drain through itself like water into a sinkhole, water seeping through broken floorboards in a flooded house, water falling off the edge of the earth and turning into mist. My fear grasped about for something to hold onto until it realized it was itself the thing grasping.

A curtain was pulled over the doorway, and a moment later, in quick succession, four sets of candles—one in each corner—sprang to life. A large, flat stone lay in the center of the room. Tran placed a golden bowl in the center of it, then pointed at a carved wooden chair that faced the slab. I sat down.

Helen had entered the room; she, Helena, and Tran had all changed into darker robes and now they wore masks— with striking lines painted across them in v-shapes, yellow, red, black—that stretched up high above their heads. But a moment later they appeared back in their old form.

"Drink," one of them said and poured liquid down my throat.

I might have been back out in the bayou at night, or lying in my childhood bed, or walking on a path, or no path. And when the room re-formed into something like it had been before, white hair like in an old photograph negative sat above her papery ancient face. Her frail hand, gnarled like an alligator claw, reached for my face.

"You have been with him," she said.

"Who?"

"We don't have long. This is why we exist. We exist to monitor him. To know when he returns, so we can stop him."

"What does he want?"

"My dear child." She touched my face, and I felt the same perfect peace I'd known when I met her on the other side, when she was young. "It's not fair to ask this of you."

"I volunteered. You didn't ask me to do anything. I chose."

"This is why I knew you were good for this." She looked about the room and smiled. I didn't see the faces of the others. "If he becomes angry with us there will be no bread on the shelves, the streets will go dark, and farmers will kill their own cattle. Fathers and mothers will no longer work and if they do they will return home empty-handed. With their children they will be thrown from their houses. Brothers will kill brothers. Mothers will hand over their daughters to slave traders."

"No. Stop."

"Then we must do as he demands. Only one who has been with him, in his primal form, is fit for the sacrifice."

Hands gripped my weak arms: Tran my right, Helena my left. They dragged me forward, seating me before the altar in front of two large goblets. Magdalena stood on the other side, a candle in one hand, a black obsidian blade in the other. With the blade, she pointed at each cup.

"Now you will decide. This one, if you drink it, you will feel peace. You will not need to fight." She ran the obsidian blade around the lip of the cup. "You will feel this way, yes, and then you will be the sacrifice." Magdalena ran the blade around the lip of the other cup. "And if you choose this cup, power will return to your legs. To your arms strength will come again. As for what your heart feels, it is not I who can say. Yes, you will feel the power, and then you will be the one who does the sacrifice."

Like a trapped animal, I struggled to get free.

"No. I didn't agree to this."

"Have you already forgotten everything I told you?"

"Is there not a third choice?"

"There is no choice at all. Whatever must be must be. You must play your part. But only you know how to play it."

Behind the cup that would make me the sacrifice, Magdalena placed a blue flame; behind the other, a red flame. Then she placed *The Aeneid* down in front of me.

"This is how you want me to decide?"

"Only you know how to play your part."

"Not yet, I don't know."

"How you play it is right. You must remember, death satisfies both divine justice and the requirements of the plot."

I flipped the book back and forth then stuck my finger down on a passage at the bottom of a page. This version was in English. I read the lines out loud: "Whom did Apollo call for? Now the man of Ithaca haled Calchas." Although Sortes Virgilinae only calls for a single line, I continued reading. "In tumult, calling on the seer to tell the true will of the gods. Ah, there were many able to divine the crookedness and cruelty afoot for me, but they looked on in silence. For ten days the seer kept still, kept under cover, would not speak of anyone, or name a man for death, till driven to it at last by Ulysses' cries—by prearrangement—he broke silence, barely enough to designate me for the altar."

I looked up at Magdalena. She smiled at me.

"So then, it's clear what I'm meant to do." I reached slowly for the blue cup as I wondered what would happen to the soul of a sacrificial victim. What if after being sacrificed there was no chance to negotiate? What if the fate of my soul was determined by a contract outside my control? And what of that day in Texas? Had my soul been anxious to leave since that failed attempt? My soul, did you betray me?

But Sinon. It was Sinon in *The Aeneid* who told this story. Sinon, The Achaean soldier, central to the Trojan Horse plot, the man who deceived the Trojans. It fell to me then to be the deceiver. So I reached for the cup that sat in front of the red flame and drank it all in one sip.

Franklin nodded, his face calm as if I were telling him about a kid's birthday party.

"Is what I'm saying on the record?"

"It's between you and me." He lit a cigarette, pointing upwards. "And the big man upstairs."

I accepted a cigarette from him, fished a serviette from the Foosackly's packet, and wiped sweat off my forehead. Franklin rested his chin on the knuckles of his left hand and leant toward me, those dark eyes calling forth the truth. We'd arrived finally at the central event. I could see it now, or at least parts of it, flickers and flashes. And these flashes contained within them the worst moment of my life. The most terrible thing I'd ever done. As I thought of it now, the world closed like a hand around me—a small bird crushed. The past seemed as it always had before—remote, fixed, a harsh witness that cannot lie.

The cross in the tangle of his grey hair; the smoke rising up through his fingers. How much should I tell this man? Remembering what happened last night—I felt a flush of arousal. How I had deceived! But it had been good in the moment.

"I'll tell you what I can remember. But there are many holes."

"We're getting closer." He grinned wolfishly. "Tell me what you can."

"By the time I stepped out of the temple the drug had taken full effect..."

The night was in bloom and my senses sharp. Like a wolf. Every breath in felt like God. The pockets of air between my joints had been replaced with magic fuel. This is how it must feel to walk on the moon. Her light—the moon's—illuminated the carved edges of the leaves, and I felt at once a part of everything and superior to it all. The most superior manifestation of this universe.

A mad horniness throbbed in me, too. I was desperate for sex. I felt completely certain that I was wanted, like a warrior king returning to his queen, the scent of enemy's blood still lingering on his freshly washed skin.

Life had until this moment been rather mediocre.

Did I know what we were planning to do? Did I know what *I* was planning to do? Yes, I believe there was some clarity. I would tell Antoinette what was going on, and somehow we'd escape, together, the two of us. But the plan was weak; it ran up to a particular moment and stopped.

Tran and Helena rowed me across the moon-shimmering bayou. We took an old car hidden in the bushes. The inside smelt of chewing tobacco and damp. The stitched lines in the seats were filled with crumbs, tobacco, and lint.

As we drove, Tran and Helena lit up cigarettes, like teenagers with mom out of sight. Tran offered me one.

The smoke felt like brilliant blue fire in my lungs, and my high intensified as I exhaled. We stopped at the gas station on the edge of Chickasaw, and when Tran returned from the shop he was folding away a lottery ticket.

We continued through the tree-lined back streets, past

the Methodist Church, and turned before the black sign with white ornate lettering—lit up now by his headlights—that welcomed us to Chickasaw Historic Shipyard District. Then we turned down Antoinette's street. Bryson's truck was the only vehicle parked there.

"We'll be waiting down the road," Helena said. "Come outside and we'll see you."

"She has to come voluntarily," Tran said.

The car disappeared at the end of the street, then reemerged moments later, facing me. The headlights turned off. Cigarette tips burned in the dark of the car. I was planning to deceive them, but their resources were extensive; their plan was deep and had roots in the mists of millennia past. Mine began here on the street and ended on Antoinette's porch.

As the screen door shut behind me and I stood in the laundry room, I saw Antoinette, in a pair of denim shorts and a white t-shirt. She turned from the stove, spatula in hand, and took a sip of her special bubbly red.

"I was hoping you'd show up, Marcel."

A drop of sweat slid down, through the white and black bandana, over her pink forehead and down past her eye. I imagined its smooth path down her chest, my ally. All her clothes off, on her back, my hand between her legs. That's how I pictured us.

"Let me have a sip of your drink," I said, reaching for her glass.

"You can have your own."

I took hold of her free hand and slipped my fingers between hers. "I want you."

She put the spatula down on the stove next to the sizzling, crumbed chicken pieces, then rested her hand against my chest. "They give you something weird, Marcel?"

"Where's Bryson?"

"He took a nap."

"Alone?"

"Yes, alone. He ain't woken up yet. You need to sit down."

"I have to tell you something important."

"What?"

I should have said—*we need to leave together, now; we need to escape.* But I believed that we had a chance right then to have everything, together, and to have it now. The world outside would wait until we were ready for it, and then it would vanish and reinvent itself just as we needed it to be. I'd invested enough in other peoples' stories, and I wasn't committed to Magdalena's. It was time to get real, to accept that the money was just that: money. We had a life waiting for us; we'd earned it.

So I said: "I love you."

"Come on, Marcel." She let go of both my hands and gently pushed me away.

"The other night you said you wanted me."

"You said it ain't wise."

"I've changed my mind. I want to be with you." I backed away from her. "If he's still sleeping, let's use this time."

"Take a seat. I'm going to pour you a drink."

I did as she said, and a glass of her bubbling special appeared in front of me.

"What the hell's gotten into you?"

She sat opposite me; chicken sizzled in the background. Skeptical still, amused even, I sensed she enjoyed my performance. Would she let me spill my heart and then throw me to the curb? Was she a cat playing with her dinner? I couldn't tell. But waves of euphoric confidence took me higher, and I felt certain that all I had to do was perform better. Like a bright-feathered bird dancing for sex, I preened myself, I cooed, I flapped, I spun in circles.

I have no idea what turned her.

She switched off the stove, pressed me against the fridge, and stuck her tongue in my mouth. I tingled madly as I ran my hand up her back then down her pants where I grabbed her butt cheeks and pulled her against me so she could feel how hard I was. Then I moved my hand around to the front of her body and with my other hand undid the button and zipper. I slipped my hand beneath her panties and my finger disappeared inside her warm, wet flesh. So ecstatic I was, I no longer felt oriented to the physical world. I could have been floating upside down. Her hand went inside my robe and she grabbed me confidently.

"Hell!" Bryson said as he came into the kitchen. "There's a room upstairs. I'm a paying guest. You two can do what you want, but come on. A little respect."

Antoinette flushed bright red as she pulled away from me, zipping up her pants. She took her pack of cigarettes off the counter, pushing the door open.

"Come back, Antoinette. Don't go out there."

I shouted after her as I ran across the porch and down the stairs into the garden, but the car was already there. Tran hopped out, grabbed her, and pulled a black sack over her head, muffling her scream. Working with Helena, he bound her hands and feet like a seasoned professional and pushed her into the trunk of the car.

"Good work," he said to me as he closed the trunk shut.

And all I could think was—*she heard those words and she thinks I'm a monster.*

"Drink this." Tran held a metal cup toward me. "That shit will wear off soon, and the night's young."

As the world tightened 'round me, crushing me, I drank the liquid. In a minute the feelings of lust and calm confidence returned to their earlier peaks; we drove into the darkness toward the swamps.

There are no lights along Highway 43. In the window I

saw my reflection, broken once by the light from the single house on the road—an old rotting, wooden shack, with a porch and a chained-up dog. Antoinette pounded against my seat. I heard her moans and screams. As the effects of the new cup intensified, I rehearsed the speech I'd give her when all this was over. It'd be funny; something we could tell our grandkids about one day. Oh, I listened to you flipping and flopping in the back there like a fish plucked from the ocean. You were panicking, but I knew everything would be fine. I imagined introducing her to my mother. We'd drive up to Charleston together and spend the weekend with my mom and Charles. By this point, of course, I'd have come clean about the money, and we'd be enjoying a great standard of living. We'd have a house in Charleston, looking out into the water and another house where Antoinette wanted to live— on the Gulf Coast maybe; and we could even keep her house in Chickasaw. We'd spend the weekends on the water, own a little beach cottage we'd rent out during our frequent travels abroad. With ten million in investments we could live off the interest. I'd finally take on those creative projects I'd left behind as an undergraduate and Antoinette could flip houses. We'd do it together—maybe get our own show like Chip and Joanna. If only she knew what was going on in my mind right now, she wouldn't be screaming.

We veered off Route 43 and I felt the sand beneath the wheels. I looked between Tran and Helena, through the windscreen to the dirt road, wrapped in thick vegetation. We went down a steep slope and turned to the right where the sand was softer. I felt the car sink, the wheels spin, and for a moment I thought we were stuck, but then we moved forward into the clearing.

"The place we came to ... was this place."

"Let's get out," said Franklin.

We walked away from the car and looked down at the tire tracks in the sand.

"Yes. Right here."

I looked up through the trees to the darkening sky. Dusk had come now and the birds raced about. Last night I'd looked up through this same patch to the dark sky. Helena, Tran, and I had stood near the car, smoking cigarettes and waiting. Tran had said we had to wait for... what had he said? He'd used a very specific word. He'd said protection. *We need to wait for protection.*

Headlights; a car arrived, Antoinette's. The driver—someone I'd seen on the island but hadn't spoken to—stepped out. A moment later another car appeared and from the passenger side stepped Magdalena. In her long white dress, barefoot, she came walking toward me, across the sand. The headlights of the car she'd been in shone bright and her shadow stretched along the ground. She moved slowly, looking down at her feet, then up at me. With her long white dress and flowing hair, she looked like a bride, one who'd shown up for her wedding eighty years too late. And I realized then how much sense it would make for her to officiate at our wedding, mine and Antoinette's. I'd have to bring this up with her, with Antoinette—not too soon, of course. I didn't want her to freak out or be scared off by my over enthusiasm. But the knowledge that it was possible, that I really could get married, that I could finance an amazing wedding to Antoinette, on a tropical island somewhere—this brought me great joy. We'd marry on white sand, like the sand here, and in my wedding speech I'd recall this moment when I'd first had the idea. I pictured all the guests at decorated tables, sipping cocktails, laughing at the story, raising their glasses to the two of us and our happiness.

As Magdalena took my hand, the final car arrived. It came down the slope much faster than the others, the solid body bounding as it straightened out on the road. The lights were dimmed, the sirens off. Magdalena handed me a cup. I took it from her and drank whatever was in it—more of the same. My body tingled, my chest felt warm, my head perfectly clear. That we were not scattered by this officer's arrival meant, I assume, that he was our protection.

Just this morning I'd had access to none of these memories. I'd had to retell my whole story for them to return, and as they did, they came not as disparate flashes from a drunken night, but in an ordered, sequential motion—up until this point. The memory continues a few seconds longer. The door of the black van opens and I see the legs appear. The door slams shut as the man places his black trooper hat on his head and folds his arms. Magdalena takes the cup from me.

This is where the memories end.

In the account I gave to Franklin, I left out the part where the patrol car arrives. But I feel I must tell you, as I suspect it's important.

"That's what I remember," I said to him. "We were standing here." I turned in a circle, arms spread out.

"Y'all were pretty confident, huh? Thought nobody would bother you?"

"I suppose."

"You suppose? You was here, son. This is you we talking about." He gripped my shoulder. "They thought someone was protecting 'em, huh? Keeping 'em safe?"

We walked to the landing, where the fishermen launched their boats. Three SUVs with trailers were parked there now, and a single fishing boat drifted in the water maybe three-hundred yards from where we stood. The others, I guess, had drifted down the streams that led deep into the bayou.

Franklin took a lottery ticket from his pocket, looked at his watch, and then up at the car-sized American flag that flew above Highway 43. A train whistled as it came in over the rusty bridge on the far side of the highway.

"This here's a new one. The drawing's in ninety minutes." He stuffed the ticket back into his pocket. "We should finish up." He lit us each a cigarette and we walked right to the water's edge. "They brought her down here, didn't they? There was a boat here at the water's edge."

"They must have given her something. She wasn't fighting anymore. She was dressed in a black robe. Her long red hair flowed down her shoulders."

And she walked with confidence and poise, just as she would on our wedding night; I remember thinking this. The images started to flow again. Tran and Helena helped her by holding beneath her arms, and the man who'd driven her to the water's edge carried a lantern. Antoinette was not in her own eyes. She didn't even seem to notice me as I took her hand and helped her into the boat. I smelt her skin; I smelt her on me. I wanted her so badly. Just as soon as this was behind us, we could be together as we'd been—as we'd started to be in the kitchen.

I sat next to her, gripping her hand in mine as our boat was paddled out into the dark bayou. I heard the oars move through the water and watched the flame of our guide torches scatter in the wakes the boat carved. I looked up at the vines growing over the narrow waterways leading into the heart of the swamp, and the brilliant white flowers that clung to the vines.

We each drank from the cups Magdalena handed us, and I felt a rush of euphoric energy surge through me. Antoinette's eyelids drooped and opened; her head rocked back and forth.

There were other boats already docked at the clearing, and several figures stood there, dressed in black robes, high masks covering their faces, torches burning in their hands. They'd pulled the roughest growth aside and laid down a wooden gangplank where we came up onto land, and there ahead of us, ten feet from the water, stood the altar.

Oh my sweet Antoinette, when this night is long behind us we'll look back and remember the smell of burning kerosene in the cool air and the way the firelight played with the bright colored zigzag images on the masks. She held my hand and we walked, slowly and with purpose, toward the altar, where Magdalena stood with the obsidian blade in her hands.

I pulled Antoinette's beautiful hair off her face and looked into her vacant eyes. What soul was there to sacrifice if none was present in that moment, if it had been numbed into catatonia?

I felt the trees rustling in me, the birds singing in me, the fire burning in me, the wind blowing in me. As it had left that day in the Texas town, so now my soul returned. I felt it wriggling back into me, hot.

Now Magdalena gave me instructions on where to cut the chest open, and how. The knife should go into the stomach, and my hands would dig beneath the ribcage and pull the beating heart loose from the sinew and muscle that held it in place.

I leant over and whispered in Antoinette's ear: "Be prepared."

Near my feet lay a wooden bucket set to catch the blood that would flow through channels carved into the altar. Once I'd ripped the heart out I'd hand it to Magdalena and she'd be the first to hold it up to the sky.

"Are you ready?"

"Yes. Ready."

I raised the blade above my head and as I brought it down I swung to the side, driving it into Magdalena's arm. Dark blood stained her robe as she fell back into Tran. Helena came at me. I stuck the blade—with the force of someone only half-committed—into his ribcage. *He's okay*, I told myself as I stepped back, resting against the edge of the altar.

"Shoot him!" someone yelled.

I cut through the ropes around Antoinette's arms and lifted her off the altar.

"You're safe with me, my love." I kissed her cold face. "I won't let them harm you."

I jumped over logs and rocks. I felt her sweat and my sweat. I heard her breathing and my breathing. Twigs snapped. The chill of the air. The extreme caution I took to place Antoinette into the boat, to lay her body between the seats and her head against the side—curled like a sleeping child. I climbed in behind her, pulling the rope from beneath the rock that held it down, my weight causing us to move into the dark water. I turned to see them standing at the edge, their flames and masks reflected in the water. Some clambered into boats and came after us. I could barely see a few inches ahead, but still each pull and push through the water I gave my all.

The boat cracked against a log; tangles of branches and vines scratched my face and arms. I'd paddled in the wrong direction. One smoky evening—I remembered now—Antoinette had told me about a place called Pirate's Cove, a small island in the center of the bayou joined to the mainland by a series of short bridges. Yes, there were shimmers of light through the thick foliage. That must be where they came from. As I pushed the oar against the trunk of a fallen tree—so we could untangle and move back into the water—I heard the splashing of the oars, the boats carving their way toward us.

Crashing into the branches, I'd lost momentum, and they'd closed in. I looked at Antoinette's face slumped against the edge of the boat, eyes closed. I ran my hand across her face and promised her that one day we'd laugh about this; but now I'd save her. Arms beneath her arms I rocked the boat back and forth, then dived to the side, splashing below the water. I scrambled to keep her head buoyed, and kicked my legs like frog's legs, face fixed on the boats as they came toward us. Thirty feet, ten feet. Weeds and sunken branches wrapped around my legs. The cold water bit my skin.

I pulled us up against a muddy bank, sliding her body over the stones and sticks. As I carried her up the bank toward the light that came from a house, I felt hot liquid on her leg. My hand was covered in blood. I'd cut her.

She felt heavier now and for a moment I worried she'd stopped breathing. But then she made a sound, a noise, I felt her turn and move. I ran along a path past dark wooden houses with gardens that went down to the water. Reaching a fence, I stopped just a moment, then climbed over it into someone's garden, a residential garden. A motion sensor came on, turned off. I ran to where I thought I'd seen a shed—yes. A chain had been wound through the handles and as I untied it, it slithered to the ground, clattering on the concrete.

With the door shut, the room went dark; I couldn't see an inch in front of me. I swiped my hand about and hit metal serrated edges, the smooth head of a hammer. Below that a wooden table—a work bench. I crouched slowly, feeling the table leg and the cavernous space beneath the bench. Seated on the cold floor, I pressed Antoinette's head against my shoulder, moving my hand up and down her back and sides to make sure she was still breathing. The drugs were wearing off, and somehow in that terrible position, cramped, cold, wet, I managed to fall asleep and dream not of horrors but of a beautiful, perfect love, the kind that struggles to take root in this barren, thorny earth, but the kind that never stops trying.

When I woke my arms were empty. The first blue came into the sky; birds twittered and shrieked. I walked along the riverbank, head pounding like I'd drunk a gallon of whiskey; legs and joints throbbing and old like I'd lost a decade in a night.

Somehow I got back to her house. Antoinette wasn't there. Neither was Bryson. In the mirror I noticed streaks of blood on my still damp pants and shirt. I feared she'd been injured worse than I imagined. Had they found her in the shed? Taken her away to complete the sacrifice? I threw my clothes into the wash, showered, and got into bed naked, gripping tight to some stupid hope this was all a dream.

CHAPTER 23

"But it wasn't a dream."

Franklin and I crushed out our cigarettes at the same time. The screeches of night birds filled the dark air. A falcon swooped in low to a tree at the water's edge. Whatever they'd given me to drink had kept the memories behind a wall that when it cracked, cracked all at once. Now I felt a cold, hollow guilt behind my ribs.

"No, of course it wasn't a dream."

"And what made you think you'd get away with it?"

"Get away with what? I told you, that was the last time I saw her."

'That's the problem, you fool."

Franklin pulled me toward him, striking the side of my head. Lights flashed, my ears rang; I stumbled to the ground and a boot caught me in the chin. Blood filled my mouth.

"That was our chance to save this town and now 'cause of you we gonna lose it."

I crouched on all fours, blood running from my mouth and nose like water from a faucet.

"If you don't got the balls to do the sacrifice, then you become the sacrifice."

I tried to catch his eye with mine, but I was slow and weak, and his boot caught me fast on the side of my head.

The ropes were bound so tight around my wrists and ankles I couldn't move an inch; my hands and feet tingled.

I saw the obsidian blade in the hand of a cloaked priest. Now the altar pressed beneath me, menacing, cold, hard, indifferent as death.

Too many bodies to count. Red and yellow flashes of masks. Firelight from flames; the sound of cloaks rustling, snapped twigs; bird wing swooshes, branches bowing under the birds' weight. Night insects screeching, and me as a child, running up a hill toward my mother and father—all of time woven together.

I'd been stripped naked but for a loin cloth. I smelt of vinegar and lard. One of the masked men loosened the ropes on my wrists and helped pull me upwards, so I sat like a sick child waiting for his medicine, and when the cup was placed at my mouth and a voice I suspect was Tran's told me that drinking would make the road smoother, I knew what he meant and I knew it was my destiny to partake of the cup. I took it all in one sip. He rubbed my back like a sympathetic parent, and even though he was about to kill me, I appreciated him.

But what had happened to Sinon, the Achaean, the deceiver? I thought I was he. Had I misread the signs given to me? In my head, these words: *I'm the one who's been deceived—all my plans have failed.* These cannot be my last words to myself—*All my plans have failed.* But the dagger was raised. I looked down its sharp nose; but—a crack like the tail of a whip breaking the sound barrier, repeated and repeated until all the trees had been replaced by flickering firelight and then fire and complete light, a white eternal circle. If I let myself go toward it, I felt perfect peace, love so bright it consumed everything. I'd be it and it me and all would be perfect.

But then... my time near it ended. I turned away, toward something familiar. A voice, a sound—Maggie, the young woman, driving my car. We raced down back alleyways past dark cafés filled with evening smokers, old men playing dice, young women in brightly colored dresses, clowns and men on stilts, elephants and white horses. A carnival. We were headed to the main act. As she skidded around the corner, crashing into a cluster of trashcans, she handed me a whisky bottle.

"You're probably upset with me, aren't you?"

"You thought you'd found a third option, a way out."

The red bird appeared from the backseat and landed on my shoulder. I took a sip of whisky and felt it warm my chest and stomach. I wiped my mouth. "You can't expect me to kill her."

"You're using present tense. That's far behind you." She turned to look at me, and the world outside the car smudged like wet paint on a canvas and then blackened as dark as the cave where first I'd met her. "You're quite lucky. Right now they're cutting out your heart and you're drinking whisky."

My fingers felt sticky from touching my left breast, but holding them close to my eyes I saw they were covered in paint. And my heart beat in my chest.

"They haven't taken my heart. You're still playing games with me."

Her bone-white skin stood against the darkness like the pale, pleading hands of a ghost on a window at night. Eyes on the road ahead, she called the town into being. The bird landed on her fingers.

"Can you feel my sadness now?"

"I felt it the first time I met you."

"But you weren't willing to step up?"

"To murder? The worst thing."

"Not murder; an honor."

The car floated above the bayous and the small town of Chickasaw. Then I stood alone on the dark street. A patch of light in a garden drew my attention up toward the source of the light, a window. The sound of hooves on concrete—click, clack, click. Sheriff Jones sat alone at his dining room table drinking a beer, leafing through the newspaper, his hat next to him, his pistol slung across the opposite chair. As I struggled to open the latch on his garden gate, the hoof sounds grew louder. Now the horse and its rider stopped on the street opposite the window. The rider's arm rose with the slow, certain ease of a windmill blade. The sound of gunfire smashed the night and the glass and Sheriff Jones's head wide open. A splattering of red, like coughed-up stars, decorated the kitchen spice rack; blood flowed off the table to the floor; his wife cried out as she fell to her knees.

Back in the car with Magdalena, I looked at my blood-soaked hands.

"Now do you see?"

"You can't blame me for this."

"You had your time."

She turned the car fast around a corner and we skidded through an empty outdoor café.

"I must get out."

"This is your town."

She sped off, wheels spinning on the tar.

The burnt tires smelt like bullet smoke and I wiped my bloody hands on the ground, muttering: Sorry, sorry, Sheriff.

Then I sat at a table opposite my father and I poured us each a glass of whisky. I told him where the bottle came from, Maggie's car.

"It doesn't really matter," he said. "We're all the same."

We raised our glasses and drank to his claim.

"Speaking of which," he said.

Around the corner came his father, the first Andries Swart, and his father, General Swart. We all drank together; I relished the feeling of connection. All the men looked at their wrist watches and said in turn:

"Must be going."

"On my way."

Even my father stood up. "Love you, my boy," he said, and patted my shoulder.

A carnival, I remembered, was in town, this floating town, and the time for the main performance drew near, but the streets had darkened, and I struggled to find my way. Then I saw an old church with stone turrets reaching up to the dark magenta sky. I paused in the nave before a bank of candles lit by mourners, dipped my hand in holy water and blessed myself. The sound of an unseen choir filled the candlelit chapel, empty but for a woman who sat near the front of the church, near the altar. Realizing it was my mother, I ran toward her.

"What are you doing here?"

"Don't worry. I'm fine. Nothing's wrong with me," she said. "Sit next to me." She shifted along the pew.

"So, what are you doing here?"

"I'm your mother; I'm allowed to appear to you, to warn you that if you travel too far the umbilical cord will snap and you'll leave the womb of this world."

"I understand why it's you who gets to tell me this, but I don't know what to do with that information."

"There's a reason for you to go back. Unless you think you've finished growing in earth's womb, you shouldn't leave."

"Unless *I* think? It matters what I think?"

The choir sang louder now and someone, invisible to me,

played the organ. Although it was dark outside, the stained-glass windows glowed.

"Of course it matters."

"What about those who leave too soon?"

"They matured faster, or they left early and have to go at it again."

"How can you know which one it is?"

"On earth we can't. I can't wait here any longer..."

I don't know if she got up or if I left, but the conversation ended and I was outside the chapel again, walking down an empty street toward an old warehouse that had been converted into a performance venue. As I got closer I heard the excited muttering of an expectant crowd. I entered behind the benches, through which I saw the feet, popcorn boxes, and drink cups of the crowd. The air was humid with anticipation. The ringmaster entered, speaking in some primal language like a baby cooing. A group of women in colorful skirts ushered me toward the entrance, pointing to the bright light in the center. The ringmaster had a lion's tale and a bright red jacket. He stepped down off the podium, a wooden tub turned upside down. His eyes flashed green and his teeth glimmered like lion's teeth in the midday sun.

A crack of the whip again and I was on the podium, scanning the crowd, the eyes overflowing with curiosity, popcorn spilling out of greedy fingers. I was to give an account of myself; my father's words—we're all the same—repeated.

So I shouted: "Ba!"

The crowd cheered.

"Ba-Wa-Ha-Ba!"

They rose to their feet. I was an infant, lying on my back on my parents' floor, feeling language birth itself inside me, pure, uncorrupted by the world. I knew just what to say. So it went, like a symphony, growing and roaring until a flash and crack more powerful than before blew it all away and I was in the sky, in the darkness above my forest.

All this time I'd been floating farther from the earth. Beyond me I felt that perfect peace I wanted to surrender to. But like I'd fought sleep in every classroom I'd sat in as a child, I fought this bliss. There were things that had to be done.

The cord from my stomach, previously slack in the air, tightened now, close to snapping. I grabbed it and pulled myself back down. Through the dark and the wind, through the flashes of light and memories of a thousand years, I swam to earth.

CHAPTER 24

My legs wriggled and twitched as I woke.

"Been praying for you, son."

Baptist Pants filled out his navy blue suit like the largest teddy bear at the secondhand store, the type you can't believe anyone would actually buy. In the pink of the evening sun, his white hair—not exactly parted or styled, just there, sitting—looked beautiful, soft, as did his smoothly shaven, round face. His shoes were freshly shone, his bowtie a shade of blue darker than his suit. A pair of perfectly manicured thumbs rested atop his blue leather bible.

"I'm so grateful you came back." He took a notebook from his inner jacket pocket, flipping through the pages. "Got the call ten days ago. Early morning, just as the sun came up. I didn't think I could handle anything more."

"I've been under all that time?"

"Correction. Nine nights you were under. Tonight would have been the tenth."

"And what's happened since I've been gone?"

"I don't want you getting all stressed out and worked up.

I'm not a doctor, and I like to stay in my lane. I'm going to fetch a doctor or nurse."

He pushed down on his knees, bringing himself to his feet. With deliberate movement of the arms, as if he had to get himself going like an old choo-choo train, he went for the exit.

"Why the hell did you take so long to wake up?"

I turned to see my mother on the other side of the bed, wearing a black and white dress, a silk scarf around her neck, hair and makeup immaculate. As always she could have been on her way to a millionaire's box at the Kentucky Derby.

"You're here."

Only as she leant forward to kiss my face did I realize there were tubes coming out my nose. She tussled my hair, pulled on my beard.

"I feel... far away," I said "Like I'm deep underwater."

Charles appeared at the door again.

"The doctors are on the way," he said. "Apparently your... uh... what's the word? Reemergence didn't show up on any of their monitors. Makes you wonder..." He stood on the other side of my bed. "We put our faith in science. But should we really trust machines?"

"Listen to him," my mother said. "Next he's going to start talking about the good ol' days."

With a practiced motion Charles took a red handkerchief from his top pocket and wiped a layer of sweat off his forehead.

"The boy's been through a lot," he muttered. "You've been through a lot."

The word *boy* cut right through me. For a moment the meaning of my prolonged blackout became clear—I'd emerged a butterfly, ready to claim my fortune and enjoy it publicly, let the world see my hard-won dollars. Turning about to get comfortable, I felt pains all through my body, and my head ached right down to the stem of my brain.

"How did I get here?"

"Somebody brought you here," my mother said, as she placed the back of her hand on my forehead. Her hands were warm, but for her cool wedding ring. It looked just like the one she used to wear when she was married to my father—I'd thought she'd changed rings when she married Charles, but this might have been that ring; my memories could hardly be trusted.

"Somebody brought me here," I said, measuring each word as I spoke.

"You remember?" Charles asked.

"No, I don't remember. Who brought me here?"

"A civilian. Didn't leave his name."

"It was a man?"

"Or *her* name," he said, and smiled to indicate that he approved of this custom, but of course we all knew the truth.

"And the election?"

"Which election?" my mother asked.

"The election... the sheriff election, here in Chickasaw."

"I know which election you mean," Charles said. "When else would a place like Chickasaw be in the national news?"

"So who won?"

"The challenger," Charles said. "Calls himself a man of God. I'm comfortable with the victory."

What did that mean? The pain in my head intensified as I thought through the implications.

"Calm yourself," my mother said, as she rubbed my hair. "You can't solve the world's problems, and certainly not in this state. Focus all your energy on getting better." She looked down at me, staring intensely into my eyes.

"When do I get out of here?"

"You get out of here when they dismiss you," Charles said. "We'll take care of the bills. I don't want you worrying about that."

"I have insurance."

"Nothing that would cover this. And you've been in a private room. I certainly don't want you tapping into government programs."

"I... um... I appreciate all you're doing for me."

"And when you're out of here, you're coming back to Charleston. We told you that you were welcome. Who knows... how much grief we might have been spared, if you'd come sooner." He wiped his eye.

"You definitely need to spend time in Charleston," my mother said. "You've known for a long time that you're welcome."

"I'll come to Charleston. Thank you."

"And the doctors still haven't come," my mother said.

"These doctors really are taking their time," Charles agreed. "I should go and call them again."

But a moment later my bed was surrounded by nurses and —I think—a doctor. Hands were all over me, lights in my eyes, needles, Velcro wrapping and unwrapping, and soon I felt much worse. I was taken from one room to another. A lanky male doctor named Jones said I'd need an EEG. They put electrodes on my skull, flashed lights in my eyes. I was told I needed an MRI, too.

My bare-bones insurance refused to cover these expensive procedures. Charles covered all the costs, and when I promised to repay him, he said, "That won't be necessary..." He squeezed my hand. "Son."

My whole body rebelled against the term and all it implied, but inside the MRI machine—a beast of a contraption that took up a whole room—with my head in a strange helmet, vibrations and beeping sounds causing my brain to ache, nausea to flow through me, I tried to summon up gratitude. The image that came to me then was of the long cord attached to my center, and how it had almost ripped out my insides; just another inch, another second and I would have been lost to this world.

They had, I later learned, done EEGs on me when I was in the coma, too. I'd shown consistent signs of brain activity most of the time, and so they weren't afraid I was close to death. But during an extended reading—they'd left the electrodes on my skull for twenty-four hours—there was a single patch of what one doctor referred to as "parallel lines", no activity at all. It only lasted a few minutes, but in that time they thought I'd died.

I wondered: How long had my journey lasted? Had the whole experience lasted minutes, hours, days? I had no idea. I remembered all the details so clearly even though some of it I'd rather forget. It seemed more vivid than anything that had ever happened in my life.

That night alone in my hospital room, hopped up on some cocktail of drugs, I pieced together the events of the past ten days. The most astounding fact of all: My article in Axan had been one of the top-trending pieces in the country—read and shared millions of times. The editor had sent me increasingly desperate emails asking for follow-up pieces.

I wrote back: *I've been very sick but I'm better now. Follow-up pieces are on the way.*

For the first time in my life, I was, it seemed, an expert on something. Sadly—and here, not for the first time in my life—I had no idea what was going on. I did my best to catch up. There was no shortage of articles—all the major news sites had covered it; there were extended think pieces in *The New*

Yorker and *The Atlantic.* Jefferson Lee III had won by thirteen votes, forcing a recount that went the same way by the same margin. This prompted an evening of demonstrations during which a woman reported as missing and suspected to have been the victim of foul play, reappeared as a leader. A short video of Antoinette leading a protest on the shore near Maggie's Island had been the number-one viewed news clip on MSNBC and FOX News' websites. The protestors had formed a human chain around the entrance, attempting to block police, whom they assumed would make an early morning raid on the premises. When the second count was completed at 11pm, Jones gave his concession speech and—as per promises made before the election—had his office cleared by midnight. Talking heads decried the weakness of Jones, his lack of intestinal fortitude. He was a coward, who'd betrayed a cause far larger than himself.

This was, I thought, unfair. Given that he'd lost the election, he was simply doing what was required of him. Side stories told of the immediate fate of Antoinette—images of her in handcuffs; charged with public disorder; released on bail.

Lee's victory speech had been given from behind a desk in his office, in front of several flags—the American flag, the Alabama flag, and some other partially obscured, dark flag. In front of him, a black plaque with gold letters: *Sheriff*; a revolver in a black holster. He wore his black leather hat and gave that smile where the right corner of the lip curls up, smooth as fried chicken, waffles, and syrup.

"Order has been restored," he said. "Tonight the people have spoken. In the weeks and months leading up to this campaign, the people spoke. We received more donations— small donations, from common, humble folk—than any other local electioneer. And as we promised, operation *Restore Order* is already underway."

All the major news outlets had covered the raid. Footage showed Magdalena, the old woman, in handcuffs. She was the queen—symbol of the rot taken hold of the town. She wore a long dress, hair loose over her face; she held her hand up to the camera, pushing it away. She was manhandled by four enormous bald men in black jackets.

Magdalena—considered a serious flight risk—had not been released on bail. There was no sign of Tran, Helena, or Helen in the arrest footage, and none of their names came up in any of the reports. In one article there was mention of Magdalena's "Top Lieutenants" slipping away, and there was a nationwide search for two men whose names and faces I did not—at first glance—recognize. On closer inspection one of the pictures looked like it could be a younger Tran with a full head of hair: Real name Marvin Stories. The other—Malachi Snopes—I suppose might have been Helena, younger and with a full beard. No mention of Helen.

And what had happened to Detective Franklin? Doors opened and closed in the night. Alarms went off. I didn't sleep deeply, for every sound turned into Franklin. Shadows moving across the wall were him coming for me, hands out to crush my windpipe, or switch my drips for poison.

Doctors came in the night, took measurements and readings; they spoke as if it were the middle of the day, a normal time to come and converse about complex medical problems. When the third doctor—or maybe nurse—left, light came through the curtains, and I wondered if my mind had reversed day and night. My hands and feet tingled as I felt my sense of time collapse around me. Wherever I looked, I saw nothing but shadows.

I feared all the symptoms that, according to the doctors, I'd been so lucky to avoid, were just in waiting. But then there were moments that came without asking and left always too soon, in which I felt the peace of that place beyond where the cord of this world could stretch. I took comfort from those moments, and their memory buoyed me when my fears rose and tried to pull me under.

Lucky—that's what the doctors said to me. My situation, they said, was atypical. Firstly, it was unclear what had put me in the comatose state. I'd suffered blunt trauma to the head, and my toxicology screenings showed high levels of potentially neurotoxic substances. They asked me what I remembered and gave me hints to help fill in the blanks. Their conclusion? I'd gotten wasted on a mix of exotic drugs with reckless friends and had an accident. My ne'er-do-well friends, afraid of legal troubles, but not so unconscionably careless as to leave me to die, dropped me at the hospital entrance. I affirmed most of what they said, but told them I couldn't remember who these friends were; I'd recently fallen in with a new crowd.

Nothing in this world is easier than convincing someone their own speculations and hunches are true. So that was it, I was a washed-up junkie who'd run out of luck. Charles seemed to like this explanation, too—there was a family connection; the Swart men needed to be careful when it came to addictive behaviors. In fact, the story made such sense I considered accepting it myself.

I'd gone forty-eight hours without checking my bank account. Why, you may wonder? I think some part of me knew the money wouldn't be there and I needed to enjoy this feeling of suspense, where if I didn't have the money, at least I didn't officially not have it. Then the two stories became connected—if the money wasn't there, the drug story was real. I'd been living in a strange town, hanging out with strange people, taking drugs, wasting my life. It had all blown up in my face and this was a chance to put things right. Of course a deeper part of me—the part that felt from time to time the touch of that perfect place—knew this isn't what had happened.

But this I kept to myself. Having a story we could all agree on made relations, between myself, the doctors, and Charles more harmonious. This harmony, and my fear of Franklin, made it easier to accept the plan put forward by both Baptist Pants and my mother—I'd move to Charleston and stay there until I "got back on my feet."

In Charles's mansion I felt like a convalescent from a nineteenth-century novel. I was given a room at the end of a long corridor on the second floor, next to the room that had been his son's. Opposite my room was his deceased first wife's haberdashery workshop in which he kept—quite creepily, I have to say—pictures of himself with both her and my mother. My bedroom had a small balcony that looked down onto an old cobbled street. On the other side of the house, where he and my mother had their room, was a large balcony that looked out toward the bay. It was an amazing location; the sea air lifted my mood, and I slept peacefully for the first time in as long as I can remember.

Dinner was had each evening in Charles's dining room, decorated like the antebellum plantation homes-turned-museums I'd visited in the South. A large gold-framed mirror hung to the side of the table, and oil portraits of Charles's ancestors, as well as one with himself, his son, and first wife, hung on the walls. A crystal chandelier—salvaged, he told me, along with the mirror, from a real plantation home in Louisiana—covered the room in a dim, speckled, golden glow.

"You like those paintings?" Charles asked me.

"I do."

"I always told your mother, and the invitation goes to you, too, you have a standing appointment with my artist."

"Your artist?" I asked.

"Charles knows many artists in this town," my mother said, smiling at me.

"Let us pray," Charles said, and raised both hands in the air.

In his prayer that evening, as in the previous evenings, Charles asked the Lord to protect and bless the souls of the living and the dead. He asked that God take especially good care of me given all I'd been through and all I'd lost. *More than any young man should have to bear.* He mentioned the charitable foundation he'd started, and recalled how it had funded my mother's literacy projects, and how without this intervention he would never have met my mother, and hence never have met me, and then I would not be sitting here. He ended, as he did each evening, with an extended Amen, that drifted into song, lowered his hands, picked up his ornate silver knife and fork, and dug into his food—white fish and asparagus, prepared by himself from one of those home delivery health food services, where everything comes ready to cook.

"Your mother got me eating healthily," he said, raising his glass.

"He's the one who's stuck at it," she responded.

"Sticking to it is easy, once you get into the habit. That's what I learned from her. Now it's all vegetables, chicken breasts, or fish, dessert no more than once a week, and even then, low sugar."

After the prayer and the reflection on the meal, he spoke about his day. He had a strange habit of addressing an imaginary figure at the far end of the table, and quite often closed his eyes as he spoke, sometimes for a full minute. Then he'd ask about my day. The first time I looked at my mother, confused, not quite sure what I was meant to say. She nodded, smiling. "Just tell the truth."

"I've been, mostly around the house." I said something about my wildly interesting life, but noticed the forcefully obvious sarcasm had not registered with Charles. Instead he nodded gently and smiled. Sarcasm, I realized, was something he simply did not get, as if the circuitry responsible for processing such comments did not exist in his brain. I felt bad then, and stopped making any kind of sarcastic comments.

It was during one of our dinners that it hit me with the force of a boot to the forehead, that my mother had never been with Charles because she needed him, but because she felt a paralyzing guilt at the thought of leaving him. At some point she'd convinced herself that without her he'd go to ruin, and she did not want to feel responsible—even if objectively she wasn't—for aiding in another man's self-destruction. This fear of hers was not ungrounded, and recognizing it, under-standing the way it had shaped their relationship, was like putting on a pair of prescription lenses. The house came into focus.

Charles was not only a strange man, but a fragile one. Although he clearly worshipped my mother, he spoke about her more than he did *to* her. Behind closed doors, I assumed, he nurtured a more intimate conversation. He spoke about his mother often, telling stories that included reference to her favorite bible verses, which often led to readings of these verses followed by tears. He drank sweet tea in the evenings and, on his large television screen, watched recordings—on YouTube—of gospel bands from the seventies and eighties. He'd raise his glass during certain lines and sing along at the top of his voice. He ate breakfast alone, standing up, often talking to himself, and brushed his hair while looking at his reflection in the microwave door. He was not quite as put together as I'd imagined, and he often misplaced important documents. Then he'd pace through the house reciting out loud all the places he'd been and in what order. I'd watch him in silence, sometimes alone, sometimes with my mother. Then she'd call out the place he'd left it, and he'd wait a few moments, say the name of the place himself, as if he'd just thought of it, click his fingers, and go pick it up. Only then would he call out a loud thank you to my mother.

He started to play the trumpet, something he hadn't done, he said, since his childhood. On Saturday afternoons, dressed even then in his suit and bowtie, he'd sit on the side porch outside his son's empty room and blast off a few notes down the cobbled streets, smiling and waving at passersby, apparently convinced that they were in awe of his performance. Tourists would sometimes stray from their walking groups and stare at him, transfixed, as if he were a standard feature of the city, an attraction not to be missed. I saw the whole situation as I imagined my mother did—the reincarnation of an old curse. Here she was, married to another eccentric with a penchant for public displays of madness. But this, I soon realized, was a projection; my mother was completely unfazed by her new husband's behavior and watched him from a safe distance, sometimes sitting outside on the balcony with him as he played his trumpet. She rubbed his shoulders, and once I saw her sit on his lap. I woke one morning to find the two of them seated on the lounge floor doing yoga together, my mother easily flexing into the most difficult positions as Baptist Pants sweated and moaned, as he struggled to reach for his toes. Their intimacy and comfort was directly disproportionate to my own. These feelings began to tug at me, and I knew my journey was not complete, that I'd have to leave soon.

Then the nightmares started, spilling over into my waking life. Sticking out from the shadows at the room's edge, I'd see the toes of those black boots, the sacrificial night's dark sentry. But worse than this, when I tried to retreat to that place of perfect love, I met a boot also. At first this kick felt cruel, but with time I realized the love was still there, only it would not let me rest. So I tried to get myself together, but the world felt far away and I had no idea how I might reenter it. I slept badly and the days passed in a haze, but still I tried to find a thread to grab onto.

Since living in Charles's house, I'd sworn off news completely, terrified that something might have happened to Antoinette, but when it became clear I'd have to leave, I tried to reacquaint myself with the story of the present.

Diving back into the world online was disorienting and painful. The political situation had taken a tragic turn. Jefferson Lee III had founded a movement to replace the lame and ineffectual Constitutional Sheriff's Movement. Members of God's Sheriffs—the new name he'd given them— had won elections across the country and now controlled fifty-one counties. Lee put forward his successful campaign as a model and traveled the country appearing alongside members of the movement at ever-growing rallies. Money flowed in from small donors, concerned citizens who, as their website bragged, "Wanted to take back the country." In every town that God's Sherriff's won, mass arrests followed. The sheriffs claimed to answer to no one but God Himself. Images of vans filled with arrestees, fathers and mothers pulled away from children, filled the front pages of news sites, and videos of the same played on repeat across television networks. And everywhere there was misery there was Jefferson Lee III.

Checkpoints were set up across the towns they controlled, and stories of people being arrested for drug possession when they swore they'd never used drugs in their lives, flooded traditional and social media.

"Of course they say that," Jefferson Lee III said from behind his God's Sheriff's podium during one of his regular *Nightly Addresses*. "These people are drug addicts who've made it their lifetime's work to lie and to corrupt." The right lip smirk-curled upwards. "The problem is far worse than the average American realizes. We have been lied to. Too many of our police forces have grown ineffectual and corrupt. Politicians only lie. The media is born of lies. It cannot speak without lying." He adjusted his hat, leaning forward with both his hands on the podium. "Our towns and our cities have become so degraded and so corrupted that only God's Sheriffs, with the mandate of Heaven, and the mandate from you the people, can clean them up and retake them. So yes, expect to read more stories of arrests, and don't be surprised when the filth claims itself innocent, and the lying news media magnifies the deceit. They want you to believe that you are living in a very different kind of world than the one you really live in. But I know what kind of world we are really living in, and you know what kind of world we are living in. That's why if you are with us you have nothing to fear, and if you are against us, you have everything to fear."

The God's Sheriffs website had a map that showed all the counties under their control. An independent website, "Fallen to Fear," kept their own count, which essentially confirmed what was on the other website. The counties were concentrated in the Deep South, but they were scattered across the country, too. I'd ignored the media for forty days and the country had come to the brink of civil war.

Thursday evening at dinner, Charles announced he was leaving the next morning for a meeting of select Baptist Lawyers in Tennessee.

"A group of us are concerned about the direction the country's taking. These Sheriffs claim to be doing God's work, but we're not all convinced."

. . .

The next evening my mother and I were alone in the dining room. She wore a blue dress the same shade as the makeup on her eyelids, and pearl bracelets that matched her necklace. She'd poured us each a glass of brandy from Charles's crystal decanter—kept strictly for visitors—and opened the windows onto the street. I imagined us in 1861 on the eve of the Civil War, and then back here again—fixed in both times.

"A country can't survive two civil wars," I said—it felt like an eternal truth, a proclamation for the ages.

"Probably not," she said, in a tone that brought the statement down to a humbler size. "But there won't be a civil war. Not over this."

"What would my father have said?"

"I don't know. He could be dramatic. He might have agreed with you."

I smiled, taking a sip of my brandy. "I'm surprised."

"By what?"

"This place. By Charles."

"He's not so bad as you and your father thought."

"And you seem peaceful. Does this place make you happy?"

"This place? It brought me..." She looked around the room. "It was a place for me in this world. Somewhere I could belong."

"And Dad never found a place like that?"

"He was looking for somewhere that didn't exist."

"What was he looking for?"

"The home of culture. A place where a truly refined, high, exquisite culture, mature and complex, thrived."

"And he was disappointed by America?"

She shrugged.

"He kept moving further west. When he reached LA

there was nowhere further to go. It made sense that he died out there."

"I just wish I understood what was going on in his mind."

"Maybe you should return to his papers."

"I don't have them anymore. Doesn't that bother you? There's so much we haven't spoken about. It's as if we just agreed that whole time never happened."

"I have faith in you. In who you are and who you're going to become. You need to embrace your mission. No one's ever come closer to that by being forced to tell stories about their darkest days, and make them sound better or more mean- ingful than they actually were."

"Is that true? Don't all the old sages teach us that we have to first go down to the darkest place?"

"Go there, yes. But don't tell *me* about it. Because when we retell our worst stories, we always spin them. We can't help it. And the more you tell a story, the more you believe it to be true. You know what happened. You know where you went. That's your fuel. Protect it. Keep it safe. And know that I love you. That we both do and always will."

Only after the conversation did I realize how heavy that time drowned in silence had weighed on us. That night my mother had given me a gift, performed alchemy, like a Catholic Priest pardoning me for all my sins without my confessing any of them. But if the forgiveness had been given, the penance had still to be done. I had to go back in and complete my journey. At the climax of it all, I'd been unconscious.

I drank whisky that night, in my room and on the balcony. Looking down those old cobbled streets toward the sea, I felt the old comfort of drunken memories that seemed to outdate me by centuries, millennia. I wanted to speak to Antoinette, but I had no idea how to get hold of her, and I was terrified of what I'd learn if I tracked her down, and afraid of what she'd say to me. She would be the true confessional. The space in which I could not hide.

That Friday afternoon, Charles arrived back with his son, Daniel, down from D.C. for the weekend. I'd met Daniel once before, at Thanksgiving two years ago. He was a few years older than me, and had his life together in a way that made me feel like a seasoned loser. For the first time since coming out of the coma I felt tempted to check my bank account, but the thought of finding it empty, how weak that would make me feel (sweat erupted on my neck at the thought, and I pictured myself stammering) kept me in limbo. Daniel had recently received a promotion at work, and his girlfriend had said, "yes" — he was getting married next year, date to be confirmed. I could expect an invite.

What did I have to show for myself? No job; no money; not even a girlfriend. How had Charles described my current state to his son? *Going through some stuff; getting back on his feet; getting his life back in order*. All of which implied I had some prior functioning state to which I could return.

The only thing in my favor was Daniel's physical appearance. Like his father, he was overweight; he had multiple chins and a balloon face. That this made me feel temporarily better about myself made me feel ultimately far worse.

Baptist Pants offered an unusually verbose evening prayer, and then his son (Baptist Pants Junior, I thought, how I wished I could have shared that joke with my father) dominated dinnertime conversation. A bipartisan committee had been established to look into the rapid spread of God's Sheriffs. Early elections had been called across the country and their members had been winning counties with diverse political leanings. That they'd taken liberal counties in the North

East and on the West Coast flew in the face of contemporary political narratives. In these rich, progressive counties, the newly elected sheriffs and their deputies went after the poor.

"It's not surprising," Daniel said. "Residents in wealthy counties often vote for zoning regulations that keep the poor out of their neighborhoods. They call the common folk in red states racists and xenophobes. And sure, far as they're concerned everyone's welcome, and if you want to live in their neighborhood it's just a two-million-dollar entrance fee. Or, you can work there as a nanny. That's fine, too. Long as they buy organic honey and remember to publicly check their privilege twice a day, everything's fine. But the poor are getting pushy and loud. This is no good. God's Sheriffs can restore order."

"But they don't say it so directly, do they?" This was the first question I'd asked all evening.

"Of course not. As I said, they know the lingo and the act. It's quite impressive, from a Machiavellian perspective."

"We're not trying to point fingers in one direction or another," Charles said. "We're all human, all flawed. We're looking for solutions."

"We won't find solutions, Dad, until we name the problem. The media is still covering this as if it's purely a red state phenomenon. And it isn't. And that's what makes it interesting, and complicated."

"I love your passion, son.'

My mother smiled at me across the table. I raised my eyebrows comically, looked down into my food.

Daniel and I sat alone after dinner. He was a very different man, all the fervor of the dinner table had gone, and he spoke to me gently, like I was a sick person, unstable, in danger of falling into the darkness.

"You've been through so much," he said. "It's no wonder you're having a rough time."

"Yes, things are looking up."

"Good. Good. I heard you wrote a popular article. I've been meaning to read it."

"Yes, that's right. It was very popular." I felt like I was speaking about a different person. "They wanted a follow up."

"Have you written it?"

"It's, uh, in progress."

"Excellent. Any other plans? What comes next?"

"Maybe going back to school. Maybe heading out West."

"Well, if you ever need to talk."

"Yes."

"What your mother did for my father... She really helped him. He was in a bad way at one point."

"Yes."

The landscape we walked came into focus; we drew visible boundaries for our relationship—we were step-brothers; we'd make the pretense of being interested in one another's lives while clearly understanding that we'd not take our relationship a step further. The questions were a formality. He didn't care if I was getting back on my feet or if I was eternally down. But if I had money, if I was worth sixteen million dollars, self-made, then he would care. All my words would have meaning, my opinions would be relevant. He'd invite me to stay up with him, talking about the work of the bipartisan committee, sensitive to my response.

Instead we called it an evening, and I watched him waddle off to bed. On my balcony I drank whisky.

It was time for me to write the follow-up article. As I sat down at my desk, I knew that this one had to be different. I needed to tell the truth. All night I worked on it, leaving out nothing. I'd tell the world about Maggie, about the work they did on her island, about the truth of gods and sacrifice. But when I'd completed it, I felt ashamed. I couldn't send it off.

· · ·

I fell asleep with a half-drunk glass of whisky next to my bed. I slipped into a dream, where I felt the dark presence all around me. I saw the boot toes and the tip of the hat. And that perfect light that had once pulled me now pushed harder, until I woke gasping for air, my chest covered in sweat. I knew I had to leave.

I struggled to find my mother that day, and when I did she was alone, in the haberdashery-room-cum-mausoleum, seated on the old white rocking chair, hands folded neatly in her lap. It was an unnatural position for her, too docile and uncombative. She looked sad.

"I know you have to leave," she said.

As there were no other chairs, and sitting on the perfectly-manicured bed that I assumed had not been made since his first wife had died would feel like committing rape, I sat on the floor, at my mother's feet. In the weak light of the room, I saw streaks of grey in her hair, and the skin on the back of her hands looked older.

She smiled. "You have my blessing, if that's what you came for."

"You know I have to go."

"I do. It's just been so good having you here. The house will empty out with you gone. Charles enjoyed having you around."

"I enjoyed spending time with you."

"He's not so bad, is he?"

"No, he's not."

"I'm just going to miss you so much." She teared up suddenly, and wiped below her eyes. "I'm sorry. We weren't always this sappy, were we?"

"Come on." I squeezed her foot. "It's not like I'm going to another planet."

"Go do what you have to do," she said, making a shooing motion with her hand as she smiled. As I got to the door she called my name. "Answers to difficult problems come slowly, and then all at once."

I nodded.

She must have said something about my plans to Charles, for that night before evening prayers, he said, "I suspect you'll be leaving us soon."

"The time is right."

He prayed for longer than usual and asked that God watch over me as I traveled through this troubled land in these uncertain times. After dinner he took me aside and gave me an envelope, unsealed and clearly packed full of one hundred dollar notes. Did he think I was too primitive for a bank account?

"Charles, I can't."

"If it troubles you, think of it as coming from your mother. Take it for her sake, at least." He paused, then spoke fast, clearly uncomfortable. "It's from Daniel, also. From your family."

"What for?"

"It's a dangerous world out there." He put his hand on my shoulder, and I caught a whiff of aftershave, a flash of bowtie. "And you, son, well, you don't have the same advantages as a young man your age in his own country, with connections and access to networks. These things, son, in the end, amount to money."

"But we're all expected to make our own way. Isn't that what this country is all about? To make our own way and have some money to show for it."

"That makes up some part of it. But you must understand, well, of course you already do understand, that we don't all begin in the same place."

"What if I told you I had money?"

"Come on, Marcel."

"Would you respect me then?"

"I respect you now."

"You pity me."

My mother, I saw, watched us from the stairwell, hidden at this angle to him but not me.

"I don't pity you. All humans are worthy of respect, regardless of... something superficial like money."

"In theory, yes. But not in practice. You know that." He lowered the hand holding the envelope. "And it doesn't matter how you get it. Money is its own justification."

"Not true, son. A man must earn his money in a noble fashion."

"What's noble to one man is a racket to another. Money speaks for itself on its own terms. It is its own justification. There are only a few... only a few ways."

"A few ways, what?"

"A few ways that don't count. A few ways that require... additional proof. The one that holds the treasure is not yet a hero. That's why I'm in the state I'm in..." I started to pace, but just then caught sight of my mother on the stairwell, making a downward motion with her hand that meant, I knew, calm down, don't rant, don't go mad like your father. "That's why all the gods need to attach themselves to money. That's how they arm you and cheer you on. That's how they break you."

"Our God does not care about money. That's not what matters to Him. What matters is your soul."

"Maybe so."

"Marcel, you've been through so much. It's not fair, I know. It's totally unfair. But life is... life can be unfair. So don't think about the money as being the primary gift. You need a solid grounding." He took a small leather bound bible from his pocket. "Christ is Lord. He is perfectly good. He entered our sin-filled, wretched world, and met humanity on our own terms. The one who preaches non-violence died a violent death. But in his death our sins are forgiven. Past, present, and future. Those distinctions lose meaning. All time is woven together through Him, and in Him all things are resolved." He placed the envelope inside the bible and handed it to me. "God offered up His son as a sacrifice."

"To whom?"

"*For* whom is the question. For us. For all of us, so that sins may be forgiven."

"But the world is full of evil. It didn't get any better."

"No Christian denies the problem of evil. God did not take away our free will. He respected us too much. To have done so, would have been to take away what made us human. But sadly, all humans are sinners."

"That's why there's evil in the world?"

"And because of the enemy. We cannot, of course, discount the enemy." He shuddered, wiping his face with the palm of his hand. "Take this gift, please."

"I'm uncomfortable taking this from you."

"It's a gift, freely given."

"What if I don't accept it?"

He paused, sighed. "We'll pray for you either way. But please, take the gift. I don't want you to be lost."

I took it from him. He wrapped his arms around me, and pulled me tight.

The next morning Daniel and Charles helped me pack my bags into the car.

"You have good taste, brother," Daniel said. "1970 Ford Torino."

It had been parked in a storage garage the whole time I'd

been here. Charles had paid for a driver to bring it up from Mobile. Daniel, apparently, did not know of its existence.

"I bought it on a whim."

My mother hung back as I exchanged handshakes and hugs with the two men, appearing at my window a moment before I drove off.

"I love you. Trust yourself," she said.

"I love you, too. And yes, I'll try to."

CHAPTER 25

I'd turned down a rural side road on the border of South Carolina and Georgia—following my GPS to a gas station—when I saw the lights flashing in my mirrors. After pulling over in the dust, I watched the sheriff's deputy taking his sweet time in the black SUV before ambling towards my car. I realized then how stupid I was not to have planned my trip around avoiding fallen counties. I had no idea who I was about to speak to.

"License and registration." He wasn't much older than me, with a unibrow and faded acne marks.

"Doing you a favor. You just about to cross that line. Our sheriff has us stopping folk like yourself as a courtesy. Look ahead."

Just short of the gas station, a few hundred feet off, were three black sheriff's vehicles.

"Them folk's a bunch of savages. They'll arrest you for nothing. Throw you in lockup with no bail. Here's the latest map of fallen counties in South Carolina, Georgia, and Tennessee. Our sheriff has us print 'em out each morning and hand 'em out to folk like you."

"Can't tell you how much I appreciate it."

"We almost come to shots with them fallen deputies a few times. Just a few weeks back we was friends. Drank beer and played pool. Now they's like a bunch a zombies."

I saw the sign demarcating the start of the new county. One of their sheriff's deputies got out of his car and stood cross-armed.

"Last county 'fore Georgia, that one. You headed ta Georgia?"

"Planning to stay the night outside Atlanta."

"Here's what you gotta do." He drew a line on the map. "Take you a couple extra hours but it'll save you a world of trouble. Some folk drive through these counties without a problem, but other folk find theirselves in chains."

I thanked the man and went on my way.

That powerful sense of freedom, that soaring joy I'd always known when driving through this country, was gone. A blown out tire or a single wrong turn could land me in prison. I felt a rush of anger with my mother, with Charles, with Daniel even. Why had they let me go? This was not the country it had been just a few months ago.

I checked into a Motel 6 on the outskirts of Atlanta at 9pm, paying for a night's accommodation with one of the notes Charles had given me.

Since she'd been released on bail, there'd been no more articles about Antoinette, but I knew where she was. Lauderdale County, home to Florence, Alabama, had not been taken by God's Sheriffs, but there was no way to enter it without passing through at least one fallen county. Lauderdale was situated in the very northwest corner, next to a fallen Alabama county and below a fallen county in Tennessee. According to the Fallen To Fear website, the Tennessee county had more arrests. The site offered a disclaimer and acknowledged its limited capacity—it relied largely on social media and reports from friends and family of arrestees. But I had nothing else to go on, and if I was going to get arrested it might as well be in Alabama, as close to Antoinette as possible.

I had a restless night, drifting along the boundary of the dreamworld and the land of the awake, never quite sure which was which. I saw boots sticking out the edge of shadows. I saw Antoinette once, sitting at a table beneath a live oak, drinking her special mixture, but when I tried to reach out to her she vanished. Then I woke up fully, filled with doubt and confusion. What if she wasn't in Florence? I had no evidence, only a powerful hunch. But no, she had to be there. It was her hometown; her father was a slain officer, which had to buy her some protection. The town had resisted God's Sheriffs. Like my mother had said, I had to trust myself.

I ate breakfast on the other side of Atlanta, bought some 5-Hour Energy drinks and a pack of cigarettes. I followed back roads through Tennessee and stopped at a gas station three miles short of the Alabama border, took a piss, splashed my face, smoked two cigarettes.

I could get through Limestone County into Lauderdale in just under thirty minutes, sticking to back roads. I drank one of my energy drinks, turned up the radio, and blasted toward the state line. My stomach tightened; I felt sweat on the lower side of my forearms and palms. Two miles along this main drag until the off-ramp. I don't know exactly what I'd been expecting, but everything looked normal—the cars, the roads, the trees, and the sky. If I hadn't known this was a fallen county, there'd be nothing to tell me. Knowing what I knew, my mind put blue lights atop every black car, and a patrol vehicle in every shadow.

Up an off-ramp, I turned left then right down a winding tree-filled lane with no other cars. This was the deepest of the Deep South. A hundred yards between each trailer home, semi-trucks parked in the yards, Confederate flags, swing tires hanging from live oaks, yard dogs on chains. I drove 30 miles per hour. I came to a very sharp curve that forced me to slow down almost to a stop. From an old white house, rotting in the ground, a man dragged a woman by her hair and threw her like a bag of trash into a ditch. My heart kicked against my chest as I heard the sound of three gunshots. And I would have stopped, I swear I would have, if at that moment a black police car had not appeared from behind a clump of trees. He must have seen the shooting, surely, but it was me he came after.

At first he kept his distance, traveling at my pace. As we turned a slow bend I saw, for the first time, the badge I'd only seen on television and online—gold letters on black, *God's Sheriffs*. He flashed his lights and sped past me, hit his brakes. My car filled with the smell of burning.

I hit the accelerator and flew to the left, past the cop. Then came the sound of screeching sirens. Blue lights bounced off the mirrors and I might have been in some strange disco, walking across the smoky room to ask a girl to dance. The car had filled with smoke; I was smoking; I'd cracked open a can of iced coffee I didn't remember buying. My wheels hit the dirt. I skidded left and right across the road, still keeping ahead of the sheriff's deputy. Seven minutes, then five. A slow car in the road. I raced to the left, missed a head-on collision with a black truck by ten feet, buying myself some distance from the cop.

The sign for Lauderdale appeared on the horizon. According to my GPS it was only five hundred feet away. I pressed the pedal right down to the floor and felt the engine's hum wrap around me. My speedometer clocked one hundred and ten miles per hour as I crossed the county line. My pursuer stopped short, and I was cheered on by the Lauderdale Sheriff's Deputies who stood outside their vans, drinking large sodas and eating chips, apparently not giving a shit about the fact I was speeding in their quiet county.

I drove slowly over the old railway bridge and looked down at the Tennessee River below, flanked by sheer cliffs; fishing boats floated in the dark water. The bridge—I'd read last night when planning my route—had been badly damaged in the Civil War, and yet, here it stood.

I felt alive, ticking with purpose, as I checked into an expensive hotel downtown. My room had a view of the bridge and river, and a street lined with bars and restaurants. I lay for an hour in the bath, the image of the woman thrown into the ditch playing on repeat. I tried to convince myself it hadn't really happened. For if it had, then surely I'd be obliged to do something about it, to report it to someone. But who the hell could I report it to? God's Sheriffs? The thought made my head rush. I imagined her crashing into the dirt, turning up to see her attacker raising his gun and firing down at her, and the policeman ignoring it. It was too much. I had to get out of my head. I drank two double whiskies and felt the intensity of the image fade.

I had dinner near the hotel and listened in on conversations —students mostly, my age and younger—talking about the route they had to take to get out of the county. Some said they never left, others suggested the whole thing had been exaggerated.

I spent two days and nights roaming the streets, hanging out in coffee shops, bars, restaurants, hoping I might run into

Antoinette. In Stagg's Grocery I walked the aisles and imagined her just a few feet ahead. I picked up a bottle of rosé, wondering if she'd taken the one next to it. I could feel her there.

That night on the balcony, drinking Antoinette's special mixture, I made up my mind. The next morning I went to the police station. Near the entrance was the wall of fallen heroes, with a few framed photographs, including one of Sergeant Waylon D. Dubois. He had her eyes, her hair. He did have a slightly crazy look about him, but then Antoinette also had a crazy look in her eyes, didn't she?

"That man over there." I pointed at his picture.

A bulky male police officer, with shaved hair, early thirties perhaps, sat at the reception desk. "What 'bout him?"

"I hear he was killed in the line of duty."

"That why he on the wall."

"I wonder if you could do me a favor."

He stared at me, silent. Blinked.

"I'm a good friend of his daughter."

"Mkay."

"I've been trying to find her. I suspect she's staying in the house she used to stay in with her father."

"Mkay."

"I have no other way of contacting her. I was wondering if you could perhaps tell me where their house is."

He turned and shouted: "Colby."

An older man with a moustache appeared at his side.

"This man here searchin' for Sergeant Dubois's daughter."

"What business you got with her?"

"I was her friend. I am her friend. I think."

He looked me up and down. "What you mean by friend?"

"I rented a room from her back in Chickasaw."

He paused a long moment. "Come with me." He led me into an interrogation room and shut the door. "That man up there was my partner. You got big balls coming down to a police station asking for a girl's whereabouts. I got half a mind to lock you up for the night."

"I didn't know who else to ask."

"Where you from?"

"South Africa. Originally."

"You a crazy son of a bitch. Who the heck comes asking police to help him find a girl?" He pulled me up from the table, slammed me against the wall and cuffed my wrists, marched me back through the station, and called out to the fat officer: "I'm putting him away for the night. Disturbing the peace by means of intoxication."

"I'm not drunk."

"You drunk if I say you drunk."

"But I'm not drunk."

I shook about trying to get free of his grip.

"Try proving that in court in three months' time."

I was locked up in a tiny cell all by myself, given a shitty meal. I got a few hours of sleep despite the constant hollering and slamming of cell doors.

The same officer woke me early the next morning and led me onto the street. He gave me a lit cigarette and handed me a box of matches. I flipped the box over and saw an address written in black pen.

"I ain't spoken to her, but I heard some rumors she was seen at her pa's old place. And maybe you a good man who can brighten things up for her, and maybe you ain't. Done some thinking last night, and reckoned it ain't for me to decide. But I'm going to tell you something and make sure you hear me real good. That gal's her old pa's daughter. Don't know if you know what that means, but let me 'splain it to you real nice. I find you floating in the Tennessee River, don't matter how many holes you got in the back of your head, I'm calling it suicide and closing the case. And she sure as heck knows that."

"Got it. Thanks for the cigarette."

I put the address into my phone. It was outside the town, close to the county line, on the opposite side from where I'd entered. I thought about the officer's strange monologue. Had he been trying to warn me not to go there? I did not doubt his sincerity nor Antoinette's capacity for shooting me between the eyes, or in the back of the head.

By mid-afternoon I'd drunk a bottle and a half of rosé and although the alcohol had suppressed my most active fears, I knew I was in no state to visit her.

I woke early from a night of nightmares—scenes of the swamp; Antoinette shooting guns; something with dark eyes watching from the murky edges. I showered, smoked, drank two cups of coffee, and got into my car. I picked up a few bottles of rosé and ginger ale, and practiced my introductory remarks out loud. A catalogue of clichés—*I can explain; it's not what it seems; I had a plan all along.*

Her house was at the end of a dirt lane—white paint peeling off wooden slats, a screen porch with insect netting so thick and dark I couldn't tell if she was sitting behind it—on a chair, gun in hand. The garden was unkempt, and I'd have assumed the house was abandoned but for the fact her car was there, parked in a dirt lot behind a black Chevy, probably from the 1950s, that sat halfway out a shed with a collapsed roof overgrown with brambles and weeds.

Grass brushed against my knees as I walked up to the black mold-speckled porch door. In the crease of my hand that held the plastic bag with wine in it, I felt my heartbeat. My whole body was clammy. Had I come back from almost death so I could be shot? I hit the back of my hand against the mangy door.

"Antoinette."

My ears rang. In the distance a dog barked.

"Antoinette."

I pulled the door open, letting it shut behind me. Two old rocking chairs sat on either side of an upturned crate. A single glass with a half inch of her special red mixture lay next to an ashtray filled with butts. I knocked on the house door, pressing my face to one of the fingerprint-stained glass panes.

"Antoinette."

I pushed the door open, stepping into a dingy room where the only light came from behind me and through cracks in the thick curtains over the windows. In front of me I saw a kitchen that led into a lounge that had been used as a bedroom; the couch was covered with duvets and pillows. To my right, a round wooden table strewn with bowls, coffee mugs, mason jars, ashtrays, magazines and newspapers. Green mold-lined cups; chunks of cereal hardened and blackened against the edges of bowls. The room had not been aired out in a long time. The stale scent of smoke and weed smell permeated everything.

I moved further into the house. "Antoinette," I said softly.

Cold metal pressed against the back of my head.

"What I say to you that night in my bedroom?"

"I don't remember."

"What I say?" she hissed into my ear.

"We spoke about many things. I've come here to talk to you."

"What I said was if a bad man ever showed up at my house, I'm going to shoot him. Turn 'round."

I turned and stepped back from her. There she was, in crumpled dungarees, hair messed, eyes red. From the table next to her she picked up a box of cigarettes and fumbled to get one out, striking the lighter three, four times before it took.

"Sit your ass down on that couch."

"The one with... the duvets and pillows?"

"Sit down."

She dragged a crate across the room with her foot and sat down in front of me as I sank into the marshy couch. She exhaled into my face, then pulled back the gun's hammer and pressed the barrel between my eyes. The skin below her eyes looked dark and crinkled, her lips dry and chapped, her hair unwashed. Three times she exhaled smoke into my face without moving the gun or opening her mouth.

"Are you waiting for me to speak?"

"Do you think..." She took a final drag of her cigarette and dropped the butt into a half empty coffee mug. "Do you think I'm angry with you?"

"Yes, I think you are."

"Why you think that?"

"That's why I came back, so we could... talk."

I instinctively moved my hands and tried to stand up.

"Sit down."

The room opened up around me as I tasted blood in my throat. I thought: She hasn't made up her mind not to kill me.

"What happened that night... it was not meant to be like that."

"What *did* happen that night?"

"You want me to tell you... the events?"

Without breaking eye contact or moving the gun from my head, she lit another cigarette. "Go on..."

"Those men... they didn't tell me they were going to do that."

"Do what?"

"Pull you away like that."

"No, Marcel. Tell it like it happened. You was telling me you loved me. Then we was making out and next thing you have me in the back of a fucking car."

Her hand trembled as she spoke.

"No, I didn't push you in. I swear I didn't mean that to happen."

"You son of a bitch."

Cigarette clamped between her teeth, she slapped me across the face. Slapped me again.

"In the trunk of that old car. Driven me out to the swamp, drugged me, tied me up. Out into the darkness. You were all going to rape me weren't you?"

"Never! I untied you. I saved you."

"Saved me?" She laughed.

"I swam with you across the water. In the pitch dark. I hid you from those people."

"When I woke up it was morning. Light shining into that old shed. I found me a hammer and I was going to smash your brain to pieces for what you done to me."

"When I woke up you were gone."

"If I killed you there, I'd've of gone to prison. Not so here. Why'd you come here, Marcel?"

"I kept thinking about you. It's true what I told you."

"Shut up."

I felt a rush of confidence like I had that night in her kitchen.

"Remember how Bryson, that guest of yours, came bursting in? I didn't plan that. How could I have? And if not for him you'd never have run outside."

"You had your finger inside me, mother fucker!" She slapped me again. "I gone to church all my life."

"I didn't plan for them to take you like that."

"What did you plan for?"

"I didn't have a plan."

"Finally, something true."

"I had other plans. I have other plans... And I'm alive because of what happened the next night. Somebody saved me."

"Sergeant Franklin dead. Tran Tran Sui dead. That piece a shit calls himself Helena, dead." She held the gun a few inches from my face, turned it sideways. "All this baby over here. I can tell you what each one looked like. Bullet holes like this." She made a circle with her fingers. "Blood streaming out nice and slow. Brains looking like shit come out your nose. Franklin still twitching like he was having an orgasm. Fact of the matter, his cock gone hard too. Pissed their pants, shat their pants. Wanna hear more?"

"That's okay."

She pointed her cigarette finger around the room. "Look at this now. I can't sleep proper, eat good, can't even take a real shit without seeing their bleeding heads, and their dead faces. After all I tried to outrun, turned out just the same as my daddy. Me and him, just the same now. Just the same."

"You're not the same as him."

Without covering her mouth she coughed hard and turned my pants speckled red.

"You okay?"

"I told you already. Don't you listen?"

She sounded coarser than ever, her accent even more Southern. She wiped her mouth with the back of her hand.

"They was all working for the same man," she said, getting to her feet. She stepped back with the gun still pointed at my head.

"Who?"

"Tran. Helen. Helena. All working for Jefferson Lee."

"That doesn't make any sense. He wanted them shut down, arrested."

"He wanted to test 'em. See if they was worthy. They all know'd it. Even Magdalena known it."

"What about Sheriff Jones?"

"He dead. Died in a *boating accident*." She made scare quotes with her smoking hand. "Died two days after the election. Real story, best as I can figure it, they took him to the station and beat him with clubs, till his head was bloody like a squashed mango, and his eyes came out the sockets."

"Holy shit. He was so sweet. I thought, at first I thought, that maybe he'd been shot. Then I found out he was alive, and..."

"Why did you think that?"

"I... had a dream. That's all."

"Pfff."

"What about Maggie?"

"They ain't killed her. She been held without bail. Alabama maximum security prison. She ain't never going to see the light of day again." She coughed into her hand, and her crimson palm became visible as she pointed at me. "You was going be a sacrifice. A worthy sacrifice."

"So were you."

"We ain't get to choose who is and who ain't. But seems like there was something about the two of us."

"We've both met him, in his... primal form. That's what Maggie told me; what Magdalena told me."

Antoinette did not respond; she walked away, turned to face me, dropped her cigarette on the floor, and crushed it.

"But it's too late for any of that now. Jefferson ain't the man folk think he is. Don't matter what they say, don't matter what they preach, most folk don't believe we live in the kind a world where Jefferson could exist. I mean, where the thing Jefferson Lee really is, could really be."

"So what are we going to do about it?"

A smile crept across Antoinette's face. "I'm glad to hear you speak that way."

I smiled. She put the gun down.

"As you know, Jefferson Lee the third is taking 'em county by county. They falling to him like plague victims. One, two, three..." She clicked her fingers as she spoke. "Now my brothers and sisters down at this station, they stand strong. They're real tough and they'll fight to keep this county. I'm safe here. But outside, well, hell, I don't know for sure, since I ain't seen nobody but you in the longest time, but I can use my God-given thinking, and I can well surmise there's a warrant for me in each state a the union. I do know that I'm a suspect in a triple homicide. And I do know I watched the brains leak out with my own two eyes. Guilty as Cain. As for the counties where there ain't no arrest warrant, well those are Lee's folk, and they sure as heck wanna see me hang."

I let the silence hang a moment, then asked: "Can I have a cigarette?"

She nodded. I breathed deeply, trying to steady my hand before I asked the next question: "Do you accept my apology?"

"How you going to ask that before you even given it?"

"I'm sorry for what happened that night." I paused a moment. "For what I did that night."

"Well, there we go."

"You accept it?"

"You wanna be useful, go buy some food. Make me a proper meal."

I jumped up, elated at the chance to work toward my redemption.

"What do you want to eat?"

"If I got to think that through, tell you what to get, I might as well do it myself." She spat into the cup-cum-ashtray, lighting herself a cigarette. "Don't forget the wine and ginger ale."

"I already bought some."

"Get more. And don't forget," she said as I stepped onto the porch, "when the gods are contrary, they stand by no one."

It was only hours later after I'd returned from the shop that I realized where that line came from.

"My father's notes. Sortes Virgilianae. How did you know that?"

"What you think happened to your father's papers?"

We sat opposite one another at the dirty kitchen table. I'd spent the last hour throwing out pounds of bad food, some rotten to brown liquid, some covered in multi-colored mold. I washed her rusty fridge and grime-stained cupboards, re-filling them with the produce I'd bought.

"I don't know what happened to his papers. I assumed they were gone. Confiscated. Destroyed. Lost in evidence at the police station."

"And you're okay with that? This was your inheritance. Your daddy left this for you. He mentions you, and you just left it behind."

"I didn't have a choice."

"*I* went back there, risked being shot or who knows what. I done it for *you*. Why'd I do that?"

"I don't know."

"Me either."

She stood up, looking around, distracted, like she'd just recalled some distant memory.

"But I did do it. I chose to do it, so I shouldn't be angry

with you. Not for that. I need some time alone. Let's eat dinner at eight."

I did my best to prepare a decent meal for her—chicken breasts, peppers, rice and beans, cooked on a stove that kept tripping and turning off.

"You done well with the food," she said, but didn't eat any. After the meal passed, mostly in silence, in her depressed living room, I had to scrape away the leftovers.

She seemed so down, so lifeless, and the longer I stayed around her the more I felt this way, too, as if the house poured its darkness into whoever came into it.

"Please show me my father's notes and books."

She'd stored them all in a spare room at the back of the house. With a bottle of whisky as my companion I settled in for a night of reading. Between patches of silence, I heard Antoinette coughing violently, weeping at times. I did my best to ignore the feelings of terrible sorrow this evoked in me— she'd lost her vitality, her beautiful vibrancy. Instead I focused all my energy into my father's notes, skimming through the books I'd seen in his apartment until I found one that somehow I'd missed. Those movers must really have dug deep when packing up the office. I felt ashamed I'd not found it, guilty even. Antoinette was right: this was my inheritance. This moment had come to me from every direction, and when every contra- dictory stream collided, finally something would make sense.

I read about Jung and Dunne. In the Boer War, my father wrote, the night before Dunne had his prophetic vision about the volcano, he had a vivid dream of an angel. This was signif- icant. Although it had been mostly forgotten to history, when fighting against Russia as a young man, camped out in the tundra, René Descartes too had been visited in a dream by an angel who told him the laws of the universe would be revealed through measurement and number. Why have we removed this from the story, my father asked? The "grandfather" of the scientific method, of rationalism, got his marching orders from a celestial being. This would disturb our world too much. But Mohammed was visited by an angel, as was Joseph Smith, and of course Mary and Joseph both.

And what about sacrifice? Not metaphorical, but real sacrifice. We have done these. We sacrifice and we compact. These are not the same thing. The good gods ask for sacrifices, and then give you something in return. The evil gods compact. They give you what you want first then demand repayment. But the good gods can cause just as much, or even greater harm. *My people*, he said—I'd never seen him describe his ancestors that way—my people were offered as a sacrifice so that the British could control the gold and continue to fund their empire. No gold no cities, no cities, no cathedrals. No place for God to rest his weary bones. But who should be sacrificed? Maybe the evil gods sometimes demand the same? Dunne had prophetic dreams, and he used his visions to invest in gold stocks back home in London. He became rich, but in the end he was plagued by demons. Why do I feel sympathy for this man? Why do I keep writing about him? I think it's because, although he's fallen out of fashion, Dunne came close to understanding the true nature of consciousness. These days I look back at all my books attempting to offer mechanistic explanations for history, and all I see is a man trying to give the world what he thought it wanted from him, and failing. These days when I sit alone and drift I have moments where I see history for what it truly is, a river that flows, a spider web covered with dew, flowers that blossom and die. Primitive attempts to break the flow, the sequence, the cycle, made more sense than do our modern games. What could stop time and history if not the creator of the universe allowing himself to be sacrificed? The greatest good sacrificed to the greatest good.

But what is my role? Do I simply have to accept and submit? Or am I called on to so something great? To show the truth to a new age? To an angry age, one that says: Come, let us find the bad one, and pluck him out.

Narratives are always bound to contradict one another, and historical narratives are no better than political fantasies, or tales spun by creative minds. Contradicting narratives cause turmoil, hatred and war. So no, I have decided, narratives will not save us. Story is not our savior. Story turns minds against one another. Here lies the problem with the metaphorical sacrifice: It is a story. The correct sacrifice must be real and it must free us from narrative, and so free us from history.

This is where the book ended. An asterisk suggested the notes picked up somewhere else, but none of the other books appeared to open with anything that might reasonably follow on from that. In the margins, in a different color pen he'd scribbled S.V. II 165. I knew that line by heart: *Who had death in store? Whom did Apollo call for? Now the man of Ithaca haled Calchas out among us in tumult, calling on the seer to tell the true will of the gods.*

Was this note for me? I wondered, as I finished my glass of whisky; I'd tried before to think of myself as Sinon, the one chosen for sacrifice who managed to escape—at least that was the story he told, even as we, the readers know it is a false narrative. And here I was, escaped from sacrifice, too, and once before that, my soul had been returned to my body after its departure time had passed. But I was not a liar like Sinon. So then, I concluded as I refilled my glass, the objective was not to focus on the lie, but to consider what came because of this lie. The gates of Troy were opened and the long and bloody war came to a violent, brutal end. I had to accept that this ending, too, would have to be violent.

In the morning I woke with no hangover, feeling powerful, my thoughts clear, my vision solid before me.

"Antoinette." I touched her shoulder and she woke, sitting and wiping blood from her mouth. "We have to kill Jefferson Lee III. No matter how risky. No matter how violent."

She nodded and smiled, running her blood-speckled hand across my arm.

"'Course we do. Why else'd we both of us live?"

Over the next few days I watched Antoinette's vibrancy return as we studied the expansion of Jefferson Lee and God's Sheriffs across the United States. Although the counties fell in a somewhat haphazard manner, they followed a clear westward trajectory. We converted the room in which she'd stored my father's boxes into a work room, with an enormous map that had belonged to her father, with all the counties in the country, stuck over two walls. We shaded in the fallen counties and numbered them in the order they'd fallen. At night we'd watch Jefferson Lee's speeches on his campaign trail. He was fluent in the language of the Second Amendment, border protection, criminal illegals, God, America, the right of the fetus and the hoax that was Global Warming. None of this was surprising, but what shocked us both was the ease with which he inhabited the inverse language. In one rally he checked his own privilege, spoke about diversity and inclusion and equity while endorsing a woman of color, insisted on the importance of anti-racism training, shook his head as he decried the dangerous myths that reproduced toxic masculinity, white privilege, male privilege; he checked himself again as he spoke about the importance of intersectionality, ending with a chant of "no person is illegal."

When asked about his contradictory positions, he denied he'd said the things he said. His words, he said, were taken out of context, deliberately distorted or manipulated. Which clips had been distorted? It depended who asked and where. These answers were themselves later denounced, and then again embraced, then denounced. No one knew what he'd said or what he hadn't said, and so it seemed people decided for themselves who he was, and that's who he remained.

Although when drawn out the route looked like the trail of a squirming snake, it was still possible to cross the country to Lee's next campaign without passing through more than three fallen counties. While he did appear at major rallies, proxies of his were able to win over smaller counties in his absence, and the longer we waited, the thicker the ivy of the fallen counties wrapped itself over the country. In nine days' time he'd be giving a speech outside Flagstaff, Arizona, hoping to win Coconino County for God's Sheriffs. Two days later he'd appear in Los Angeles for what was the most anticipated sheriff's election since the movement started.

"We need more guns," Antoinette said. "Two days' time, two counties across." She pointed at the map. "Biggest gun show in North Alabama. I'll give you a list of what we need."

"How much will it cost?"

"For what we need? Five or six thousand. You still broke?"

"I'll make a plan."

"And you need to restock the house again. Get a carton a cigarettes."

"Yes, ma'am."

Although working together on this scheme had brought us closer again, I felt like my every action was also an apology. I'd bring her dinner (which she didn't eat) and drinks, clean up afterwards. Once in a while she'd sigh loudly, say, "I'll do that," then rinse a plate, wipe it down with her hand, and leave it on the counter. One afternoon I saw her wriggling her shoulders and offered to massage them.

"It's all right," she said, and went to smoke alone on her porch.

I wanted her to give me something to help make sense of what we were, but I had nothing to call her toward. We'd never been anything with a name; we'd never belonged to one another.

One evening as we sat together—as we usually did, in silence—I ate, and she picked at her dinner. The weight of the dark house pressed down on us terribly. Her father's ghost. Her mother. Antoinette as a child. I asked if we could smoke our evening cigarettes on the porch, and we drank 'til midnight.

"Are we doing the right thing?" I asked her.

"Why else're we both here?"

"There could be many reasons. I could help us get away, live a better life, without worrying about... anything."

"Not yet, you can't."

"What if I told you... I really could?"

"People everywhere are like you and me. They're all living like this."

I looked through the screen door at the bugs swarming around the porch light. They'd all be dead by morning. I'd read an account once of Stalin sitting at his desk reading a long list of names of men and women sentenced to die, and him asking, who will remember these people? No one, no one, he answered. No one will remember them.

"They can feel the shadows pressing down on 'em," Antoinette said. "But they don't know how to peel 'em off."

I was silent for a few minutes as I finished my drink. In the distance, a siren wailed.

"I'm so sorry for what I did that night."

She was quiet as she finished her drink.

"You can come sleep with me tonight," she said. Blood raced through my body.

She cleaned the dishes, threw away the cigarette stumps. I brushed my teeth, splashed my face. Her bedroom smelt damp; the unwashed sheets had been sweated into. We lay close together, fully clothed, and once I tried to kiss her neck and run my hand down her stomach, over her pants. She rolled away from me, clutching her pillow. In the night she coughed and once I heard her crying. I put my arms around her then, and she held my hands in hers.

I dreamed I was with my father on a hill, like the place we'd sat together for the last time; the sea was visible in the distance, but it was blood red, the sky black. Then a hand with a knife came through the sky and someone was stabbed, and I looked to my father, but he'd gone and my hands were covered with blood.

In the early dawn light leaking through the cracks in the old yellow curtains, we lay face to face, Antoinette and I, our toes and fingers touching, our breath mixing. My heart pounded heavily.

"This is a crazy thing to do."

"Sure is. Also, it's the right thing to do."

"I don't want others to get hurt. I thought I could see past that. But I can't."

"We're gonna do our best."

"Where will we find him?"

"I known him forever. I know where he'll be. Old silver trailer. He's gonna be in there. He needs to recover sometimes. Needs his time alone. That's where we going to kill him." She pulled herself close to me, rubbing herself against me and breathing into my ear. "We'll be much better soon. We'll have everything we want."

On the way to the gun show, driving along a quiet country lane, I pulled over. I was in a safe county; I'd be okay. I had the cash from Charles and that would be enough to buy the guns, but that didn't matter. I needed to know I had the money—I needed a sign. It'd been so long since I'd checked, I couldn't believe it would still be there. My toes crunched up in my sweaty shoes as my eyes closed, and when I opened them it was there. Fifteen million, nine hundred and ninety-seven thousand dollars.

Heart flaring, I drove like a demon along the winding roads to the gun show. I revved my engine in the grass parking lot and walked to the convention center with mechanical springs in my knees. So full of life, I chatted to men in the line around me. Most of them were middle-aged and podgy, with jeans, black or checkered shirts, and NRA Lifetime member hats. One man in front of me sat in an electric wheeler, others waddled, a few were young, some skinny, and there were a few women.

Inside, the spirit of glee had me whistling through the massive hall past hundreds of tables and thousands of guns. Armed with two AR-15s (and the basic knowledge of how to convert them into fully automatic weapons), two small handguns, a long-distance high-powered rifle with scope, and enough bullets to start and end a war, I left the show in higher spirts even than I'd arrived. I drove home at a reasonable speed, windows open, country music blasting.

Antoinette was pleased. We sat in the long grass of her garden, drank her special mixture, smoked cigarettes, and laughed.

That night we slept together, our faces close. After hours of play and innocent rubbing, our tongues met; I tasted the blood in her mouth. She pulled away quickly, coughing into the pillow. I held her from behind and in that way we fell asleep.

The next morning I bought eggs and bacon, bagels and champagne. We opened the curtains, letting the light stream into the dark house.

"We can be happy," I said to her.

"So close now."

The next morning we set off at dawn, sun at our backs, car filled with the hot stench of burning flesh.

"Dad," I said when we'd stopped at a gas station and Antoinette was out of the car. "I hope this sets you free."

We drove west then south, criss-crossing over the Tennessee River, before taking a sharp north up towards Jackson, Tennessee, and then northwest towards St. Louis.

There was no way to program the GPS to do what we wanted, and so Antoinette had a map folded out across her knees. Although it was only a half day's drive, we stopped outside St. Louis—we'd leave the next morning at 3 a.m. so we could pass through the first fallen county, Crawford, Missouri, at dawn. According to sources online this was the time you were least likely to get pulled over—cops were changing shift, falling asleep, or not yet quite woken up.

It poured with rain that evening as we lay by the pool underneath a small thatch umbrella, smoking cigarettes, picking at the hotdogs we'd cooked on the gas grill.

"Can I say thank you to you?"

"For what?"

"Saving my father's books and papers. Like you said, it's my inheritance. I nearly lost it all. Now I have his notes, his thoughts."

"You came back."

I rubbed her hand, kissing her cold fingers.

We slept only a few hours that night, together, her back to me, my nose nuzzled up against the nape of her neck. The alarm went off at 2.30 a.m. and by 3 we'd already bought coffee and were driving numb into the darkness. Antoinette had acoustic guitar music playing on her phone that rested on the dashboard, reflecting off the dark windshield.

It was predawn when we entered the fallen county. My flesh knotted, but I kept driving.

"Forty minutes and we'll be out of here."

A single road took us all the way to the end, and I tried not to think about time, but time was all I could think of. The image of that woman in the other fallen county played again in my mind. My eyes darted from side to side, waiting to see something, hear something. Every guitar chord lasted a day. A red light suspended by electric wire across the street bounced in the wind. I took her hand as the light turned green. At the horizon, the sky cracked orange.

"There was a moment," I said to her. "A moment when they had me out there in the swamp, in Chickasaw. I'd seen all these dead people, but then I saw my mother and she told me I'd see the umbilical cord that attached me to this world. I'd know then I'd have to turn around. And then I saw it, just as she'd said I would, and just in time. Otherwise I'd have gone too far, and snapped the cord of this life."

"Yes, you would have."

"But how could my mother have been there? She's not

dead, and so that could just have been my imagination. And if I imagined that then maybe I'm imagining this mission has meaning, that I have a purpose. How do I know?"

"What your mamma told you is true." She coughed and covered the back of her hand with red specks. "Look up there."

A dull orange glow lit the road up ahead. Flames leapt up from a burning building. Outside a crowd danced, hands in the air, as others shoved a family into the back of a black van. As we passed a man brought a club down against an old lady's back as she was hauled up from a wheelchair by her hair.

"What the fuck?"

"We can't do nothin," she shouted. "This what happens when they fall. I seen it in Chickasaw. There was beatins and beatins after the raid. All them protestors came back. I seen teeth, and swirls of blood thick as red liquorish. I seen hair pulled up, still attached to the scalp."

I instinctively spat to get some foul taste from my mouth, and I would have slowed down, I swear, but watching from the other side of the street was a black sheriff's vehicle.

"You gotta go, Marcel. We got bigger things to do. Can't stop. You drive fast as you can. But if it comes to the worst, we got weapons. And I got this on me at all times." She drew a handgun from her purse and pointed it at the windshield. "Push it."

My foot went down on the accelerator; the whole car embraced me. The cop stepped into the road and I swerved to the right then left, heard the tires screech as we swayed to one side. Then came an explosion of glass. Had the bullet come from us or him? I couldn't tell, but the passenger window had shattered and we'd crossed the county line.

I drove two more miles, pulling over onto the dirt. Her hands were covered with red specks and there was blood on her chin, but in this pale morning light she looked beautiful.

"The ones of us who got this cough. Turns out there ain't no way to get better. It took us all." The car seat, it seemed, opened up beneath me, swallowing me, and my ears rang. "But somehow you can still see me. You can touch me. No more games, Marcel. I don't know how long this is going to last. Let's stop wasting time."

Our fingertips touched and I looked at the point where flesh met flesh. I saw it and felt it—life flowing back and forth between us. Fingers slipped between each other until our palms met, both wet. Then her leg moved over me and her tongue entered my mouth, tasting of blood. Together we took off her top and her bra. I ran my hand across her breast, around the side to the nipple. As I moved my hand up her neck, I thought about all the moments like this I'd wasted, hastily trying to get to the next phase, or otherwise worrying I'd set in motion something that couldn't be stopped, even though I wasn't ready. Now all I did was marvel at the freckles on her shoulders, each one its own shape and color, speckled apart at secret distances filled with meaning like a code in the stars left by a playful creator. She took off her pants and underwear and lay herself across the two seats, back on me, legs towards the shattered passenger window. As I moved my hand between her legs I watched her watching me and I knew just what to do with my fingers; the movement of her eyes, a breath held a moment longer, a deep exhale, a stretch in her legs. When I ran my hand through her hair, touched her breast, slipped my finger deeper into her, I felt all of it so intensely. I sensed her sensing my desperation for her; she pulled off my pants, climbed on top of me. All my thoughts and memories, confusions and regrets, were converted into an intense pleasure. Like calories and sunlight power the muscles of a fighter, but in the ring he knows nothing about the process inside him, he simply moves and surrenders; so with me—all my life had come to this.

When we'd finished and changed back into our clothes, we smoked on the hood of the car. My hands trembled as I dialed my mother's cell phone. Nothing. Charles answered the home phone.

"Can I speak to my mother, please?"

"Ah, Marcel. I was afraid we'd let you go to soon. How can I help you?"

I hung up and looked at Antoinette, smiling as she smoked, radiant as she'd been in our Chickasaw days.

"Once the cough started, it was just a matter a time."

I climbed off the car's hood, running my hands through my hair. My heart echoed in my chest.

"But you're not... how long are you going to be here?"

"I told you, I don't know. But while I'm here, Marcel, I'm going be your best help."

She smiled, shadows over her eyes, and suddenly she became as distant as the sun that lit up her red hair so the strands at the edges, the loose ones, glowed golden. I needed her to comfort me, but she could not. I sat down on the sand, eyes closed; I pictured my mother on the stairwell just out of sight, at the table, smiling at me only, Charles and her talking around one another. Why had she not told me?

"When did you find out? How long have you known?" I pressed my hands into the sand and struggled to my feet. "How could you not tell me? And you were angry with *me?*"

The small stones I picked up pierced the skin of my hands. She exhaled from a freshly lit cigarette, un-crossed and re-crossed her legs, as carefree as the first time I'd laid eyes on her. I walked toward her, heart kicking, as my anger, like a wave, surged, crashed, dissipated.

"I don't know when I first known, Marcel. It's like falling in love. One day you realize you already known for a long time."

"When I stayed with my mother. She didn't have the cough."

"I felt mine getting better, too. Maybe that's the first sign, that we getting ready."

"So... I'm not crazy."

"Oh, you're crazy all right. Look at you." She smiled.

"But I caused this, then. I put the curse in motion."

"Maybe you didn't and maybe you did."

"I didn't want things to turn out this way."

"You think this is what I dreamed of for my life?"

"I would undo it if I could."

"Well, you can't. So stop moaning like a little bitch. Stop feeling sorry for yourself and try to make things as right as you can make 'em."

I sat on the hood, and as Antoinette put her hand on my back I felt my whole body turn cold with pain.

We ate dinner that night in a motel outside Wichita, Kansas. We shared a bottle of whisky, and with the batteries out of the smoke alarm, we worked our way through half a pack of cigarettes, flipping through channels, our bodies rubbing together. We laughed, we shared stories of our lives, we kissed, made out, made love. It was a night of perfect romance.

At a gas station the next morning, I drew money from my card; the receipt assured me the rest was still there. I ran the notes between my fingers, touching them to my face. The smell comforted me.

I bought us coffee, donuts, and cigarettes. That afternoon we passed through a fallen county so silent it seemed all the residents were dead. No cars on the street, no pedestrians, shopfronts closed and boarded up, others nothing but charred black skeletons. We passed through another fallen county the next morning. Trash piled up on the sides of the road and the air smelt heavy with piss. We saw a few pedestrians moving along the sidewalks, but like cockroaches they scuttled off at the sight of us. At the very edge of the county a group of men had formed a circle, and as we approached I realized they were all pissing on a man with a raw beaten face.

"What are you doing?" I shouted at them.

One ragged-faced man turned from the group, drawing a gun from his side.

"Go! Go!" Antoinette shouted.

I pushed my foot down on the accelerator as the sound of gunfire echoed down the street. He was, apparently, too out of it to aim properly, and all his shots missed the car.

"This is what will happen," she said. "Everything's going to be this way if we don't stop him."

❦

"Don't forget to breathe out before you aim." It was mid-afternoon in the Arizona desert, and we'd pulled down a dirt side road Antoinette had found on her map. "There you go. Now boom."

The watermelon blew to pieces. Somehow, under her guidance, I became an excellent shot.

"You're a natural."

"Only when you're guiding me."

"I'll be there."

"You can't say that for sure. And what if we get caught? Then it's only me who'll go to prison." I looked at the cloudless blue sky, wiping sweat from my forehead. "But what does it matter? My mother's gone now, too. You're gone. Everyone I know... has vanished."

"Stop feeling sorry for yourself."

"I'll do my best."

"No, do it. Stop feeling sorry for yourself. It's the most pathetic thing a human can do."

"Okay. I will. I'll stop feeling sorry for myself."

That night, on her insistence, we went for a drink at a nearby restaurant and bar, where we (where I) had to wait thirty minutes for a table. She knew I couldn't answer her in public, yet she talked the whole time about the fiery energy.

"Something's going on here. You can feel it."

From reading Jefferson Lee's posters plastered all over the walls, it was impossible to tell which way he'd lean. All they said was: "Good ol' Sheriff."

We slept close together that night, our faces inches apart. Her hot breath on my lips. When I woke she was standing by the windows, beautiful in the first light of day. She wore her dungarees like she did back in Chickasaw, hand on her hip, long hair resting on her shoulder.

"You look beautiful."

"Don't look too bad yourself. Now you got a big day ahead."

"What... exactly am I doing?"

I stretched and rubbed my eyes.

"*We*. We're doing this together. I ain't leaving you. Got to go do, what's the word? Reconnaissance. Figure out what time he leaves, how he leaves, when he goes to his trailer."

For a moment I felt peaceful, but this feeling was fast attacked, as if it were a viral invader, and sadness the white blood cells. I sat in the empty bathtub, fully clothed, and dialed my mother's cell phone, listening over and over to her voice message. My whole body was a bruise, pressed down on by a malevolent thumb.

Antoinette's smile brought a moment's warmth. She held in her hand an old Bluetooth headset.

"Put this on your ear, then when we're talking folk won't think you're crazy."

I couldn't help but laugh. She put her arm around me and kissed the side of my head.

CHAPTER 27

On screens outside the highly guarded open-air arena, was the image—broadcast from the stage inside—of the American flag, the Arizona flag, and the God's Sheriff's flag standing like sentries behind a podium on a platform in the park beneath a perfect blue sky. Near the entrance a group of protestors—who looked like students—stood with placards, shouting: "He's a liar. He doesn't care about you."

The attendees—older mostly, dressed in boots and hats—seemed to enjoy the attention.

"If this county falls, we all fall!" a protestor shouted.

"We've already fallen," a big man in a Stetson hat called back. "Only God can save us."

Passing through security, I had to take off my head piece.

"Better not talk to me now," Antoinette said, kissing my neck.

"Stop it," I laughed.

"Sir, I'm going to need you to cooperate," the guard snapped. "This is standard procedure, sir."

"Sorry. I wasn't talking to you."

"Sir, I'm going to need you to move along. Sir. Sir."

I apologized again, and retrieved my belongings on the other side of the x-ray machine. I found a seat three rows from the stage.

"I'm going to sit on your lap. 'Less you want somebody sitting on mine."

"I don't want that."

With my arms around her waist, I closed my eyes.

"You best be more alert when he leaves. We gotta be prepared. I'm gonna follow him out of here. Marcel? You hear me?"

"Yes."

"Excited to be here," said an old man in a cowboy hat as he sat down next to me.

"Me, too."

"You look half asleep, son. Want some coffee? I brought a flask and two cups."

"That's very kind, thank you."

"You ain't here to make friends, Marcel."

"I'm just trying to blend in."

"Well, you fit in just fine, son," the old man said as he gave me the coffee.

Thankfully he didn't expect conversation as payment for this kindness, and we all three sat in silence until Lee made his way up onto the stage.

In front of the podium, a sign read: *A people-funded movement. Bitcoin Donations Accepted.* The crowd yelled and cheered, some spun about in adulation, unable to contain the excited flow in their bodies. Camera crews dotted the edges of the arena. Lee raised his black-gloved hands, clapped them together, and smiled. Bright white teeth. Leathery skin.

"Take a seat."

We all sat.

"I see America's finest here in front of me." Cheers and

hoots rose from the crowd as he pointed at us. "Outside is the enemy. Holding those signs, saying: liar. Are they referring to themselves?" A roar of laughter. "We know who the real liars are. Those people outside who would stop the good we're creating. These people here." He pointed at the media. "The ones who twist our words, and make it seem we've said things we ain't never said or done things we ain't never done. That's why I always say, if you want the truth, ask: What is the opposite of what those liars are saying? That'll be the truth. That's where you'll find it. As for me, I only speak the truth. So you don't have to worry, or be confused, or doubt. You don't ever have to question. I speak only the truth. The truth is the only language I know."

"He lies," Antoinette hissed into my ear.

"You know, folks, God spoke to me the other night." He raised his hands in the air. "And he said, Jefferson, I like what you're doing, but I need you to do more. I have chosen you for this. And I said, tell me Lord! I am your servant. Your humble servant. Take my hands and use them for your purpose, Lord. And he said: You need to *win 'em all*. That's right, folks, God speaks with a drawl." The crowd cheered and clapped. Lee raised his hand to silence them. "But seriously, that's what He said to me. Win every county. Then, and only then, can we restore justice to this nation."

They all stood up, screaming. Antoinette jumped off me and ran through the crowd.

As I walked alone down the street outside the venue, violence broke out between protestors and the faithful. A fat man in a leather wife-beater, the loose edges of his hairy arms swinging like jelly-steak, smashed the sign of a lanky protestor and punched him in the face. A younger man, similarly dressed but in better physical shape, pushed his way through the crowd and smashed his fist into the side of the protestor's head, painting the sidewalk with a fat slash of blood. A boot toe hit the stumbling protestor's chin, causing a sick thud. At first it seemed the protestors were scattering, but then they regrouped and came at the cowboy-dressed faithful. I'd been backing off slowly, but now turned around and ran away, bashing into a cameraman running toward the fight.

Waiting for Antoinette in the hotel room, I pressed my hands against my heart. Sharp, hot pain radiated out from there through my chest, down my arms and back. On my phone, I streamed a live interview with Lee. He'd changed into a pair of jeans and an inoffensive white-collared shirt.

"One of the major challenges we face," he said to the interviewer, "is trying to free our boys from the grip of toxic masculinity. For too long, we Americans have been held captive by toxic myths. These deeply problematic ideas are tied to the hegemonic forces that reproduce white privilege. These toxic masculine myths of conquest and expansion need to be challenged, and intersectional feminism is our most powerful tool. That, and anti-racism training. We need to unravel the nexus of intersecting oppressions through constant vigilance. We must call out problematic behavior wherever we encounter it, and actively unravel the intersectional web of oppression. That's why I'm supporting female candidates across the country, and endorsing a woman of color for sheriff in this town."

"That all sounds good and fine," the interviewer said, "but what do you say to critics who claim you speak out of both sides of your mouth?"

"We all speak out both sides of our mouths. That's human anatomy."

He raised his hand when she tried to interrupt him.

"Excuse me if I seem like I'm mansplaining."

"Well, more like manterrupting."

"Ha-ha. I really do need to check my privilege. I'm sorry. The fact of the matter is the corporate media has vested interests and much to gain from maintaining the current hegemony, so they portray me, highly inaccurately, as a liar."

So the interview continued.

By the time Antoinette got home, I was desperate and paranoid.

"I thought you'd disappeared," I shouted at her.

"I've been watching him. He's in his caravan. But he's guarded."

"I saw an interview with him on an LA television network."

"They done that one here."

"Can't you get close to him?"

"Might be he can see me. I don't know. Can't take no risks."

"Why can't you kill him?"

"I can't. I just can't. Has to be someone who's living. I know that much."

"I don't think I can go on with this. I feel weak. I've lost so much."

"Many people have lost much. That don't mean you can be weak."

"You're just promoting... toxic masculinity. You're trying to push me... to reproduce toxic myths of conquest and expansion. We should embrace intersectionality to free ourselves from the grip of the patriarchy."

"Shut the fuck up, Marcel." She sat on my lap, kissed my face, and rubbed my heart. "I'm sorry you feeling sad. Soon this all gonna be over and then you can feel everything. You won't have to do nothing else but feel."

We left at dawn. We drove through the desert for hours, in silence. The GPS led us through the heart of downtown LA; past the sprawling Skid Row where miles of tents lined the edges of the streets—the detritus of the city of myths.

"Forgotten people," I said. "They're as bad as the folk in the fallen counties."

"Not by half, they ain't. Things gonna get a whole lot worse for 'em if God's Sheriffs win, I can tell you that. They're gonna be rounded up, locked away."

I spat out the window.

As planned, we rented an RV trailer.

It was late afternoon when we turned up the Pacific Highway and I finally asked her: "Do you know how you died?"

"Don't remember when. Don't know how, neither. After I saved you from the swamp; after I been back to Magdalena's. I know that much for sure."

"What about my mother?"

She shrugged.

"And where is she?"

"I'm sorry, Marcel, I don't know. Don't know why you can see me or how long things are gonna stay that way."

"I'm afraid. A time might come when you're all gone. When I can't see any of you."

She took my hand. "Don't let that get you down now."

We set up our RV in the parking lot above the beach where I'd taken that final swim with my father.

"I'm going to take a walk along the beach. Do you want to come with me?"

"I'm gonna stay here. You enjoy the walk."

I walked where the water met the sand. Anxiety dissolved in the sea air; watching the sun on the water, I caught myself thinking of nothing. How beautiful was an empty mind.

Back up the stairs, as the sun hovered above the water, I caught a whiff of meat cooking over flames. Meat grilled on a BBQ in front of the RV. And then, there was my father. He'd poured himself a drink and smoked a lit cigarette.

"Dad."

"Come here."

He put his arms around me and I felt his body, meat and bones. I smelt the sweat from his shirt and the smoky hair on the back of his head. I closed my eyes; time slowed to a blissful hum, and when I opened them again my mother stood there before me. I felt then how the unity of a single life was no more or less illusory than the unity of many. They must have held me like this once, and looked at me this way when I was a baby, but I could no more remember that moment than I could the moment they first met. Yet I was there for both.

There were the important matters that needed to be discussed—the fate of the soul in eternity and the true form the universe took beyond the observable. But when my father brought the meat off the BBQ, and we all tore pieces of freshly baked bread and dipped it in garlic butter, I understood that if this moment didn't matter then no explanation about ultimate purpose ever would. Did I come to this conclusion first, or only after I began to describe in great detail, the most trivial matter—the size and color of Baptist Pants' s bowtie on the last night we ate dinner together: Yellow, the size of a baby's head. My father laughed so hard; my mother did, too.

"Why did he wear those things in his own house?"

"It was his fashion," my mother said, and hit my father's knee, playfully. "And he wasn't such a bad guy. Right, Marcel?"

"To be fair, he was, he is, a nice man."

"We're just having fun with something silly," my father said. "We don't mean him any harm. And, come on, how am I supposed to feel? He stole my girl."

"You always had my heart." She rubbed his chest, kissing his cheek. "You crazy man."

Antoinette took my hand and kissed my fingers.

"I never had nothing like this."

"We must just enjoy it." I kissed her cheek.

As the setting sun turned the water bright orange, it drew the hidden shadows from our chairs and cups; and when the moon rose, coloring us silver, all I wanted to do was remain. But I felt the restless forces, the energy that powers both the moon and the meaning of the moon, clawing at us all, ripping our perfect sanctuary to pieces.

"You must sleep now," Antoinette said. "You have a big day tomorrow."

I kissed both my parents. Although I sensed that if I ever saw them again as I had now, it would be when I was dead, I resisted a tearful good-bye. They looked so happy, heads resting together, drinking wine.

When I lay down, regret surged through my stomach, my chest; the words I should have spoken flooded my mind: Why hadn't my mother told me the truth? What did the asterisk in my father's notes point to? Had he died on purpose? Had my mother? How had I wasted the conversation on trivialities?

"That was pure love out there, Marcel. I ain't never seen such a thing."

"Really? I didn't waste my time? I had so much to ask them."

"Asking all that can't be answered, that would be a waste a time. Sitting in love. Now that's something worth living for."

"You're right... Yes."

"How many times I have to tell you: I always am."

She climbed into bed next to me and my mind quieted, even as my body remained full to bursting with discomfort.

She ran over the plan for tomorrow. The stage was already set, and just a few feet away from where we'd had our dinner offered a perfect shot of the podium. In the panic certain to follow, Antoinette would help me escape, leading me down a path she'd scope out tonight.

"And then?"

"We'll have ridded the world a darkness."

"I'll go to prison for murder."

"It ain't murder."

"To the world it is."

"You ain't never getting caught. So it's just in your head. And you know the truth."

"Fine. Let me sleep, please."

I turned away from her, so my face was just an inch from the RV wall.

At 3 a.m. she shook me awake.

"He's in his trailer. He's awake. He's waiting to die. He knows he has to die now."

I tried to resist, but she pulled me from bed and led me to the edge of the garden where we'd had dinner. On the sand lot right by the water's edge stood a silver RV, covered with God's Sheriffs insignia. A few feet away, his aging black horse dozed on her feet. The light inside the RV was on, and Antoinette was right; I could see the shadow of his hat moving back and forth. Clearly he was pacing. Perhaps he did know. Perhaps some part of him accepted his fate. This thought had a narcotic effect on me, quieting and focusing my mind, dulling my nerves.

Back inside our caravan, Antoinette loaded the handgun and gave it to me. I slipped the gun beneath my belt and followed her across the moonlit parking lot down a side path she'd scoped out earlier that evening, taking her hand to make sure I didn't lose my grip. We walked down a flight of stairs toward the sand lot that ran to a cliff, beneath which the ocean waited.

And there his caravan sat, maybe twenty feet from the edge. A single guard on a chair sat half-asleep at the door. We started to run, and as we got closer, she told me to smack his head with the butt of the gun.

"What are you...?" the lanky man said.

But he never finished his sentence. I smashed the gun handle between his eyes and watched him fall like a heavy suit from a broken hanger. The old horse raised her head and let out a half-hearted neigh. Antoinette pulled the door open and shut it behind us. It was an old model caravan with wooden floors, faded leather seats. The center part was empty except for a single chair (on which Jefferson Lee III sat) and a wooden table (on which he'd placed his hat).

"Mar-say-al. Weyl-come. I wondered when you'd show up."

"You've missed me?"

"He ain't missed you," Antoinette hissed in my ear.

"I sure have. I thought we had a good thing going." He smiled, the lip-curl-smirk, baring the pearly whites. "You were going to tell the world about me."

"You didn't need me to."

"That's right."

All this while I'd pointed the gun at his head. I took in my surroundings. The walls were covered with God's Sheriffs posters, pictures of Lee with fans and other politicians, newspaper headlines, all manner of papers big and small, and rows of lapel pins fastened to a cork board next to banknotes, gold and silver coins, stock market graphs. Notebooks lay spread out across the table next to bars of gold, old coins, shells, and gold-plated collectors' Bitcoins.

"Don't let him talk to you," Antoinette hissed in my ear. "He can convince you of anything. Shoot him in the stomach, so he don't die right away. We gotta get him down to the beach."

"Your hand is shaking," he said. The room seemed at once too bright and too dark. "You've come to kill me. And I've worn my best suit. Now I've got some things to say to you first."

He wore black leather gloves. His thinning grey hair was gelled straight back over his sun-spotted scalp. Now the right corner of his lip crept upward like a scoundrel sneaking off to do filthy business. With his ivory-white teeth on full display, he pointed at the couch.

"I've invited you to sit."

"Say to him, I've come to kill you, not to talk to you. Then shoot him in the stomach. What are you waiting for?"

I looked at Antoinette: wild hair on pale cheeks; violent eyes. Then I looked at Lee, back at Antoinette. Was he truly unaware of her existence, or did he just refuse to acknowledge her?

"Are we two here alone?" I asked him.

"You're wondering where Haylee is?" He slid open a metal slat covering a window. Moonlight touched the edge of his cluttered desk. "She had her own trailer. But I don't think she's there tonight. If you know what I mean?"

"Does that make you angry, you filthy fucker?" Antoinette hissed at him.

"She's a rock. But she's her own woman. Come on, take a seat."

He closed the shutter over the window, sat down behind his desk. I did as he asked, taking a seat on the old couch. I lowered the gun.

"Marcel," Antoinette hissed in my ear. "Don't get comfortable with him. He going to use this against you."

"I've got this."

"That's right," Lee said, and rubbed the underside of his chin. "You've got this."

"I've watched you on the trail, Jefferson."

"Had I had it my way, Mar-say-al, you'd have been along for the ride." He raised his hands, as if in prayer. "But you abandoned us. Time and tide wait for no man."

"But there'd be no way to tell a coherent story about you. Not anymore."

"Mar-say-al. You offend me."

Antoinette sat down beside me and gripped my arm.

"Don't reason with him. Shoot him."

"I have to have this conversation."

"Go on, then," he said.

"One day you're talking about God, guns, and country, the next you're checking your privilege, and going off about inter-sectionality and anti-racism."

"That's because I can only speak the truth."

"He can only speak lies."

"That doesn't sound incredibly truthful to me. Preaching from different gospels."

"You make my point for me, Marcel. There're four gospels. Which one is true?"

"Don't you dare, you... blaspheming... slanderer!" Antoinette slammed his desk.

"Some say they're all true, even when they contradict. Some folk say they're all false. But hey, Marcel, let me write you a check. Will ten million dollars do the trick?"

"What are you talking about?"

He took a checkbook from his desk drawer, wrote on it frantically, tore a sheet off, and handed it to me.

"What's the meaning of this?"

"Cash at your own discretion. You've done it before, haven't you?"

"When you finished flirting with him, wake me up." Antoinette sat on the couch and pulled her legs up to her chest. "We got to kill him before sunrise."

"I've earned money before. A large sum, yes."

"Earned or won?" he asked.

"Earned." I paused and looked at his hat, sitting alone. "Won."

The room lay in silence for a few minutes.

"Without the beautiful second amendment, let me tell you, son, you wouldn't be holdin' that pistol in your hand right now. Gosh darnit, boy, you should tie a flag around your head and sing the National Anthem. Don't you care about the men and women who died for your freedoms? This is America. The greatest land on earth. *Individual* freedoms. Here, let me write you a check." He wrote hastily, tore off the top check in the stack, and handed it to me. "Am I the only person who sees how problematic gender reveal parties are? Let me write you a check. Here take this one." He handed me another signed check. "The very idea reinforces the normative position of white patriarchal cis-normativity. Here, another check for you."

"He's breaking down," Antoinette hissed. "He's coming undone."

"We need to have more conversations around the intersection of fatness studies and queer studies." He coughed loudly. "God bless America. This is the finest nation on earth, and we need to reclaim it from the radical leftists who are trying to force our children to swallow their Marxist ideologies." He wiped sweat off his face. "Don't try pull *both siderism* here. I..." He coughed again, pouring himself a glass of whisky and knocking it back. "Here's another check for you." As his eyes rolled back, he massaged his temples.

"My apologies. I don't know what came over me there."

"He slipped up," Antoinette hissed. "He shown his true self."

"You want some whisky, Marcel?"

"Don't drink it," Antoinette hissed.

"I'm okay. I don't need a drink."

"Suit yourself." He threw back another shot. "In an ideal world," Lee said, "I'd ride my old horse one last time." He re-lit the knobby, broken stump of a half-smoked cigar, taking a few puffs. "But we live in a broken world.."

"What do you want?" I asked him.

"Nothing." Resting on his elbows, he leaned across the desk. He looked focused now; life had returned to his eyes. I felt Antoinette rustle beside me. "Nothing at all." He pointed at me with his smoking hand. "That's what frightens folks. I'm as happy to see a life saved with a fancy new gadget, as I am to see a building blown to pieces with a hi-tech rocket. That's why folks think they can bend me, and twist me to their will, 'cause I don't want nothing. I speak like a man who wants nothing, and I preach the gospel of nothing. And because I want nothing, I attract everything, and because I want nobody, everybody loves me. How about I write you another check, Mar-say-al? Twenty million this time?" He wrote another check, tore off the sheet, and handed it to me. "But from time to time I'm forced to take form."

"He ain't forced to do nothing. He chooses," Antoinette called from the couch, her arms crossed over her body. "Don't let him talk you out of what you got to do."

"And when I've taken shape, then I have desires. You're no one special, Mar-say-al."

"I know that."

"If you kill me, you'll be prosecuted for the murder of Jefferson Lee III. When you're in prison, men stronger than you will rape you. Is that what you want?"

I shook my head. "You're not only Jefferson Lee III. You've admitted it to me. You confessed to your true nature."

"Try that in court."

"I'm not a fool. I know they won't believe me."

"You want to sacrifice me as a metaphor, Mar-say-al. That's all I am, a metaphor."

"Then let me kill you, as a metaphor."

"But I'm a man." With an offended look on his face, he put his hand to his heart. "You don't want to kill a man, do you?"

"Listen to him lying, again," Antoinette hissed.

"You were the one who demanded a sacrifice, a real human sacrifice."

"I'm a metaphor and the world suffers because it believes I'm real. So I became real, to free y'all."

"You didn't care about freeing us. You've come before, but you won't come again, because I'm going to kill you." I said the words again, and let their meaning flow through me: "I'm going to kill you."

"Before we do that." He put on his black hat, poured himself three fingers of whisky, and knocked the drink back in one shot. From his desk drawer he took out a badge and held it out toward me.

"Sherriff Jones? He gave me one like that, too. You killed that kind, old man, didn't you?"

"Oh, you have one already? Then I guess you don't need this one." He dropped it back into his drawer. Now he retrieved a different badge, a sheriff's badge. "See this one here, it has a few extra star points." He clipped it onto his shirt. "I call it: the asterisk."

"You're the continuation of my father's notes."

"Hmmm." He smiled without baring his teeth, looking down at the badge and carefully adjusting it. "Very poetic. But don't confuse poetry with reality."

"Don't listen to him. He's gonna get in your head."

"Don't confuse metaphor with truth," he said.

"Metaphors have betrayed us."

By the time he looked up, his shirt had turned red and blood dripped heavily against the floor, flowing towards me in a straight dark line. My ears rang from the explosion. My hand no longer shook. I put the gun in my pocket.

"Good shot."

He dropped to his knees and wiped his forehead, leaving a thick red line above his black eyebrows.

"You fucking done it, Marcel."

Antoinette pulled my face to hers and kissed me with her tongue. I tasted blood. I smelt blood. As we carried him from the caravan, his body slumping, blood trickling from the edge of his mouth, he seemed to smile. The moon had fallen far and sat just a few inches above the ocean. As we stumbled down a rocky path I looked at the sky and found my mind searching not for excuses if I was caught, but rather for the perfect metaphor to describe the first hint of blue in the sky. A corpse, I decided, was the night, and the blue that came through that blackness was the flushed skin, returning to life.

Three shadows danced around a fire on the beach; I knew who they were—my mother, my father, and Jones.

"Good job," my father said, patting my back as we dropped Lee onto the sand. "You understood, dear boy. I knew you would."

The old Sheriff pulled his knees up to his chest, heaving and coughing, blood flowing from his mouth onto the sand.

"Everything needs to be perfect," Jones said. "Thank you, Marcel." He drew a knife and cut the old sheriff's suit, ripping it off his body. Lee had started to shake and convulse. "He's running a fever. We need to be quick. He must be wrapped in his own God's Sheriff flag and the flag of the country. Marcel, you will cut out the heart. First hold it North, then to the South, then West, and then East."

We waded into the water, keeping Lee at the surface. Waves splashed over him until both flags were as wet as his face and hair. His eyes rolled back. Our movements were aligned perfectly, like we were a single organism, and now that we were nearly chest-deep, Jones handed me the sacrificial knife.

"Good luck, son," my father said.

"You know what to do," my mother's voice encouraged me.

It was Maggie who'd explained to me exactly how to slice a body to get the heart out, and the one she'd been preparing me to sacrifice stood next to me now. Yes, this moment was truly perfect. I drove the knife into Lee's stomach. The water turned red as his intestines slipped out of him like fat spaghetti into the ocean. I felt the grit of blood and sinew beneath my nails. Finally, I found the heart, still beating. I struggled to get a grip, then ripped it free and held it up to the sky. Some primal energy in me knew each direction— North, South, West, East. Blood flowed down my wrists onto my body as the waves came stronger.

Then I heard cheering and screaming. A huge crowd had gathered on the pier to watch the ceremony. But they vanished from view as salty waves lashed my face. Lee's body was pulled beneath the water and I heard a scream that came from the belly of the earth, and all four of my partners, my fellows in this sacred crime, turned to mist and slipped into the dark, red water, leaving me alone. I dipped below the surface and let go of the heart. Even with my eyes closed, the salt burned. Submerged still, I turned myself around and swam toward the shore until I could hold my breath no longer.

I came up gasping for air and wiped my face. The water's

dark surface reflected bright flames that tore skywards from the wooden pier. The crowd, come to see the sacrifice, ran and screamed. A man jumped off the edge, falling fifty feet to the water below. The wind blew in from the sea and the fire raged, consuming the boardwalk, concession stands, and pillars. A wave dragged me under. I resurfaced in deeper water; a current pulled me away from the shore. I looked up through salty eyes to the burning planks above me that fell like brimstone, hissing and bubbling as they hit the water's surface. Bodies fell, planks, shaded awnings, fishing rods, tackle boxes.

Somehow I managed to turn myself around and make it through the surf; I stumbled to the beach where I fell to my knees. A cuttlefish lay in front of me. Holding it, I turned to the burning pier. The first fire engine had already arrived and sirens wailed from every corner—North, South, East, West.

Lee's checkbook—it must have been in his pocket—had washed up onto the beach. I picked it up along with the checks he'd written me, which I'd left on the beach; I ran fast. I passed paramedics and police officers, as I took a flight of stairs up to our RV and car. Of course, I avoided the sand lot where Lee had parked. In the RV, I changed out of my wet clothes. I took all the belongings I had with me and threw them into the trunk of the car.

I managed to get out of the city in less than an hour. The car was without smell, without sound. I filled up with gas, bought coffee, energy drinks, and cigarettes. At first the LA news was all about the burning pier, but then came the first wave of stories about Lee. He was missing, his guard found unconscious outside the caravan.

I drove and drove, weaving across lanes. The desert burned hot. The edges of the road were strewn with dead animals and exploded tires. At a gas station, I checked my bank statement. Yes, I had all my money. I still had it. I had it and it was mine.

Late afternoon I arrived in Van Horn. I bought myself three nights at the Motel 6. Not a typical location for a millionaire who'd earned his money, but it would do for now. By the hotel pool, I waited for the day to end; I waited for something to happen. Each time I heard sirens I expected them to grow louder, for armed men to drag me away in chains. But it didn't happen. According to the news, the police knew nothing. No suspects, no body. I spent the whole night awake, pacing in my room, drinking whisky, waiting for someone. I called out Antoinette's name. I called for my father and my mother.

The next day I read the paper again; still nothing, but by the evening the news had changed. The fire—caused by an electrical fault—and Lee's disappearance, were not related. Tributes to Lee poured in. A war veteran, a hero, a patriot. Who would do such a thing? Ha, I laughed. This was a good thing we'd done. The best thing that had ever been done. Did they not see how all the stories were about the one who'd called himself Lee? Every paper, every channel, every chat show. Where was the horror of the world now? We had cleansed the world and nobody even knew our names.

I know what you're wondering, and yes, I did cash those checks Lee gave me, and no, they did not bounce. They added up to hundreds of millions of dollars. I wrote myself more checks from his book, and these too, no matter the amount, always cashed. And yet, I still needed my article to be published. I had to tell the full story, and thankfully at this time I had limitless energy. I survived on just a few hours of sleep each night, ran miles every day, quit drinking and smoking.

I needed somewhere to work and the Motel 6 had lost— in my eyes at least—much of its former charm. So I bought a property on the Malibu beachfront, right near to where it all went down. Lee's horse was still living in the area, and I put her out to pasture in my garden. Lucy Lae is a good horse, and she shouldn't have to suffer because of who her master was.

Each morning I'd rise at dawn, run five miles, and then write at a desk that overlooked the ocean. It took me a few months to complete my article. I made sure every line shone. I left out nothing. And when I sent it off, a supercharged rush of joy passed through me as I slammed my laptop shut and ran out into the garden. There sat the RV at the very edge of the property. I could smell the meat cooking, and I knew that when I rounded the edge of the vehicle I'd see my mother and father again, and Antoinette would join us.

As I turned the corner I anticipated my laughter melding with theirs, but instead I ran into silence, like a boy crashing into a wall. Soaked grey ash caked the edges of the barbeque stand.

My article was not an incantation, just a wish. I sat on the chair my father had sat on that night, or was it my mother? Or did I sit there? Or Antoinette? The wind blew harder, all their memories ripped away from me.

That night I received the response from Axan.

The email began like this:

Marcel –

Right away I knew something was off, like the stench of rotten meat. The arrogance of the M-Dash in a greeting; the lack of "Dear" or even a simple "Hi". As I scanned through the condescending rejection email, in which I was told that I'd clearly given in to delusion, that I needed to seek psychiatric help, that I was chasing demons, I felt my heart fall faster and faster, and then... soar again as I reached the bottom.

All these thoughts occurred at the same moment: *This*

email is from Martin Huffman; Huffman, my one-time supervisor, has left academia to become an editor; I can buy Axan and fire Huffman; I can force them to publish my piece.

The next morning I dismissed the idea and crashed for a few days; but as I reaffirmed my commitment to the project, so my energy returned. I had much to learn, but within a month I had a sleazy, predatory lawyer who stank of after-shave and mint candies, working to help me acquire Axan. I insisted that my name not be brought up until the purchase was complete.

We acquired the publication through a hostile takeover, and I moved the offices to a new building just a few miles from my home. My office—on the third, and top floor—still had clumps of wires sticking out of the walls the first day I inspected it.

"We'll have those taken care of," the project manager assured me.

True to his word, the room was in pristine condition when I moved in a few days later. I positioned my antique executive mahogany desk facing the glass walls that overlooked the ocean. I had my secretary send up Martin Huffman, the editor.

The hefty man stopped dead in the doorway.

"Huffman," I said. "Is there some kind of force field blocking your entrance?"

"Marcel?" He glanced from side to side, up and down, as if looking for a hidden camera.

"Come on in. Sit down." I smiled as I turned on my chair. "Do you like my office? What do you think of the view?"

I lit a cigarette as Huffman sat down. His face had grown a few shades paler, and contrasted against his neatly kempt dark beard.

"Your hair has thinned out," I said, pointing at my own and then his.

"I... um... You allow smoking inside?"

"Why not? I own the building. What are they going to do?"

He took his vape pen from his pocket.

"Oh, no. I'm afraid vaping is strictly forbidden."

"Huh." He tried to gauge my seriousness. "Oh."

He put the pen back into his pocket as I took a drag on my cigarette.

"Shall we go over the rejection letter line by line?"

"We'll publish it."

"Oh, we will? Hahaha." I leant back on my chair, hands in the air. "There is no *we* here. The world is not as you think it is, Huffman. Your cynical, reductionist, either-or, black and white thinking will not stand. You replaced mystery and wonder with cleverness and irony, spirituality with pedagogy. You don't understand nuance. If I said to you: *love is a burning fire,* you'd say, *er, I don't see any smoke, idiot.* Get out of here, Huffman."

He rose slowly to his feet, like a cow shot with a tranquilizer dart.

"And it's time to give up on the elbow patches."

I persuaded Dr. Virgil Rose to take up the position as editor.

"We'll run my article and gauge the response. I'll let you figure out how to take it from there."

"If I want to clean house?"

"Clean it."

We ran the article. It received even more reads and shares than the first, but this time the audience was morbidly curious: A man who'd lost his mind; but how did he have so much money? Was there something to it all?

"Most folk, even those who work here, think you've... uh, lost it," Dr. Rose told me.

"What do you think?"

"I don't think so."

"We have a good readership. I'm not interested in the day-to-day work here. I'll leave you in charge; I'll check in... every now and then."

"I appreciate the faith you place in me, Marcel."

He shook my hand and we walked out together, his hand on my back.

❦

My bedroom overlooks the ocean, as does my office. I rise at dawn each morning and run along the pathway as the sun comes up and paints the water gold. Time stretches out before me and above; evenings give way to mornings. I stretch my limbs, content as an old man with a full life.

The first visitor is a young woman, probably my age. She has hair the color of Antoinette's; her name is Alice. Then an older woman; then a young man.

"We'll be happy to work to earn our keep," Alice says. "We believe you speak the truth. We know you do."

"Stay. Yes."

More come. They set up tents.

One night I deliver this speech to the crowd: "We must learn to live beyond the material. We should accept many propositions and also reject them all. A being or a truth can be both itself and also its opposite. And stop trying to reduce metaphors to propositions. But neither should you categorize them. Angels live amongst us, but you cannot dine with them. They shed feathers, but only a fool would try to gather these up and make pillows. If I tell you, I am in love and love is a burning flame, do you run to the fire department? Or, do you say, well then, if there's no fire he must be lying about his love? Two factions form, one that says, this man claims love is fire and we must accept this; wherever we see a fire that is love and where there is no fire there is no love. The other faction says, this man speaks obvious untruths, everything he says must be rejected. Only the rare person listens carefully and then feels the warmth of love inside and sleeps at peace, knowing it must not be analyzed and turned to ashes."

I retreat to my room.

As the congregation grows I spend less time amongst them. Occasionally, I take evening walks through the camp and listen to the chatter. I am known as Marcel, although some say I prefer to go by Marcy. One night I meet the first arrival in my dream. She sits at my feet and I explain to her again: It is possible for one to be more than a single thing. You are you and also everything.

"Must we be on the lookout?" she asks.

"Yes."

"The world is peaceful since you did what you did."

"That is true. But he can return at any time."

"Yes. I will make sure we remain vigilant."

Two nights later I stand at my window and watch Lucy Lae as she grazes at the edge of the property. When the night deepens and the fires go out, I leave through the rear door, sneak back into my own property by jumping the fence, and hastily saddle the old horse. Her breath is hot and grassy.

Although well beyond her prime, Lucy Lae gallops effort-lessly along the cliff-side pathway. Soon these midnight rides become a nightly event. I buy a Smith and Wesson, a leather gun holster, and always make sure I'm armed when I leave for my ride. We return before dawn and I sneak back inside, shower, and slip into bed. I move Lucy Lae's paddock to the back of the house and install a special door that only I have access to. When they ask about the sounds at night, I tell them not to worry. No, nighttime sentries won't be necessary, but yes I am taking the threat seriously. I install extra cameras, and set up a control tower in my office so that I, and I alone, can see who is coming and going. A few nights later I tell them I've apprehended a suspect and he's been taken care of. If such an event should occur again? Again, I'll take care of it.

We leave the matter there.

Sometimes I receive visits in my dreams from members of the ever-growing community.

"Can we weave large spider webs?"

"Yes."

"Can we make music and dance?"

"Yes."

"Can we look for signs?"

"Yes."

"Is he coming again?"

For how long had they known I was the nighttime rider? The black rider? Of course I'd suspected that they suspected me. I'd often considered abandoning my nighttime self. But I could not.

So, no, I am not surprised when they smash down my door.

"Why do you refuse to commit to a definite answer?" Alice asks me. Her hand trembles as she points the gun at me. "The world is a mess. You've made everything vague, hazy. No one knows what's up and what's down."

"Let me pour you a drink," I say. I light myself a cigar.

"No, you're only going to try talk me out of it. We know who you are."

More burst in.

"Say something real," one shouts.

"He can't. He only speaks in riddles. He only knows metaphors."

"He's betrayed us," one screams.

Another takes the checkbook off my desk.

"The living are already ghosts," I shout. "You're all ghosts already."

"Listen to him rambling."

They drag me out the room, through the garden and down to the beach; my back slams against the wooden stairs, still cold from the night. In the dawn light, I see the crowd along the pier. As they drag me toward the ocean I grasp behind me, trying to save myself, but my fingers slice straight through the wet sand and the waves eat up the scars I leave behind. The pain of the first knife stab digs into me like hot ice; and then I hear the sounds of flesh and sinew ripping, and I plead as fractured thoughts go off in my mind like popcorn.

But then I see the spirits waiting for me on the water, and the pain instantly softens and flows from me. Antoinette laughing; Mother and Father reaching their hands out toward me. The perfect peace pulling. This time I won't resist.

ABOUT THE AUTHOR

Michael Rands is a South African born writer who lives in Alabama with his wife and toddler. He teaches college-level English and Creative Writing and is the author of several works of fiction and non-fiction. He holds an MFA from Louisiana State University.

ACKNOWLEDGMENTS

I would like to thank everybody and everything, but especially the following people:

My wife, Elizabeth, for being my brilliant, amazing partner in life, as well as in writing, editing, and Bayou Wolfing.

My mother, Jennifer, for supporting my writing dream, and reading my work over the years with a laser-sharp eye.

My father, Jonathan, departed from this world, but very much with me all the time.

My son, Johnny, for teaching me everything about the world, and being the smartest, cutest, and funniest little stinker.

All my friends, colleagues, and fellow writers who have read my work over the years and given me feedback.

Hanneke Mackie, Mike O'Brien, Erin Beth Langille, Ikuko Takeda, Nick Bradley, Bronwyn Clarke, Frances Slabolepszy, Ruarri Rogan and Matthew Van Onselen have all read and critiqued manuscripts of mine. Thank you!

BAYOU WOLF PRESS

Bayou Wolf Press is an independent publisher of quality fiction. If you enjoyed this book and would like to support us, the best thing you can do is leave a review on Amazon, Goodreads, or wherever you review books. If you'd like to learn more about our press, sign up for our newsletter, and stay informed on upcoming books, please visit our website.

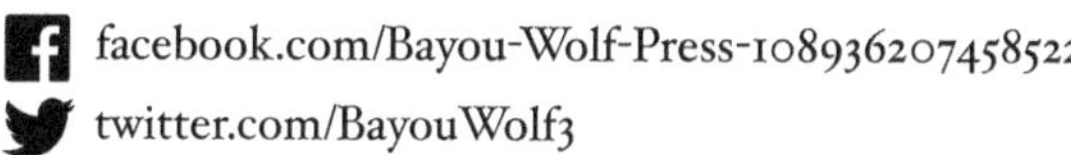

facebook.com/Bayou-Wolf-Press-108936207458522

twitter.com/BayouWolf3

www.ingramcontent.com/pod-product-compliance
Lightning Source LLC
Chambersburg PA
CBHW072053190726
48294CB00005B/1500